The quest for truth continues in the next two books, Time of Dreams and The Lost Prince. Be the first to read the entire trilogy! Sign up now for release notifications at thegiftedonestrilogy.com.

PARADISE RISING

PG SHRIVER

Paradise Rising by P. G. Shriver
Cover Design by MiblArt

Previously published as *The Fairytale*
ISBN: 978-0615600734
ISBN: 978-0-9963778-2-9

Address comments and inquiries to the author:
Gean Penny Books: author@pgshriver.com
URL: https://www.pgshriver.com

ACKNOWLEDGEMENTS

I would like to acknowledge the following in spurring me to complete this trilogy, some of which helped get my creative juices flowing again after a long dry spell.

First and foremost—my family. They tolerate creative me so well. I could not write without them.

Next, thanks to Jay Boyer and his team at Children's Book Formula and Apex Authors for giving me back my creative flow through the wonderful courses they've created.

And for their great work on the back cover blurb for this book, Bryan Cohen and Best Page Foreward, you have inspired my brief writings and taught me so much about ads and copy.

Last but not least, Miblart for their beautiful work on the cover designs for the three books in this trilogy. They did a wonderful job bringing my teens to life and together with some wonderful design work.

There's so much involved in producing a great book independently. I'm happy and honored to have worked with all the aforementioned on this journey.

DEDICATION

It's taken me 20 years to write this trilogy. Various obstacles presented while I attempted to complete this idea that began as a conversation around the table between myself and the three special ladies below. Those conversations sprouted more animated conversations that developed this once unique idea into a plan for a series of books. I cannot express the difficulty of completing this trilogy. It's as if the end of the written words would terminate the strong connection, the bond, that I've had with them since birth.

An endearing thank you to my mother, who I have loved since birth and will love forever.
Anna Marsh Velin
1943-2011

My heart aches with lost love and eternal endearment for my only biological sister,
Cassandra Velin Wachsman
1964-2004

Last, but not least, my first precious angel, born on my birthday, my first niece
Jennelle Fuller Boen
1983-2003

As these ladies rest in their eternal homes, they've patiently waited for me to tell the story we began so many years ago, whispering in my ear while I dreamed, leading me gently to the keyboard, but never taking me away from the precious moments of life. Mom, Candy, Jennelle, we have finished telling their story.

Screams... were they part of the dream? A tiny wet caress on her bare shin, her elbow, and then her chin, attempted to wake her.

Trying to shake off both the dream and the licks, she rolled away hoping to stay asleep, hoping to see him this time, the faceless man. Her need to see his face was strong, though she wasn't sure why. She felt, in her semi-awakened state, that he connected to her life, to the tragedies that had occurred, the loneliness, but she had no factual assurance, only intuition, and the dream.

More screams pierced the sleep induced silence, stirring her—distant, torturous screaming that had never before presented itself in the dream.

She rolled away from more intermittent moist tickles, a cool dampness running over her arm, and in her sudden urge to remain asleep, she fell off the hard metal park bench onto the dew soaked grass beneath it.

No staying asleep now. She raised up on her elbows, wiping wet grass from her face while frowning at the little mutt, her companion in hiding for the past few days. He shook the dew drops from his multicolored coat, spraying her with wet dog water.

Not fully awake, she stood—wiped fruitlessly at

dampened skin—and rubbed at the chill on her bare arms.

"Thanks, buddy!" She scoffed at the dog.

Glancing beyond the early dawn, darkness still surrounding the park, street lights sparkling the dense fog, circular areas of grass glistening with moisture, she stretched her cold, stiff muscles. The chill of the morning seeped under her skin, gripped her muscles and caused tiny tremors throughout her body.

Damp to her soul, she looked down at the pitiful dog. Screams echoed through the dark background. Her vision tunneled, blackening around the edges. "Not again," she whispered.

The screams, the moans of pain, the weak cry for help, called to her, chose her course, started her in motion, running, building speed, though she didn't realize it; she was already gone, drawn within herself into the darkness.

It was happening more and more frequently, the screaming, the black outs, the memory loss. Physically, she ran; mentally, she stood silent, in that all too familiar place of shadows.

Led without control to an unknown destination, as always, she followed.

Returning to the early morning light of a

world her body never left and to the sounds of the city around her, she blinked repeatedly, focusing her eyes to the dim alleyway where she stood. Crammed and filthy, homeless people slept about her in cardboard boxes, under newspapers and tattered, worn coats; rats scurried over motionless bodies; the sound of sirens echoed in the distance, police sirens.

She shook her head, regaining some of the lost clarity, shaking away the shadows. Her vision sharpened.

A hand held hers; a rough, arthritic, dry, callused hand that reminded her of someone. Sadie?

Her last safe place, her last foster mother, the cook from the Home who took her away from that depressing, unforgiving place to give her a real home, the first she had known in some time.

Sadie? She dared hope in her semi-conscious state.

Even knowing the risks, knowing her life's story, Sadie had taken her in; in spite of the dangerous truths that came with the young girl's past, Sadie dared to love her.

A smile grew within the girl's heart; a buoyant bubble burst by a moment of memory.

This was not the hand of Sadie holding hers. It couldn't be Sadie's hand, because Sadie was dead.

Guilt flooded her, chasing out the smile of hope, spreading to every chilly limb—tiny bottle rockets exploding beneath her skin—returning the trembling to her body after the darkness had left it warm and forgotten.

Flashes of Sadie, the short time they spent together as a family, replayed in her mind in various minuscule moments.

Sirens in the background; the little apartment Sadie shared with her.

Six months of memories replayed like old movie scenes, short clips leading to the last time she saw Sadie, lying on the kitchen floor, coffee cup shattered, shards spread atop dark spots that speckled the linoleum, as if the older woman's own skin had been cast in various sized pieces among the kitchen. Sadie's death was her fault, just like all the others who had tried to love her.

The camera of her mind replayed the image of her own body running out the front door, away from the scene of death, death she caused, wearing only the pajamas in which she had awakened that morning, a budding actress fleeing the suspense thriller that was her life.

She shook the memories away; her burning eyes blinked to check the tears that always followed; her body racked with shivers.

Someone sitting before her repeated the same words over and over; a dry, croaking voice echoed into the depths of her inner ear; someone else unashamedly dripped his own hot tears on her big toe, its hiding place given away by a hole in a trashcan, cross trainer.

She let her eyes move up from the hands joined before her, over the arms, across the face of the old woman standing there, to rest upon the young, rough looking boy; a toboggan fitted over the crown of his head; greasy golden spikes poked out over his too large ears; baggy, ripped clothes hung on his body; dry, cracked lips moving; tiny streams followed two freckled white lines down a dirt-encrusted face, drip... drip... drip.

"Thank you!" His thin arms reached out to her; his dry hands, palms partially concealed by time worn gloves, rested on her boney shoulders, as if to pull her into a hug.

She tried to shrug away, but his hands gripped her shoulders firmly while tears continually splattered her toe. "Thank you for bringing him to me, my little brother..." His voice broke with emotion.

Cheater searched beyond the old woman, the boy, her eyes questioning. Him who? What brother? Without success, her eyes sought another boy, the one he mentioned.

Why this tobogganed boy was so grateful she didn't understand; she never understood.

She... or something... changed people this way every time the darkness came. No memories of heroic acts remained.

Although no visible reuniting of family members presented itself, each spoke of another family member, as if she had pulled them from the depths of Hell and returned each to their long lost brother, mother, sister, aunt, uncle, spouse, but all she knew, all she remembered, was the darkness; all she ever remembered was the darkness.

From a pool of Sunday school memories, she learned that Hell was a dark place, but it was also filled with flames, so Hell couldn't possibly compare to the total darkness she encountered, no matter how warm she felt when stashed away there; it was a different type of warmth, a safe warmth, an infant swaddled in blankets and loving arms warmth.

And the people, the admiration, the changes, the after effects of the darkness, she remembered those. Not knowing what happened or where she went during these mindless times scared her as much as the faceless man dream ever did.

Sirens ripped the morning air.

Closer!

Louder!

They shrieked through her thoughts. The dog yipped his warning. He understood.

She looked down at the homeless woman, gray hair sticking up about her drawn face, a bruise darkening her left cheek, one hand holding a dented, half full can of black label green beans.

Standing beside the old woman, the young man, his face frozen in that look of awe, still spoke, "Thank you."

Every blackout left her in the same scene, different people, and different places.

Every time she blacked out, the same ending, changes for the better.

“I’ll make it up to you. I promise.” She heard as she tore herself from them. “I’m going to get a job, somehow, somewhere, take care of both of us. I don’t have anyone e...” Cheater fled; she couldn’t listen; she had to run. The sirens were too close. She couldn’t chance the police catching her; they continued to search for her, missing person posters up on every corner, on every wooden pole, some now only corners of paper stuck to staples, ones she had ripped from their perches.

They’d take her away if they caught her, take her back; she couldn’t go back, because this time they would send her to a worse place.

She had a mission to accomplish first. She had to find him, the faceless man, and she couldn’t do it locked up in a youth home or a correctional facility.

She ran, an out of place gazelle bounding down the dirty city sidewalk, wiry frame leaping tumbled trash cans, fire hydrants, small animals—the sirens closer, the little dog padding behind.

She breezed past a restaurant with the King's face in neon sticking out over the roof of the building, soles slapping the cracked concrete.

The King smiled down at her, mocking her from above the outdoor tables where half-eaten food littered two or three of the bolted down wrought iron surfaces, the aroma from within calling her stomach to breakfast.

Cheater grabbed hopefully at a slightly crumpled bag left behind, the newspaper stand worker just rising from the table and walking back to his job, his disgust for the cheap meal apparent.

As she ran by him, she prayed he would ignore her, that she wouldn't be caught, that she wouldn’t trip over the soles of her old sneakers as they gaped with each slap against the concrete. The little dog ran at her heels, ears bouncing, curled tail stiff.

Huddled beneath a sprawling, almost bare pecan tree, hidden by green shrubbery and fallen logs, early morning sun speckling knobby knees that rested her chin, Cheater listened intently, barely breathing as the police officer talked into his radio. Her mouth was dry from the crumbly half eaten biscuit sandwich she now shared with the small dog who didn't mind eating the already bitten parts.

She didn't think the officer had seen her, but the car rounded the corner, red and blue lights flashing, shortly after she had, chasing her until the road no longer led her.

Now, while the sun rose, peeking through the only bit of clear horizon in the city, two cops searched.

Probably someone she breezed past had identified her from the poster and called the police; perhaps the newspaper hawker—or some other stranger that she couldn't be warned of while nestled safely in her dark place—saw her last school picture in black and white plastered on a pole or in a nearby window, glanced her face as she passed, assumed she had assailed another.

There was also the reward of a thousand dollars which she couldn't understand.

She may as well have made the FBI's most wanted list. A thousand dollars would go a long way in helping most people today, and it meant more chance of getting caught.

When she first arrived, she hadn't noticed any of her posters in this large city where so many other missing or desperately wanted people must be harbored. That's why she'd made the decision to stay around for a while.

Of course, her intuition begged her to stay, too. Something was happening here that required her special skills. She hoped it had something to do with the faceless man. A shudder crept up her spine at the thought of him, his horrible laugh, his terrible implied acts in the dream.

He was evil; she knew that, felt it, but she didn't know who he was, or what he had to do with her... not for certain.

What could she do about it anyway? Evil was everywhere, and she was no heroic vampire or machine-like mutant.

She remained under the pecan tree until the warming sun pressed through to her scantily clothed arms, humidifying the chill in the little wooded area. No noise from police cars or police radios met her ears, only the noise of the city awakening, those who still held occupations racing to be the first on the bus, in the taxi, on the sidewalk.

She tossed pieces of biscuit to the little dog, stealing bites for herself in between. One for you, two for me played in her head, a memory of a little boy from her past, hand reaching into an off limits cookie jar. She shook the memory away and peered into the eyes of her furry friend.

He sat on his haunches smiling, licking his lip, baring small teeth, waiting for his next bite of biscuit. She tossed him the rest. The busy city commotion quieted. Cheater watched the dog chew the remnants of biscuit then stand and stretch. He trotted toward a small stream winding through the wooded area.

"Good idea!" She praised the wanderer, rising from the safety of the log to follow him for a drink.

Creek water left a bitter taste in her mouth, but she had become less picky about drinking water the past several weeks, since she had no money for other options. In her jumbled years of schooling, she remembered that a body needed water to survive, and as much as she wanted to give up, she needed to survive and find the faceless man.

Dipping her hands into the stream, she brought the water to her nose and sniffed it first, a lesson she had learned in the first week of being on the run. The water was cold from the extremely chilly nights. The little stream rushed down hill to a larger source somewhere beyond the horizon filtering through stones along the way.

She didn't know if the little dog sniffed the water, because when thirsty, he seemed to drink from the most stagnant of puddles, and she couldn't understand why animals didn't get sick, like she had.

"You should smell that first," she reprimanded. "What if it's polluted?"

The little dog cocked his head at her, then returned to the stream.

After drinking, she splashed the cold water on her face, rubbing it around to free the grime of the city night, the park bench, the homeless lifestyle that chose her.

Multiple times she inadvertently eavesdropped on conversations between elderly homeless people about how good the natural waters used to be when they were youngsters. People had ruined them, ruined everything, with this, their arms passing over the recycled trash that was now their warmth, their homes, their livelihood.

After walking through garbage-lined ditches and alleys for the past two months, hearing the stories, she made a vow never to throw down another bottle, cup, or wrapper that would add to the already polluted waterways. She looked down at the greasy yellow wrapper under her knee, crumpled it and stuffed it in the bag, then bag and all went into her back pocket to later find its future home in a dumpster.

Following the creek, Cheater picked up fallen pecans, filling the front pockets of her ragged, worn cut offs. The pecans would fill a hunger later. Cheater focused all her attention on her surroundings, now scanning the area, her ears tuned toward any disturbance in the ordinary crunch, crack or pant of her small friend and the natural sounds surrounding her.

Being on her own had stimulated her already powerful intuition. She had always had good intuition, and lately she trusted it more.

Whole pecans lay scattered about, so plentiful after the wet summer—untrammeled by pedestrian traffic, yet often stolen by fat little squirrels that now drew her canine companion's attention. Pecans floated above and below damp, fallen leaves, rich, brown shells gleaming. The nuts brought a memory of Sadie's pecan pies that Cheater had loved so much. Sadie used to make one every month on the anniversary of the day Cheater had moved into the tiny apartment with the lonely old woman. Cheater could eat a whole pie in one sitting, but Sadie never allowed it.

The young girl's mouth watered, thinking about the firm, sweet texture and incredible flavor cradled by the flaky, buttery crust. Sadie would have been thrilled at the plentiful crop of pecans this fall. Cheater picked another handful, knowing the pecans alone weren't a substitute for the last pie that she had never gotten to taste.

The bulges of pecans tightened up her loose denim shorts while the added weight of the nuts struggled to tug the shorts downward at the waist. In one motion, she looped her index fingers into the belt loops on each side and lifted the shorts.

She'd have to find some winter clothes in the

next few weeks, but that was just one of many tasks that demanded her attention. Solutions for those types of problems seemed to appear when she most needed them, so she learned not to worry too long on them. Worry was a negative energy that sapped her hope.

The faceless man, however, that was something to dwell on. The blackouts, the people whose lives differed from moments earlier, that, too, was worth dwelling on. Her brows furrowed in thought of them now as her slightly crunchy steps followed the small stream farther from her hiding spot beneath the log.

The faceless man had become a constant mystery in her life the past few months, since Sadie's death. Waking, she could not hold on to details of the dream, but she remembered the strange feelings, the fear, the dream left behind.

Who could he be? Was he related? Her father's brother? Her mother's brother? She hadn't known any uncles. Based on the little information she learned in her dream state, no conclusion could be drawn. Perhaps he was just somebody she struggled to remember from her past, someone with a lot of power. Whoever he was, she awoke with the sense of an inner struggle between good and evil, as if he was struggling to do the right thing. Or maybe, it was her struggle to do the right thing. She just didn't know.

Beyond the little wooded area, the creek led her to the opposite end of the small forested sanctuary, where it disappeared under the bridged roadway. She searched the area for future resources.

She'd entered the city from a back road, which didn't provide a great amount of details, no city signs with population postings announced locations on windy dirt roads.

She spoke as little as possible to the myriad of homeless people, only overhearing their rants and ravings about the change in times, sad faces filled with lost hope.

She ghosted among them, and they, being of the same mindset, accepted her without conversation. She easily deduced, by the large population of poverty driven people, this city was much larger than she normally liked to be in for any period of time. Although larger populations afforded some positives, such as getting lost in the crowd, it also had negatives— more people, more need of money, more chance of getting caught.

When she had arrived that night, her only concern had been finding a safe, dark place to rest that stood above the humidity soaked ground.

Around the small woods, back toward the area she burst through early that morning, were the distant daily noises of cars, buses, trains and busily smoking buildings.

She wondered about its solitary existence in such a largely populated place as she allowed her hand to drag down the rough bark of an Oak; belonging seeped through her immediately, as if their single natures blended and became one. She could hide away in its heart, safe from the world, forever, if a force stronger than her safety weren't tugging at her to leave the small secluded woods.

The gentle breeze carried the aroma of exhaust and pollution, mingled with cinnamon buns and bacon, topped with oak and pecan trees, and moist earth. Glancing beyond the edge of the trees, memories of her home town of Eden brought an ache to her chest.

At the forest's horizon, far on the other side of the creek, she made out the backs of several buildings. The row of buildings appeared to be one of those little strip malls similar to those where Sadie had liked to shop.

Cheater scanned the buildings as she moved toward them. She took note of the huge dumpsters behind them, hopeful of nearby restaurants, thinking about her next meal, her next minute, hour, and day, while moving toward a destination her life and instincts led her toward, an unknown place where she sensed great danger, where evil awaited her, a place her curiosity wouldn't allow her to ignore. She buried any fear the thought brought to her stomach.

As her gaze moved from building to building, a nicely dressed, slender, blonde woman in a dark business suit exited one, carrying a briefcase, heels clicking to an expensive car. The tall woman reminded Cheater of Mrs. Barston, one of many foster mothers from her past.

Two other people, employees, casually dressed

in jeans and business logo tee shirts, stood behind another building, smoking. Cheater wrinkled her nose, remembering another person from long ago who smoked, an elderly family member, since passed on, whom she had dreaded visiting, hugging, because her house and breath always smelled of musty, old cigarettes.

A man dressed in white—a tall, fluffy, white hat bouncing on his too round head, matching the bouncing rhythm of his too round belly beneath a jostling apron—carried out a big silver pan and dumped the contents into a dumpster.

She could only think of two professions identified by white coats; a doctor, or a chef, and the doctors of her mind didn't wear a fluffy white hat or carry a large silver pan full of food.

"Well, fella', looks like we found the perfect place for lunch later," she whispered, her stomach momentarily satisfied, yet unfilled from the leftover biscuit.

The one adjustment she'd had to make that took some time and slight starvation was dumpster diving.

She preferred to make money for her meals, and offered to work many times, for the cafes, restaurants, and small grocers she traveled near, risking recognition, but she found that not many people today were interested in helping the multitude of poor, even fewer had time to notice posters stuck to poles. They were too busy surviving their own lives.

Poor people—now the majority in everyday life—and missing people now long forgotten, without compassion. Life in Cheater's world had become survival.

Restaurant managers and their assistants shook disapproving heads at her and sarcastically told her to go back to her cardboard box, judging that was exactly where she had been; lost in the oceans of homeless people keeping her safe and hidden, she was free to fulfill the mystery mission of finding the faceless man whom she was certain held answers that were related to her tragic situation.

She had almost starved after the first three days on her own with no food before finally deciding to tame her pride and take matters into her own hands, and feet, and knees, literally.

Extreme hunger and thirst had reduced her to little more than a rat, making it much easier to lower her expectations and take food and water from sources never before explored. That was when she had learned about the water.

She grimaced at the thought of that first time she climbed into the smelly, fly infested dumpster, searching for freshly added edibles that contained no maggots. Having survived that first trip in, she found subsequent trips less gross.

Silently wishing before every dumpster she stepped in—her stomach roaring—there were more people in the world who cared didn't feed her. There were few who did help, but most people seemed to have little compassion at all anymore.

When had the world become so self-absorbed? She remembered times when she was younger when people helped each other, telethons, fake Santas, food drives, soup kitchens. What had happened to stop all of that?

She remembered Sadie complaining about some higher ups—that's how Sadie referred to politicians—making changes, changes for the worst, but she hadn't listened at that time. She had been too busy being a twelve-year-old girl. When she asked Sadie later what she meant, Sadie had told her not to worry about it. She said it would be over soon. They would be fine, the two of them, with or without work because they had each other. Those kids at the Home would be fine, too, Sadie added with her always chipper tone. Smiling she drilled into the young girl that Cheater had Sadie, and Sadie had her, that Cheater's future was sound, nothing to worry herself about.

"Now look at me, Sadie," Cheater's sad whisper carried in the breeze. "I wish you were here."

Why hadn't she listened, asked more questions about that guy? Maybe he was the one, the man without a face in her nightmares.

Behind the last strip on the corner, a group of kids skirmished.

Cheater moved closer, peering around the naked autumn trees, her eyes taking in three bigger, older, tougher looking boys; she guessed they were about sixteen years old. The three boys tormented a younger boy. Forming the points of a human triangle, they shoved the boy back and forth between them, ignoring his pleas to stop, pleas soon becoming painful screams as the three hoodlums shoved the kid to the ground, laughing.

Something small and shiny fell from the victim's hand. Wires swirled from his ears to the ground, a treasure stolen with his pride.

Cheater watched curiously, smirking at the baggy, sagging jeans of the tallest boy. He appeared to be the leader. As she watched, the boy stopped and made a futile attempt to hike up his jeans, which immediately slipped back down when he bent to pick up the gadget that had fallen to the ground. His sleeveless, dingy white tee shirt revealed lean, wiry muscles, and his dark, bare arms glistened with sweat in the morning sun.

Sadie would tell Cheater that this boy was a 'wannabe gangsta.' The label she reserved for one of the boys similarly dressed at the Home; a boy who always wound up in trouble because of his choice of activities and attitude, which usually confined him to a solitary room during most of his stay. Sadie would roll her eyes every time the boy came through the food line, "Boy be thinkin' he has some power!" She'd scoff under her breath.

Cheater had known kids like him were pretty street tough, or at least they acted it.

She also knew from experience that they had no respect for other people or their property. In this current time of apathy, boys like this took full advantage of others.

As the human triangle scene played out before her, Cheater had wandered to within twenty feet of the mugging, the darkness swirling in her peripheral vision, the circular view growing smaller and smaller as she drew near them.

"What else ya' got?" One of the others, his head shaven, asked as he kicked the groaning boy in his side.

"See 'f he got some money!" the tall boy ordered. The injured boy's whimpered as he rolled from one kick into another. He tried to control his sobs, show that he wasn't afraid.

Nobody moving about behind the buildings stopped or called for help. The businesswoman drove away, eyes focused on the road before her; the two smokers quickly closed the backdoor behind them; the chef took his silver pan and quietly slipped back into the restaurant, unwilling to become a target.

Cheater was used to that response from people. Their apathy towards the rest of the world didn't startle her anymore.

No real heroes existed in places such as this, only people struggling to survive. This was the way of her world, and the mugging was the last thing she noted before darkness descended upon her, moving her physical body into the open sunlight just beyond the mugging.

Within five feet of the scene, it appeared to the gang of older boys that she watched as they took out their anger and pain on the younger boy, but the scene through her eyes wavered away, the bullying bodies withering from feet to head as if each stood on hot pavement in the July heat of Texas.

Staring at the taller boy, the leader, as he disappeared from her view, the only one of the three facing her, her eyebrows drawn into a puzzled, sympathetic angle, she felt no fear for herself. She was in the darkness. The ending would be the same as always, as every other time she returned from that safe place.

The first time that she blacked out was at the age of twelve, right after she had moved in with Sadie. It scared her then, but not anymore, even though she still didn't know what happened to her, what she was doing that caused the sudden changes in people.

She discussed it with Sadie, who told her it was a gift from God himself, yet neither of them knew anything about that gift. Sadie just knew that if it made people better for having experienced it, then it was a gift from the Good Lord.

The older woman smiled, her contagious

features glowing, as she told Cheater about the report of that first dark time.

Sadie's great nephew had in part been the one to experience the change, the first incident in a now growing list, an incident lacking much detail.

Sadie retold the reaction of her nephew's childhood friend after he had cornered Cheater on her way to the market to get corn syrup for Sadie; Sadie was making Cheater one of those special pecan pies, the first of five.

The older boy, the friend, drug riddled and withdrawal shaken, had tried to take Sadie's money from Cheater, but had received more than he ever imagined when he reached his quivering, desperate hands toward the preteen girl.

Sadie had listened intently to her nephew's account, interrupting him with, "M-hm" and "Oh, yes" leading to "I remember that" intertwined with several stories of times that he had tried to help his friend.

Excitedly, she retold how her nephew talked about rounding the corner where Cheater stood facing the addict. He'd first noticed the trance-like state of the two, like a paused video, and how immediately after the change in his friend came, his friend who suddenly began to attend school regularly, who held a steady job to help his mother pay bills, his friend who talked of college.

Sadie's great nephew called it a miracle, an idea Sadie agreed with, because his tenth grade pal no longer needed fixed. But nobody ever told Cheater exactly what or how it happened; nobody mentioned the details, especially not the friend. She wondered if they even knew or remembered.

In the here and now, the dark eyes of the present day abuser turned her way after catching a glimpse of her blank, sympathetic stare.

"What's wrong with you, you stupid little b...?" he started, but something about her felt familiar, halting his warning. He stared hard at her, giving her the look he used to buckle his victims, pushing away the rush of emotion filling him, but, looking into her eyes, he couldn't hold on to his fear inducing look, couldn't block the flood of emotions from hers.

As he stared, for moments seeming like days, into her melancholy gaze, she drew him into her mind somehow; she seemed to see through his painful charade of Mr. Tough Guy, down to his very soul, his deepest secrets. He knew of only one other who looked at him that way, and she was dead. Had it not been for that simple fact, he might have believed this crazy, poor, homeless white girl was his sister reincarnated.

His discomfort with her eyes, the depth of them, the sadness, the disappointment, the hurt, burned deeper into his soul than a warning from his boyhood minister.

He recognized it, the sensation, and wanted to turn away, but he couldn't.

He wanted to run to her, kneel before her for absolution, but he couldn't; it wasn't right.

He longed to hug her, but he didn't.

His silent behavior alerted his followers, and within moments, all was quiet, the girl before him no longer appearing herself.

"Jaz, man, what's up with her?" asked the shortest of the three, a handsome younger teen. "What she doin', man?" Puzzled by no answer, the teen watched the facial transformation taking place in his leader's eyes, and the abnormal stare of the young girl.

Jaz, the apparent leader of this small band of brutal boys, who had been just as puzzled, took in the sight before him, a sight lasting only moments, and then he nodded once at Cheater and turned away, trying not to let the shame filled tears burning in his own dark eyes come to fruition on his awestruck face.

"Come on, let's git outta here. It ain't worth it!" He jerked his head, dropping the small wired item next to the pale hand of the abused boy, pretending to wipe away sweat as he lifted his dingy tee shirt instead of the tears on his cheeks.

Any other day, Jaz wouldn't have moved away slowly; he would have been running from the crime.

Any other day, he wouldn't have looked back over his shoulder. Life had taught him not to look back.

Any other day, he wouldn't have believed what he had seen. There wasn't much he believed in anymore.

But today was not any other day; it was a day unlike any other he had encountered in his tragic life, and when he glanced back at the scrawny, stringy haired girl with burning brown eyes who had stood there, staring him down, that's not what he saw, and a bittersweet smile softened his face of stone; for the first time in five months he felt like floating.

For once in his lifetime, he didn't even think about his stepfather, the Beast. What he saw that day was amazing, ethereal, a dream, yet not. She was right there before him. He turned back to his confused friends and motioned them home, intuition telling him that he would see this girl again, soon. Suddenly unafraid of everything that had brought fear to his last few years, he felt the urge to go someplace he hadn't been in a long, long time.

"Wow, you gotta gun or somethin'?"

Cheater looked into the tear stained face, unaware that she had moved. She stammered, shaking the darkness from her consciousness.

In a blur of mental confusion, she squinted at the face below her. Another ghost from her past surfaced, a young boy, her brother. "Stevey?" she murmured painfully.

"Who? No... Hey, do you know your name? Are you okay?" The boy frowned at her.

"Um, what, no... where... are you okay?" She stammered when his face focused and her mind cleared. She picked up the small blue and silver, wired object lying on the grass, remembering the situation. "Here, I think this is yours."

"Thanks. How'd you do that? Those guys were some of the meanest kids in the complex. How'd you chase 'em off? Wha'd you do?"

"Hmm? Do... What? Hey, come on, I'll walk you home or wherever you were going." She held her hand out to him, noting his grunt of pain as she pulled him up. The young boy resembled Stevey.

Is it possible? No, it's not. You know where Stevey is, what happened to him.

"You okay?" She asked again, shaking off the

memory.

What am I doing? This is not a good idea! Just walk away from this kid, she told herself as she followed his lead.

What if somehow Stevey had survived? What if this kid is...

"Well, my side kinda hurts where that boy kicked me." Tears of pain shone in his wide gray eyes as he felt the area with his fingertips.

"How old are you?"

"Ten. I just turned ten! I got this mp3 for my birthday last month. I hope they didn't break it." He hooked the headphones around his shame reddened ears and turned it on to check it.

They walked a few steps before he pulled an earphone from his ear and handed it to her, "Wanna listen?"

"Uh... sure!" She fumbled with the earpiece, glanced over at the one hooked around the boy's right ear, and finally adjusted the half-moon arm over her left ear. "Cool," she nodded. She had never owned any music player, although she had seen others with them.

"You remind me of someone. He would have been about your age now. What's your name?" Her sullen tone, her use of past tense, halted his next step. With his right foot hanging in the air as if in a game of freeze tag, he frowned up at her. She had opened that door, but he wasn't quite rude enough to walk through with the question in his mind.

"Thomas, well, everybody calls me Tommy. It's not Stevey..." He looked down at his shoes, then his eyes moved to her flappy shoes and her ragged clothes. His frown deepened. "I sure would like to know what you did to make them boys leave. You do some martial arts stuff or something?"

"No, I don't know any of that stuff. I guess they just got scared because I walked up on them, you know?"

"Uh, unh. That wouldn't scare them! Last month, they attacked a kid walking to school, and they stole all his money, his laptop and his tennis shoes! There were three people watchin' it all happen, too, and those boys didn't get scared. You musta done somethin'! If I knew what it was, I could keep them from doing it to me again!" he paused, excitement leaving him breathless, his shaggy, blonde hair swinging from side to side, his eyes searching her hands for weapons. "Is it whatever ya got in your pockets? A chain?"

"Pecans." She brought one out and showed him. Cheater wished she could tell him what she did, but she had no idea. Apparently, it was her 'gift' again, as she had learned to call it, though she thought of it more as her curse of loneliness.

"You threw pecans at them?" his eyebrows rose in surprise.

"What? No!" She stuffed the pecan back into her pocket.

"Did something happen to Stevey, that other

boy I look like?" he went through the door anyway, unable to resist the nagging sensation of nosiness eating away at him. He glanced up at her solemn reaction. His face reddened with embarrassment. He shouldn't have asked! His curiosity wouldn't allow him to mind his manners.

"Yeah, I think. But that was a long time ago. I guess it's possible that he could be okay." She shook her head slightly. "I don't want to talk about it." She couldn't mask the tears in her voice, the trembling, so she quickly changed the subject. "By the way, just so you're not walking a stranger to your house, my name's Cheater. So where are we headed?" She glanced left, and then right, at an intersection.

"Cheater? That's a weird name!" his eyebrows drew together. "We go this way to my apartment!" He motioned left, leading her in the opposite direction of the strip mall. "We live in a complex down there. It's for poor people. I was at the diner where my mom works, eating breakfast. I can eat for free there, three times a day, 'less I'm in school. Saves on groceries. My mom works hard there, and she works all day. I'm glad those boys didn't get my MP3 player. She paid a lot for it, and we don't have much money. Since my dad left, it's just me and Mom, and I don't see her much. We can't afford a whole lot, at least, that's what she says..." His nervous voice rambled.

He continued, anxious and confused, checking out her worn, dirty clothes again, "But, I guess you know about not having a lot, huh? Why'd they call you Cheater, do you cheat in games or somethin'?"

"Yeah..." she laughed "...or somethin'." The memory of Sadie nicknaming her Cheater resurfaced, "'Lucky li'l cheater, cheatin' the big one so many times." She heard the gentle voice of Sadie as it conjured the image of the woman's smile, warming Cheater's heart.

"Here it is." Tommy turned into the parking lot at the end of the next block. "Ya' wanna come up? We could play cards, or a board game, or something, or get on the computer?" Fear still wrinkled his forehead as he scanned the parking lot and nearby apartment buildings quickly, his left foot resting on the stoop.

Sadness filled Cheater as she looked up at the tired old brick building before her, cracked in places, tagged with gang symbols here and there, cold and dreary in appearance, like the world they lived in. What had happened to her and Stevey, living like this?

"How do you know I'm not some nutcase that's gonna steal everything you have and leave? Technically, I am still a stranger, you know?" She wanted to say no, but she stalled instead. Her intuition fought with her conscience over leaving. After what had happened to Stevey the last time they were in the same house? He could have survived, been adopted. She didn't want him to go through it again.

"If you were a nutcase, you would have joined in with those boys instead of running them off." One corner of her lip raised, and she shook her head at his logic.

She didn't want to put the boy at risk by staying with him. She knew what happened when she got too close to someone, but he winced in pain as he stepped up the stoop.

And, he was still afraid. With his mom working, she decided to maybe hang around and keep an eye on him, in case he passed out, or worse. After all, he could have some serious internal injuries. Plus, it would give her a chance to find out about him, too, where he came from, a little of his background. Maybe he's adopted. Maybe by some miracle he is...

Certainly staying just long enough to find out wouldn't bring danger; she wasn't moving in with them, like she had with the others. She would never live with anyone, again.

An excited, soft whimper interrupted her thoughts.

"Stay here!" She called to the homely pup. "Maybe I can come up for a while, if you think it's okay with your mom. You sure you're okay? Maybe I should just go get your mom for you?"

"Nah, I can't make her leave her job. She'd get fired for sure. We can't afford that. I'll be all right. That your dog?" Tommy gritted his teeth through the pain and stroked the dog's head, scratched him behind his ears.

"Yeah, sorta, for now I guess."

"He's kinda skinny, like you." Cheater looked

down at her slender, seemingly shapeless body, then at the pitiful, scraggly dog, and shook her head again at the boy's bold, yet accurate, comparison.

The two, hero and victim, stepped lightly up the three flights of creaky stairs, and then turned right down a long dim corridor.

Yelling.

Loud, angry words seemed to float through the walls and down the halls before them.

A hungry baby screeched.

A television blared vulgar music videos.

A radio with booming, bumping, banging sounds filled their ears.

Two men at the end of the hall turned toward them, and then back to each other, resuming their heated, yet quiet discussion; one man—thinning, dark hair greasy and unkempt, his rag clad body hunching forward, his gapped smile displaying few teeth—counted the cash in his hand; the other, taller and dressed in street best, gold jewelry dangling and flashing, his fair complexion masked with a sly street tough expression, held a bag full of some substance.

Cheater knew what was happening. She'd seen drug deals happening in every corner of the poor and destitute that she'd passed through in life.

A memory pushed up through the heavily burdened soil of her mind, at the edge of her consciousness, of a trip she had taken with her mother, at age five, to the mission shelter at Thanksgiving, back when people still cared, before 'that man' had changed everything. Her mother volunteered at a church to help serve the holiday meals every year, and her own family would share their meals, cooked by her father, later in the evening.

That year, the charitable mom took young Sara, now Cheater, with her, and allowed her to help in the kitchen. After gathering her own dark hair up in a hairnet, she twisted Sara's hair around and wrapped a net around the small head, brown strands trying to poke through here and there. The too big white apron she tied around Sara's waist touched the tops of her shiny black Mary Janes in the front.

Sara watched her mother, eyes sparkling and smile gleaming, scoop mash potatoes and gravy onto each tray that passed before her, wishing everyone in line, each poor, homeless, or lonely person, a cheerful, "Happy Thanksgiving!" no matter how angrily, bitterly, or hatefully they responded to her.

Young Sara smiled brightly, placing a golden brown dinner roll on each tray as it slid before her, wondering what had happened to all of these people to bring them here.

Once, when she followed her mother through the kitchen and out the backdoor to take out the garbage, she saw two people in the dark alley, two very unkempt people, their hair too long and smell too strong, sitting in the shadows, passing something back and forth.

She thought they were sharing a cigarette. She knew about cigarettes because of the great aunt her mother checked in on every other day; she smoked about a gazillion cigarettes in the short amount of time it took Sara and her mother to clean and cook for her. The young mother had seen the two people in the alley and quickly ushered little Sara back into the shelter kitchen.

A grave appreciation of her far from chosen, lonely, unstable lifestyle versus that of Tommy's suddenly filled her. Concern for him creased her brow. Helplessness swirled within her as she considered this sweet kid, and who he might become, being swept away into a dangerous drug world for lack of money and worry over his mother during his teen years.

In such areas as these, drug lords constantly sought out the young poor kids of their communities, tried to turn them into pushers and killers. She silently prayed that she could help Tommy somehow, keep him away from such a disastrous ending. A growing responsibility filled her.

Having been approached herself several times by such characters on the street, she allowed her strong faith, her strong intuition, to lead her to resist the powerful temptation of the money the strangers flashed before her for 'running a little errand.'

Evil was evil. It came in many forms, but the form of drugs and violence were most prevalent in places such as this, places Sadie quietly referred to as 'slums' or 'ghettos.' Cheater heard Sadie's strong, husky voice in her head, "You stay away from them places, them people. They're no good and no good will come to them." But how could they be avoided when they were cropping up everywhere?

She frantically led Tommy into the apartment as the two men parted like her mother had done with her. The one with the bag walked toward them, a bad business deal smile turning his face into an undesirable, drug-pushing malady.

Cheater pushed the door closed behind them, the deceit filled, singsong salesman voice calling to them through the disappearing crack, "Hey, kids, ya' wanna lose your troubles?"

Cheater clicked the dead-bolt lock with a sigh, leaning her ear to the door and listening for his departure.

"You musta looked at him. Mom tells me to ignore them, act like they're not there, and they'll leave me alone. They do most of the time.

"So where d'ya live?" His words ran together as he picked up dirty clothes and threw them in a basket in the bathroom to the right.

"Not around here. I'm just passing through." Cheater glanced at the faded, dingy, striped wallpaper, torn and peeling away from the walls, the original colors indistinguishable. The stain-laden, once blue carpet below her feet unraveled in spots near the walls and corners, suspicious stains scattered throughout.

She wasn't appalled by their situation, just sympathetic. She'd already figured out the living arrangements, seen it hundreds of times: the single mother, living where she can, trying her best to bring her children up in what seemed a hopeless, never ending battle against the society she could afford. Tommy was one of many latchkey kids she had met in her travels during the past eight years.

She had also seen love, hope, and faith prevail in very wicked environments, but not too often recently.

She helped Tommy pick up around the apartment, following his lead as to where everything belonged.

"Runaway, huh?"

"No. Well... yeah... kinda."

"Howdya kinda be a runaway?" he smirked, rolling his gray eyes toward her and giving her that I-wasn't-born-yesterday smirk.

"It's a long story," another avoidance. "Hey, d'ya think I could use your bathroom to clean up a little?"

"Uhm, sure, that would be a good idea!" He wrinkled his nose and fanned his hand before his face jokingly, then laughed out loud as Cheater lifted her right arm, lowered her pointy nose, and sniffed her armpit. Strangely, they fell into a sibling-like comfort.

"I'd say you could take a bath, but we only

have cold water in the bathroom right now. The Super hasn't come up to fix the hot water heater, yet. Ya' need some clothes? My cousin... She's a girl... was here last month from California, and she forgot some clothes. You could have them if you want." He disappeared in a flash.

She glanced again at the tattered rags enveloping her body, the holy green tee shirt with a big 4-H logo on the front that she had snatched off an untended clothesline, the cutoff denim shorts she had found lying near a river bed during the end of summer, just after she ran away, so faded the only blue could be found at the seams; they seemed to have loosened more each day of the two months she had been wearing them. The bulging, pecan-filled pockets barely helped keep them up.

The tattered, splitting cross trainers she had found atop a banged up trash can in the wealthier part of some neighborhood she had passed. She traded the shoes for the pajamas she'd been wearing when she had left Sadie's.

The shoes had been less worn two months ago, but now the big toe on one of her feet poked through the top after twenty-four hours a day of wear, half the time spent walking. Stiff and holy socks washed daily in creeks or rainwater—without the desperately needed soap she couldn't afford—and dried on a rock lined her shoes on the inside, another clothesline run-by.

She couldn't remember all the cities she had

traveled through that had absently donated to her worn wardrobe because she focused only on the one destination embedded in her mind, the one place she moved toward, the one place that called to her, the place her late mother repeated every night, that magical place in the fairytale where hopefully she would find the answers to events of her past. It had to exist.

"She doesn't want them back?" Cheater nodded toward the folded clothes draped over Tommy's thin arm.

After scanning over them, first lifting the shirt, then taking the folded jeans gently from his arm, she concluded that they probably wouldn't fit. They appeared too big.

"Nah. She said give 'em to Goodwill or somethin' anyway. She couldn't wear 'em anymore by the time we could send 'em to her; she's pregnant. That's why she was here, talkin' to my mom. They always stayed real close, and she thought Mom could help her make a decision or something."

"How old is she, your cousin?"

"Mmmm... 15, yeah she's almost 6 years older than me. Her mom and dad are mad, I bet. They're strict.

"They got lots of money. Mom doesn't talk to them at all 'cause they don't care about family or nothin', just the 'almighty dollar' as Mom puts it." His blonde hair, slightly greasy strands falling just above his ears, swung side to side as he shook his head, imitating his mother.

Cheater turned away. She's only two years older than I am. I've never even had a boyfriend! Of course, I've had other things to worry about.

She took the clothes that Tommy had retrieved from somewhere down the hall and went into the bathroom. She located a washcloth and bar of soap; a cold birdbath awaited her in the deep, chipped white porcelain sink.

Tommy had been right about the cold water; it was like ice. The rusted goose neck faucet came up high enough that she could wash her stringy brown hair, so she found some peach scented shampoo and took care of it. She hadn't been able to wash her hair in a couple of weeks, as all the roadside restrooms seemed to be out of soap by the time she got to them, so she could only rinse and scrub with plain water.

It felt good to have soap and water, even cold water, and scented shampoo, running over her head, down the long, wet strands that would be clean again for a couple of days. Baths were definitely something she missed while being on the run.

She recalled her last real bath, a little over two months ago, the night before her first day in eighth grade when she lived with Sadie in her tiny one bedroom apartment, Cheater's bedroom doubling as the living room, her bed as the sofa. The water in the deep tub was always warm and fragrant, full of crackling bubbles and fun. As the evening sun set into the tiny bathroom window, it sent rays down upon the tiny bubbles, prisms of various colors dancing and floating before her. Of course, that memory led to one much more horrifying, the one in which a teenage girl dialed 911 because the woman she lived with had passed out and quit breathing, leaving fingers pointed toward a young girl killing yet another person that she loved, yet again running away, too scared to remember to take clothing or food.

She shook away the burn in her eyes and wrapped her hair in a towel, trying to avoid the tiny medicine cabinet mirror before her. As her head came up, towel turban style, hiding her wet hair, she accidentally glimpsed her reflection in the mirror.

Mesmerized by the picture before her, she stared. She hated mirrors, seeing what she had become over the past few months. Her pale cheeks were drawn; her brown eyes were slightly sunken from lack of sleep; a worry line creased her forehead.

She thought of her mother, whom she resembled so much now, except for the thinner face and frame from weeks of travel and lack of proper nutrition. Very little differed the two— age, size— and perhaps the fact that mother never carried the death curse like daughter. Cheater would not be here if that were the case.

Tearing herself from the mirror image of the unhappy girl, she sized up the donated clothing against her body, laying the shirt over at her shoulders, holding the jeans against her waist.

An article of clothing dropped to the floor when she opened the jeans. She bent now to pick it up after laying the stiff denim over her arm.

She snickered quietly to herself. Tommy had brought a pair of underwear, apparently his—boxers, a red and blue superhero she recognized as Spiderman, covering them, front and back.

A smile dawned her face; she shrugged her shoulders and nonchalantly slipped them on. She would be the only one to know what kind of underwear she wore anyway. The jeans, slightly faded on the thighs, had looked a little big, and the light blue ladies tee shirt with cropped sleeves, bearing the logo of some designer, seemed huge, but when she put the clothes on, they fit perfectly.

The cooler weather wouldn't be a problem now. She had guessed that it must be around the beginning or the middle of November judging by the change in evening temperature that she felt outside last night, but she wasn't certain. Although she usually tried searching calendars for dates when passing offices or store windows, sometimes bank signs, she wasn't always in direct sight of them. Trying to stay in hiding on back roads and small avenues away from business districts and police cars offered very few opportunities to satisfy curiosity. She'd lost track of time.

Her focus remained on the location she remembered from the fairytale her mother always told; it tugged at her. That was the only time and day that seemed important anymore. It was there she would find what she longed for, but she didn't know why, or when, or what it was that she would find once she arrived.

She wondered several times when the desired destination popped into her mind, if she would find family again, or fearfully just another unexpected tragedy.

She did know this: as she traveled closer to that destination, the pull strengthened, the name of the city popping into her mind at every corner, on every sign, on every piece of paper that floated past her feet with the breeze. It twisted through her thoughts, and it was that guiding sensation that brought her here, to this city, this much too big city full of risks and dangers.

She carefully relocated the pecans to her new-old jeans, which happened to be a little more in style. She slipped into her holy socks and worn sneakers and left the bathroom, combing the fingers of one hand through her hair to untangle it, while carrying her old clothes in the other.

"Where's the trash can?" She called when she didn't see Tommy.

"In the closet in the kitchen!" His voice carried from down the hall.

She pulled open the partially unhinged door that barely clung to the frame at the bottom. The inside of the sparse closet was dark. When she flipped the light switch, nothing happened.

Wondering what Tommy was doing, she dumped her clothes in the bag-lined trashcan that held little trash.

She was still trying to remove the tangles from her long hair when he came down the hall with a box. "You need a comb? I have a spare comb. Mom always buys the big pack like at the dollar store, 'cause I lose 'em outta my pocket all the time. Cheaper that way, too." He reached in his pocket and handed her a comb.

"Uh... thanks. Watcha' got there?" she tugged the comb through sections of tangled hair.

"Just some games. Card games mostly, 'cause they're cheaper and easier to store. Hey, how 'bout Uno, you ever played that?"

"Uh, no, I don't think so. I'd like to learn, though."

"It's an old game. My mom used to play it when she was a kid, and she saved the cards. Sometimes, when she has a day off, we play it. She's not that good at it, though. I always win."

Facing the old, scratched coffee table, Cheater sat on the lumpy couch, Tommy opposite her perched on a floor cushion; he dealt the cards. From below her brows, her eyes search the tiny living room that consisted of the worn couch, a chair with balls of fluff popping out through holes, the scratched up coffee table with little to no finish left, and a warped and worn computer stand holding an old computer.

No television, she thought curiously. That's

odd. Of course, it wasn't so odd since they were poor. Too bad, she would have liked to watch television, see what was on the news, or laugh at some stupidly insane comedy show.

She hadn't watched TV in over two months, except what she saw passing store windows. It was probably better that she couldn't watch anyway. There may be some local news on about her disappearance.

She fondly remembered some shows from when she lived with Sadie. One show Sadie would absolutely not let her watch. She attributed it to the fall of children everywhere, the disrespect, the apathy. It was a cartoon show that, at that time, had been running for almost twenty-five years.

Skimming through the channels one evening, Cheater had come upon that show. She found it funny, but upon hearing the main character's voice, Sadie grabbed the remote control and calmly told Cheater that she would not allow that show in her house, ever.

That memory led to movie night at Sadie's, where she would rent a movie for Cheater. Sadie would fix a huge bowl of popcorn. They would drink almost an entire two-liter bottle of root beer on movie nights. She thought back to the last movie night they had, the week before Sadie died, and remembered it was the third Spiderman movie. Sadie had been into Superhero movies; it was the third time they had rented that particular movie. Her voice filled

Cheater's mind now, "This sad excuse for a country needs Superheroes now more than ever. Don't nobody care about nothin'."

In spite of the sad feeling reeling in the pit of her stomach, the thought of Spiderman made her smile, and then Cheater giggled, thinking about the underwear she wore now. Sadie would have gotten a kick out of that.

As if reading her mind, Tommy explained, "Sorry about the underwear. My mom always buys them for me on sale. I don't wear them anymore, those are fresh out of the bag, and I keep telling her that, but she still thinks I'm just a little kid, or something!" His face reddened when he realized what he had just told her. If not these boxers, then what? "I mean, I have to wear them," he mumbled.

The smile on her face grew bigger, and she burst out, "So do I!"

Laughter filled the small living room, rolling, belly holding laughter; she hadn't laughed since Sadie, and she did so now until she felt her abs start to cramp. She relaxed. She could let her guard down a little, yet she found it curious that he seemed to know her as well as she knew herself.

Could this be Stevey? She hadn't seen him since he was three. She glimpsed him through joy-filled tears. Maybe subconsciously he recognized her. He was so little when...

She decided she must be here for him, that he was supposed to go with her, but she needed to be sure.

Their faces damp and eyes still blurry Cheater glanced again at the computer in the corner. Tommy turned his blonde head, following her gaze as he dealt the cards.

"The school gave that to me. Some new program for poor kids without computers. We even have internet through the school, so's I can do my research and stuff. It's an old computer, but it works real good."

"Can't you find places on those things?"

"Sure. You can go to MapQuest and find directions, too. Sometimes I do that when I start dreaming about having the money to move me and Mom away from here."

"Hmm. Think maybe later you can find a place for me?"

"Sure. We can research it. I like to research stuff on the computer. I would probably be doing that now if you weren't here to play cards with. You ready to play?"

He briefed her on the rules and objectives of the game before they played a round. The computer kept pulling her concentration away from the game, though, and Tommy won. He taught her some more card games: solitaire, tens, and even five-card draw poker, without betting. The next time she looked at the clock it was noon. Her stomach growled loudly enough to make Tommy chuckle.

The thought of Paradise, of the fire, and the humming of the computer, reminded her of the only foster family she had lived with who had a computer in their home, the Barstons.

They had lived on Eden Street. They were a middle-aged couple, and they had died shortly after Cheater moved in with them at the age of five. A drunk driver broadsided their minivan.

For the safety of the children, the Barstons hadn't allowed anyone under the age of ten to use the computer, which left out Cheater and another younger foster child.

She had never gotten to use computers at the Children's Home, either, because the few old computers in the lab were claimed fast, and she always seemed to be one of the last ones to get to the tiny room.

Sadie hadn't had a computer; the only technology Sadie wasn't afraid of had been the DVD player and television.

Cheater waited now as the paper churned from the printer, and within a few minutes, she was reading over a list of cities with the name Paradise, or another synonymous name to that reference. There were at least ten different cities in different states, the first on the list in the state where she had been born and now stood, Texas.

"So, do you want to look up directions for all of them, or just the first one, or what?" Tommy's question jarred her back from the past, away from the list, into the present.

"Well, I don't think the first one can be what

I'm looking for." Truthfully, she didn't know, but given her past, it would be too easy. She scanned the list, allowing her intuition to take control.

After a few moments, her eyes focused again on the first Paradise. She told Tommy, "Yeah, just try this one, after all." She pointed at the one on the top of the list, and Tommy typed it into the MapQuest destination bar. Another paper rolled out of the printer and Cheater studied it, folded it up with the list, and slipped them into her back pocket.

"That's a long way from here. You sure that's the place?"

"Uhm..." she began uncertainly "...yeah, I'm pretty sure. Thanks!"

"Hey, let's go down to the diner and get something to eat!" Tommy brightened.

"Uh, thanks, but I forgot about my dog. I should probably bring him some water or something. You can go to the diner. I gotta leave anyway. Seems like you're doing okay." She stood and stretched, glancing at the computer.

"Do you have to go?" His sparkling grey eyes pleaded, hoping to stall her leaving; he wanted her to stay. He liked having another kid around. She felt like a big sister to him.

Looking at her bulging pockets of pecans, he realized she was probably embarrassed that she didn't have any money.

"Ya' know, I never eat the whole special. It's huge at lunchtime. I could share it with ya'. My mom will want to meet you, anyway," he continued. "I mean, since you practically saved my life and all, or at least my mp3 player."

His face reddened again, and he stood up, bending to pick up the cushion; he winced and grabbed his side, leaning away from the pain.

Feeling sorry for him, and still a little curious, she compromised, "Tell ya' what. I'll walk with you to the restaurant, to make sure you're safe, and then I gotta go, or I won't get to where I'm going in time.

"I'd like to stay, but I can't. Besides, your mom's a grown up and she'll feel sorry for me and call somebody or somethin'. She'll probably realize she's s..." She quickly looked down at the carpet. Yes, even if he was Stevey, it was best to wait and watch from a distance. The last time they were together didn't turn out well.

Tommy bit his lower lip. "Yeah, you're probably right. Well, let's look up that place you wanted to find first." Sadly he moved over to the computer and shook the mouse. The flat monitor awakened, and he immediately double clicked on the blue 'e' at the top of the screen.

"Okay, what's the name?"

"Paradise is the name of it, the name I've heard M..." she stopped short, realizing she was about to say mother, "That's what I've heard it called."

"Whaddya mean? Does it have another name?"

"No... I just... I don't know why I said that."

Tommy looked up at her, no recognition in his

eyes. Maybe he doesn't remember the story, she told herself.

He noted her expression, the panicked look in her eyes like she let a bad word slip, and he didn't ask any further questions, but his powers of reasoning knew what she had intended to say. "So, Paradise, like the street we're on, Paradise?" he pointed out the dingy window that faced a green street sign. Glancing out the window, she nodded, thinking how many coincidences she had experienced with that name, the many signs she had encountered with the word Paradise written on them, the impressions left on her at each location.

Recently this incident, the young boy who happened to be the same age as Stevey, and who just happened to resemble him, and whose apartment building just happened to be on Paradise Avenue. She wistfully longed to kiss the top of his head at that moment, thinking it would comfort him if he had gone through all the horror she had since that night. She had seen and felt her mother do the same so many times.

Click, click, clicking on the keyboard brought her attention away from the window to the computer monitor. She noted his quick typing skills as he entered into the search field: Paradise.

While the computer pulled up the list of sites related to the search, she wondered briefly of the street's name, its meaning to her immediate future.

What does this mean for me, meeting Tommy?

What is going to happen here? Will it be bad again? I just wish I knew before it did.

Obviously, she had been led here, just as she had been led to all of the other Paradise Avenues, Eden Streets, and Heavenly Lanes of the past. Could he be Stevey resurrected from ash? If so, it was just another reason for her to disappear, and soon... with him?

Outside, the noon sun beat down between the buildings, warming the city to an almost stifling temperature, even for November. So much for the cool November evening she had experienced last night.

Tiny beads of sweat formed on Cheater's forehead as she glanced across the parking area toward an adjacent apartment building, spotting the three boys who had beaten up Tommy. Apparently, Tommy had spotted them, too, his fear almost tangible, his pace quickening. "We'd better hurry, or we'll miss the lunch special."

Cheater felt his fear as if she had been the one who had taken the beating, and she glanced back at the three teens, their eyes following her and Tommy out the gated driveway.

The stray dog trotted behind them, stopping to drink from a puddle of water formed beneath an air conditioning unit. He glanced back at the boys, too, and gave a quick, low growl, a warning of defense; then he licked his nose and followed Tommy. Cheater expected the three muggers to follow as well, had actually hoped they would, but they didn't.

Across the distance, she made eye contact with the taller boy, and she thought his head nodded in acknowledgment, a barely traceable smile tilting the corner of his mouth, as if to reassure her that they were safe from harm.

His sudden change of heart, because of Cheater didn't puzzle her. She received the same reaction every time. Whenever she came upon someone in need of help, whenever she slipped into the darkness, the result was the same. She didn't know what wonderful event came upon them to caused those moments of change. She thought it strange that nobody mentioned it afterward, other than a simple thank you, before leaving with a complete reversal of attitude.

She fell in step behind the boy, peering closely at Jaz, feeling a connection unlike any other she had known before, sensing they would cross paths again, hoping they would. She would like to talk to him. Alone. Maybe he would tell her what happens when she blacks out.

Looking at him now, she found the searching in his eyes, too. That was the link. Like her, there was something, someone, he was searching for. He was being pulled and called like her. He was also alone. She could see that.

What had happened to him?

How many tragedies had he suffered?

Perhaps he knew why they'd suffered so much.

Quelling the urge to turn back to him and pull him away from his gang, talk to him, get answers to her unasked questions, she forced herself to turn away.

She couldn't go to him now. She couldn't do it for the same reason that she shouldn't be hanging around with Tommy, too many lives at risk. She couldn't add another.

Although this guy wasn't the nicest person she'd ever met, she didn't want to see him die. She didn't want anyone to die.

But they always did.

Still, why the connection, the feeling there's more?

Why was she drawn to this teenage mugger?

The reason lay in a corner of her mind, melting away behind a frozen glacier of memories into the turbulent waters of doubt. There was definitely something different about him, something drawing her to him. She'd never before met anyone who filled her with such a compulsion. While she stared, a segment of her dream, her nightmare, rolled up with a foamy wave, the faceless man...

Pulled from the verge of revelation, Tommy's voice, an echo in an underwater tunnel, prodded her on, "Hey, why'd ya' stop? Let's get outta here, quick. They might come this way. Come on!"

"Coming, Stevey." She squinted toward Jaz one last time; her lips tightened and eyes searched. "My name's not Stevey! Come on!" Jaz nodded again, knowingly, and made no move to follow. He turned away from her, back to the conversation with his mugger buddies.

A few littered blocks away from the apartment building, at the small diner, Tommy held the door open, and although Cheater could see business was slow, she shook her head timidly, waved, and walked away, the little dog tapping his nails on the cracked concrete walk behind her. Even if this was Stevey, he had to be safer now than he would be with her. She had to think of him, protect him.

Before she reached the barred, glass door of the next business, her profile matching her sluggish pace in the spotless plate glass window next to her, a woman's soft voice called out in a questioning lilt, "Um, Cheater... Won't you come in here and join Tommy for lunch? I'd like to talk to you."

If she had been a cursing girl, she would have flung out a few choice words right then, but at the same time, she had learned from experience that there was a reason for everything and to follow the paths of open doors, this door being that of a small diner with the incredible scent of a lunch special wafting up the sidewalk to her flaring nostrils, and with the half sausage biscuit long gone, her stomach growled again. She looked down at the little dog.

"I'll get your dog a bowl of water, and some scraps from the kitchen. Come on, before we start to get busy." She motioned with a tilt of her head. "I'm Tanya Wilkins. Why don't you sit at the counter with Tommy?" the touch of her hand on Cheater's back as she led her through the door sent a warm tingle up Cheater's spine and drew from somewhere deep within Cheater the almost lost memory of her own mother's touch, years ago. She wondered if this young mother would have touched her before Cheater had cleaned up, or if she would have turned her nose away in apathy. Knowing Tommy, she doubted Mrs. Wilkins would have turned away.

Cheater self-consciously settled at the counter next to Tommy who, head bobbing, held a big grin on his lips. While waiting for the Salisbury steak and mashed potato plates, he nibbled on crackers from a little basket, taking sips, between bites, from the sweet, cold cola sweating on the counter before him.

Cheater hadn't had a cola since her last movie night, and she took her time enjoying the sweet treat set before her, glancing back now and then at the little dog standing outside the window greedily eating the scraps and lapping the water. The moment of near normalcy brought a wishful smile to her face. Having a dog, a family, a place to be, a life shared by most other girls her age... and then she frowned, releasing the plastic straw from between her sweetened tongue and teeth, because she knew that it was an impossible dream for her to live.

Even if Tommy was Stevey and he had found a new home with Mrs. Wilkins, Cheater couldn't be a part of that. She knew. The only reason she'd remained this long was to find out if this boy was Stevey. It didn't matter, though. He couldn't go with her. She couldn't risk losing him again. It didn't make sense, why she was drawn here. Certainly not just so she could suffer his loss once more.

"So..." the woman's husky, gentle voice edged through her thoughts, "...you saved my son's life, huh? And saved his birthday present to boot. That much he told me in thirty seconds without taking a breath. Now, you two can tell me the rest of the story, more slowly, please." She smiled teasingly, and Cheater looked up from the soda she'd been staring into and up at the soft brown eyes of Tommy's mom. She was very pretty, Cheater decided, and she was a good person, with a strong, gentle heart. That much Cheater could see through the 'window to her soul,' as Sadie always used to put it. And this young mother loved this boy very much, no matter who he was.

A hesitant, shy smile played the corners of Cheater's mouth, as they looked at each other. She felt Mrs. Wilkins had learned all she needed to know by holding her gaze, and she quickly glanced back down into her cola.

The older woman turned to her son, "Say, aren't those Nina's clothes?" an eyebrow arched at Tommy suspiciously.

Tommy shot a sideways glance at Cheater, then tilted his blonde head at his mom, "She said to give them to Goodwill, Mom."

"I thought you said her name was Cheater?" Mrs. Wilkins whispered, smiling playfully at her son, and winking at Cheater.

"Mom, you are sooooo lame!" Tommy rolled his

eyes and shook his head.

He told the story of how Cheater had saved his life, embellishing the size of the boys. From his point of view though, his size and position on the ground, and the amount of fear shaking his limbs, they must have seemed larger than Jack's giant.

"Ten feet tall, huh? Wow!" the woman joked, interrupting, eyes huge.

When he mentioned the kick to his ribs, she rushed around the counter and lifted his shirt to check the bruise. Tommy leaned and moaned with embarrassment while Cheater giggled.

"Did you get a good look at them? Maybe we should call the police and have them..."

A bell rang from the kitchen stopping her mid-sentence, and Mrs. Wilkins floated over, spoke softly to the man who was cooking, gave him a pretty smile, and returned to the counter with two heaping plates of steaming brown mushroom gravy covering a mountain of mashed potatoes and a steak half the size of the plate. She set the plates down in front of them, followed by two small bowls of green beans, and rushed off to take out another order.

Before Cheater forked some creamy, steaming potatoes into her mouth to savor the rich, buttery thickness of them by holding them on her tongue and working them around her taste buds, she leaned toward Tommy. Gravy dripped from her fork as she whispered, "We can't let your mom call the police."

Tommy, sucking in food like a human vacuum

cleaner, nodded and continued bite after bite without breathing, until his mother told him to slow down.

"So, this the young hero?" a man's deep voice floated toward Cheater while he refilled a clear, red tinted, plastic cup with cola. Cheater's eyes moved up and up and up until they rested on the clearest, bluest, gentlest eyes she had seen since looking into her own father's eyes. She thought briefly of Tommy's ten feet tall description.

Tommy nodded, swallowing his mouthful, leaned over and said loudly, "That's my mom's boyfriend, Danny!" and a hand flew up out of nowhere right into the back of his head, almost pushing his face into the half mound of potatoes on his plate.

"Be quiet and eat your green beans!" his mother scolded.

"Just between you and me, Tommy, you know I would like to take your mom out on a date..." his voice lowered to a whisper, "...but I don't think she likes me."

"Don't you start, too, Danny!" She threatened, wound up the damp towel in her hand, and playfully popped it within inches of his hip.

"I'm retreating to the kitchen, now; don't shoot!" Danny pushed his backside into the swinging door to the kitchen, one hand in the air, the other shielding his face with the cola, then he winked at Tommy and Cheater through the little order window, "Maybe she does like me!"

They laughed and continued their meal.

"So, Cheater... That's an unusual name. Nickname?" Mrs. Wilkins glanced up while wiping the counter in front of them.

"Yes, Ma'am. You could say that." Cheater used a soft, golden dinner roll to mop up some extra mushroom gravy on her plate, and then bit into it closing her eyes savoring the flavor and texture.

"Last name?"

"Mom, don't be nosy!" Tommy spoke up, wide eyes pleading an urgent reminder to their previous deal.

"Okay, I was just having a conversation!" She stuck out her tongue and nosily continued, "Where do you live? Around here? I haven't seen you before. Did you just move here or are you visiting? People seem to move in and out of this neighborhood all the time." The questions streamed out, one after the other, and Cheater stared down at her plate, familiar with the routine, the look, the prodding. Her stomach knotted with uncertainty, and she slowly pushed her plate away.

"Mom, stop it!" Tommy's eyes grew.

"Okay, okay! I was just showing you what nosy is!" she flung her hands up and backed away from the counter, her elbows leaving smeared prints on the freshly cleaned black Formica.

"Anyway, it doesn't matter who you are or where you're from, thank you for helping my son. I would appreciate it if you would walk him back to the apartment and stay with him until I get off, if you can. Just in case something happens or he starts feeling sick. When I get home, I want to hear more about those boys. We should call the police." A concerned hand reached out, wiped at the too long bangs, touched the boy's forehead, as if feeling for fever, and then flipped the loose strands of hair out of his eyes.

"You need another haircut, buddy!" She smiled warmly at him and slid Cheater's plate back into place. "I'll be home around six tonight. I know he would enjoy having company!" Her eyes pleaded with Cheater. How could she say no to that motherly command?

"Unless she has a date!" Tommy teased. "I don't think we need to call the police, Mom. They didn't get anything, thanks to her!" He bobbed his head toward Cheater, whose relief came out in a large whoosh of breath she hadn't realized she was holding in.

Mrs. Wilkins thumped Tommy in the exact spot she had so lovingly touched moments earlier. "Well, as long as you're okay. If you have to go to the hospital, though..."

"I'm okay!" Tommy reassured her.

"Still, I would feel better if someone stayed with you until I got home!" She pleaded with the young girl again.

"I don't know... I should..." Cheater looked down into the sad, gray eyes of her new friend, and remembered another pair of gray eyes she couldn't say no to.

Stevey.

She thought about Tommy's attackers hanging around the complex. What would she do if she found out he was her brother? She wouldn't let him wander the streets of a city this size by himself.

Besides, what was her connection to that tall boy? She wanted to talk to him a little, and see if she could understand why she'd felt such a strong connection to him. Hanging out would put her that much closer to a place where the tall boy hangs out, giving her an opportunity to talk to him. But, it could also put Stevey—or Tommy—in danger. She needed more information about both of them. She had to take the risk.

"Okay, but just till you get home. Then I have to go." Cheater returned Mrs. Wilkins' grateful smile and finished her lunch.

Back at the apartment, Cheater sighed, slightly disappointed to find the small gang of muggers gone, but at least the drug dealer in the hallway was gone, too.

The cold, dim room saddened the visitor upon entry. Immediately, with a slap, he flipped the light switch up, drew the shades back, and placed the cheerful pot of daisies in the center of the shelf. In that location, the daisies sat in view of the shallowly breathing patient, should she awaken. He knew better, though.

He seated himself next to the hospital bed, in the uncomfortable wooden chair, the seat cushion so well used little padding remained, lumps forming beneath the green plastic coating. Reaching out, he took a slender, limp, dark hand in his own, and then gently began stroking the forehead and hair of the sleeping beauty before him with his free hand. Tears pooled in his dark eyes while guilt flooded his heart.

"Momma, I'm here. I know you already know that, and I realize I haven't been here in a while. I haven't exactly been doin' things that would make you proud the past few months, either, and I'm sorry.

"I hope you don't know too much about that, but I've just been so angry.

"Just be glad I ain't in jail!" He paused, waited, hoped that her eyes would flutter and he would see that disappointing look she always gave him when he transgressed. Her silence pushed him onward in the one-sided conversation.

"You'll never guess what happened to me this morning,!" Excitement brought trembling words, dimmed only slightly by a guilty tone. He continued on hopefully, sounding almost chipper. "I was doin' one of those things I shouldn'ta been doin', one of them things you wouldn't be proud of? And this girl walked up, ya' know?" he paused again, this time not for a response from the comatose woman before him, but out of fear that what he was about to tell her might be overheard. As he remembered the event, disbelief almost stopped him from retelling it.

Anyone listening outside might think him crazy when they heard the description of what he saw that morning, what he wanted his mother to know. After raising his eyes to the open door and the slatted window looking out on an empty hall, he leaned forward, close to her left ear, her light, slow breath warming his cool forehead, "I saw Bree this morning, Momma.! I saw her, and she told me I had to come see you. She made it sound important, Momma... you know... like you might wake up today or somethin'. She knew I hadn't been here in a while, too. Her smile, Momma, man I sure miss her smile. Remember how pretty she smiled, Momma? Remember the sparkle in her eyes? I saw her today, Momma, and it made me so happy, but it made me feel guilty, too." He stopped, stood nervously for a second, leaned forward again, and gripped the motionless, slender, brown hand, a sense of urgency filling his heart.

"Wake up, Momma. You can wake up now; you can come back to me; it's safe,. I need you, especially now. At least give me a sign you can hear me, Momma, please?" a tear rolled down his cheek, a drip of condensation slipping down a plum. Her eyes were dry, still and tightly closed. When no sign came, he scooted back in the chair, folded his hands together, set his elbows on the edge of the bed and bowed his head in silent prayer, something he hadn't done in months, since he had given up on her... on life.

"Hey!" A soft female voice called from the hallway, interrupting his repeated prayer, first causing a start of joy, and then anger as he turned away from the face.

When his face fell at the sight of the young dark complexioned nurse in the doorway, she quickly apologized, "I'm so sorry for interrupting. I just wanted to let you know there's been no change, no movement, except spasms. Have you been okay? We haven't seen you in a while!" In spite of her sad countenance, her eyes crinkled with a smile as she moved into the room.

"Yeah, I been busy." Jaz switched to the tough-guy facade he often used these days when talking to girls. At one time, he'd had a crush on this pretty nurse, but he soon realized she was engaged, and much older than she appeared, therefore, uninterested in him. He had taken it personally. He still held an emotional grudge, mostly out of embarrassment.

"Oh, sure. I imagine school keeps you busy. You're probably involved in various after school activities, too. I used to be that way!" She smiled broadly.

"Yeah… after school activities… sure." His voice dispelled a coolness he had not intended to use. If she only knew about his after-school activities! If she only knew about his during school activities, the ones he took part in when he didn't go to school, which was every day.

"Well, everything is reset." She said more to herself after pushing the buttons of the various machines that monitored the unconscious woman; His terse reply distanced her from the emotional side of patient contact. She sensed that something troubled the young man, aside from wanting his mother to awaken, but she didn't pry. "I hope we'll get to see you more often, now!" She sadly turned and left the room.

He glanced after her, making certain she was beyond earshot before continuing, "Momma, if you come back, I bet Daddy would, too, just like Bree did. He would come back to you, Momma, and he would help you, make you see that you need to leave that man, Momma. Please come back, so we can see Daddy." His heart ached at the thought of his father, the painful death he suffered years ago, the cancer that had eaten away his young body when Jaz was only ten. He could hardly picture his father anymore, but he had wonderful memories of times he spent with him in their old home, on fishing trips, tossing a football in the backyard, reading a book together in the spacious study.

Weeks of sitting by his father's fading side with his heart broken mother and angry sister—his seemingly unanswered prayers floating in the air in search of The Great Listener—overtook the happy memories more often than not, which made sitting in the hospital now with his mother, hands folded, head bowed, even more difficult. At least with his father's long-term stay, he had his mother's and sister's hands to hold, their strength to lean on. Now, while he sat here, tenderly speaking and holding his mother's lifeless hand, he had no one to lean on. This time he had given up on prayer, but after this morning, he found himself slowly starting to believe again, somewhat. Because of that girl, that scraggly homeless girl who had just happened to stop him from adding another crime to the list of many he had already committed.

No movement followed his pleading speech, and comparisons of past and present made him angry again. He released the delicate, limp hand, laid it back on the bed at her side, and moved toward the window, slamming his fist down on the solid brick ledge, and then shaking the pain out of it. When the view out of the barred window offered no comfort, he moved back over to the bedside.

"Momma, I don't know how much longer I can

handle stayin' in that apartment. I can't leave, not while you're like this. Please wake up, so's we can move on, Momma. I'll get you outta this place! I will, Momma!" No answer. No movement. No sign. Never a sign.

"Well, I gotta go, now. When I come back, I'll tell you the story, Momma, the story you always told me, remember? About Paradise?" He leaned forward and lightly kissed her soft, cool, cheek; stroked her fine, dark hair; touched the white, gauze bandage on her forehead, an iridescent ghost on a moonless night. His fingers gently stroked the teardrop pendant at her throat, her favorite necklace. He'd brought it up to her two days after the accident, hoping it would magically wake her, the only item the staff allowed him to keep on her. He quietly left the once dark and dreary room that now seemed to shimmer with light, hope and floral fragrance.

He had to find that girl.

He had to talk to her.

He needed to find out how she did that.

He needed to tell her a secret that he hadn't told anyone else.

"You should just stay the night. I mean, it's already so late. Honestly, I didn't mean to work this late, but the evening waitress had car trouble. Look, it's so dark outside!" Mrs. Wilkins pulled the flimsy curtains back and swung her hand toward the blackened window, a slight flip of fingers for emphasis, reminding Cheater of the times she had watched Wheel of Fortune with Sadie. Just like Vanna White showing prizes on The Wheel, Mrs. Wilkins smiled revealing her perfect white teeth. "Surely one night won't put you off schedule too much? Besides, where would you sleep? I would worry after all you've done for Tommy."

Cheater hoped Mrs. Wilkins didn't see the glimmer of relief on her face before she steeled herself against the offer. She dreaded another park bench. Besides, by this time of night she had found her safe place to settle in, whether it was woods or a lone concrete slab well away from the rest of the world, or a bench in a non busy bus stop, she was always settled at dark awaiting daylight. Plus, she hadn't gleaned any information from Stevey, or Tommy, about his past. She wanted to know if he was her brother, if somehow he had survived.

She also felt the unrelenting compulsion to stay. One night here might actually buy her enough time to talk to that mugger boy, too.

Doubt filled her mind, though. Doubts that included memories of all the families she had stayed with for short times or long, and all the deaths that had taken place, the alleged death of her own brother.

She told herself that she didn't have to stay in this apartment to see that other boy again. She could leave right now, and she would probably find him in some other forsaken act.

No, she knew better than that. He was changed now, just like the others. And there was something else about him, something she couldn't quite finger.

A night in a real bed versus the hard, dirty ground outside, or the chill of a metal bench; a wonderful breakfast, instead of a dumpster meal; a loving family, instead of a deep, cold loneliness were necessities she longed for, necessities that tempted her to stay.

Since the fire, she hadn't known those familial comforts. That fire she believed took her little brother; he would be the same age as Tommy. It took her mother, too, a mother as loving, or more so than Mrs. Wilkins. Cheater shook her head, as much at the past as in answer to the woman before her, but Mrs. Wilkins was already taking out extra blankets from the hall closet.

"I will not, absolutely cannot, as the mother of

a young child, let you go out into the dark toward some unknown destination at this time of the night! No, ma'am. Especially not after what happened to my son today, and what you did for him.

"And besides those muggers are probably lurking out there, waiting this very moment for you to leave this building so they can attack you while you least expect it. Gangs are like that, and they probably belong to some gang. You'll stay, and that's final. You can have Tommy's bed, and he can sleep on the floor in my room for tonight. That's final, young lady!" She glared firmly, a smile tilting her eyes as Cheater shook her head.

"But, my dog..." Cheater started. "Tommy?" Mrs. Wilkins questioned.

The boy grinned, and then opened the door to the hallway. The little dog trotted by him to stand next to Cheater.

"You're staying and that's that!"

Having been ordered as a mother would order, Cheater had no choice but to accept the invitation. She had been taught early in life not to be rude, to respect her elders, but she was genuinely afraid of what might happen if she stayed, and with good reason. Regardless, she would be on full alert throughout the night, probably sleep less than if she were curled up in the woods, and leave as soon as she could in the morning.

Perhaps that mugger boy would be coming in from his nightly pursuits about the time she left in the morning. She hadn't seen him at all since their return to the apartment. She glanced out the cracked window several times hoping to see him in the courtyard.

She was tired. For now, a warm, soft bed, called her name and she was being prodded to accept it by a very caring person. She didn't encounter many caring people these days. Caving to the invitation, she thought to sneak away after a short power nap. After she helped Mrs. Wilkins make the bed and prepare Tommy's pallet on the floor, she went her separate way to the land of dreams, the little dog padding behind her.

Cheater wanted to stay awake, tried to stay awake, but her clown-in-the-box eyelids kept closing and popping open at every sound.

She lay on top of the covers—fully clothed and ready to run—listening to the loud noises of the city, of the apartment building, always jarring her awake, but never for long. She'd grown used to noisy places at night. The little dog's warm, sleeping body against her leg didn't help either.

Sadie's voice was the real culprit stealing her sleep, "History repeats itself, baby girl, always."

Sometime after one in the morning, once she had drifted away again to the loud, booming music of a radio in some apartment room below her, and just before the 'faceless man' dream could steal her into its paralytic terror, she heard the floor creak at the foot of the bed, felt the little dog's head raise, and was jerked awake, again. Tommy stood there, pallet of blankets in hand.

"You awake?" He whispered peering into the darkness at her. There was no security light outside his window, so the room was dimly lit by the waning moon. Cheater could only make out his silhouette.

"Uh, yeah, what's up?"

"Mind if I sleep in here on the floor? Mom sometimes snores loud. She has bad allergies."

Cheater giggled, picturing the pretty, blonde, freckled mother with her mouth drooped open and her nose roaring. "Sure. Come on in."

He placed his blankets on the floor and lay down, the little dog leaving Cheater's side to lie next to him. "You know Mom didn't work late, right? She was out with Danny. He likes her. No, I think he loves her. He's been trying to get her to move us in with him, but Mom won't do it."

Tommy leaned on his elbow and peered up from the pallet on the floor toward Cheater's light breath, the only object he could focus on in the shadows. His other hand stroked the little dog—who now lay next to him—to sleep again.

"So, how would you feel about that? Do you like Danny? Would that bother you? Him not being your dad and all?"

"Shoot no! Danny has this humongous house that his aunt left him, out in the country, on lots of land. I would love to live there. Mom just won't do it, though. She likes him, but I don't know why she won't get together with him. He would make a great dad. He's fun to hang out with."

Cheater had hoped to be alone in the room. It would have made sneaking away so much easier. She was glad Tommy came in to talk, though. She just didn't know how to question him about his real identity.

"Maybe your mom's feelings about that have something to do with your dad? Maybe she still loves him.

"Or maybe, you know, sometimes it's hard for people to trust other people when they get hurt," she offered with real conviction. "What happened between her and your dad?"

"I don't know. He left when I was two, and she didn't have a job or nothing. They got married right out of high school, and he got a job, but one day he just left for work and never came back. We had to move before the rent was due again. Mom says he was bipolar or something."

Stevey was two when I was five, when the fire happened, Cheater puzzled. "Well, then she probably doesn't want to be left without a home or money again. Do you think your dad will come back?"

"Nah. We haven't heard from him, and Mom doesn't want to, either. She says she's afraid for me to get close to him and then him run out again. I look just like him, though. She showed me a picture."

"Can I see it?" Cheater perked up.

"No. It's gone now. I don't know what happened

to it. I remember it, though."

"Hmm. Do you think your mom loves Danny?" How could I ask him whether she's his mother? He probably wouldn't remember, anyway.

"Yeah... maybe... I don't know. But she could still work if we moved in with him, just not as long of days. Then, she could be there when I get home. Danny would work, too, but I could hang out with him more," silence again. Then, "He's cool! We could go fishin' and stuff. And I could go to another school. And no more drug dealers and gangs. I'd like that."

"Yeah, that would be nice. Hey, Tommy? Do you remember anything about your life before your dad left?"

Tommy's voice had trailed off with the last sentence as his arm relaxed, his head resting on it and the pillow, and he quietly drifted off to sleep. Cheater doubted he had even heard her question.

She thought about the happy picture Tommy had painted just before conking out, wishing she could be a part of it, but it would never happen. She couldn't risk it.

For one slight moment, she fell into a well of self-pity, another of Sadie's phrases playing through her thoughts, her sad memories of the past, "What goes around comes around... what goes around comes around... what goes..."

She wondered what had gone around in her own life, what she had done, to have to suffer the events that had happened to her.

What did all of the other people she met in her travels do to deserve what they had gotten? She wished she could tell Tommy that her dad had just walked away from home and never came back, but that wasn't what had happened. She wished now that it were. He would probably remember what happened, if he was Stevey, but she wouldn't find out tonight.

Her dad had been her hero! But, at what expense to her? She was the one still here, the one who had lost everything. Yes, she wished he was just bipolar instead of dead, and then she could search for him and maybe live with him, get him some help.

Not usually prone to self-pity and why-me thoughts, Cheater soon grew tired of thinking and turned her attention to the one who haunted her, the faceless man in her dream. Soon she felt herself falling into the dream, tossing, turning, trying to see the face, the face she held responsible for all the bad things that had happened to her.

On the verge of recognition, the face floated into her view, featureless as always. A familiar voice called out, "Look at him!"

The voice repeated the message.

"You must find him!"

As she turned toward the hovering face, the edges of his features beginning to clear, a familiar smell wormed its way to her nostrils, prodding the recesses of her sleeping brain, startling her awake. The little dog sent up a sharp bark and turned anxious circles in front of the door.

The pungent smell grew stronger as she blinked her heavy eyelids open with the sound, and she jumped from the bed, waking Tommy as distant sirens filled her ears.

8

Boom! The slamming door rattled the thin walls, echoed down the hallway into the closet sized bedroom, and startled Jaz to action. He had been lying on the bed, staring up at the dark ceiling, contemplating where he would go, could go, how soon he could leave, what would happen if he did. His canvas bag lay in wait in the locker like closet, but his ideas shattered with the reverberating sound.

He wasn't supposed to be in his room; he was supposed to be in the kitchen, making sure that dinner was ready.

"Boy! Where the hell are you? You better get in here! Is my food ready you lazy little punk?" A voice more terrifying than the roar of a predator resounded from the kitchen as Jaz entered the living room. Inner quakes worked their way to his skin, prickling goose flesh. He knew what was coming next.

He feared what was coming next.

The slurred words struck and bounced off the thin walls around the teen; the big burly man turned slowly, staggering circles in the middle of the floor, as if lost in an unfamiliar environment. "I... uh, you were late... I... your dinner's ready!" Jaz rushed around the large man, hoping to avoid the iron hard fists hanging from muscle bound arms the size of tree trunks, but the man's reach was too long.

Jaz felt the blow to the back of his head before he could pull open the door of the microwave oven. Tripping forward, he gripped the counter to keep from falling, biting his tongue to avoid the cuss word at its tip, the word that would bring a worse beating.

Tasting the familiar bitterness of his own blood from his swelling tongue, he pushed the button to open the microwave. The back of his head throbbed, and before the big man could strike again, he turned toward him, plate in hand.

"I thought I told you never to use that damn microwave for my dinner, boy! Ah... give it here! You're about a worthless piece of crap, you know that? I ain't never met a kid so damn stupid!" The man challenged, standing eye to eye with Jaz, who quickly looked to the floor in mock agreement. The breath of The Beast smelled of cheap liquor, his uniform of cheap perfume.

"And it's none or your damn business when I come in!" He backhanded the boy hard on the right side of his face before jerking open a drawer, yanking out a fork, and sitting down.

Heat stung Jaz's face, the heat of anger welling up like the torrent of steam building in a teapot about to explode.

Jaz squinted at the knife rack. As much as he wanted to, Jaz couldn't strike back. He knew better, knew if he did, The Beast would bull him over, and he'd wind up next to his sister, or worse, next to his mother. Momentarily, he believed that not to be a bad result for striking back. At least he wouldn't be here; The Beast would no longer be a threat. The stringy haired homeless girl flashed into his mind, and he remembered their earlier meeting, knew he wanted to speak to her about what she had done that morning.

She could solve some of his problems, probably not this one, but some of them. He capped his anger, standing tall.

"What is this crap, anyway?" His stepfather forked the food a few times before bringing some to his lips. "Shit's cold! Ah, never mind!" He flung the plate behind him, spinning it to the floor. "You iron my other uniform, or are you too stupid to do that right, too?" His temper bounded again.

"Yes sir, I ironed it. I can make you somethin' else for dinner." Jaz cowered—fear distinguishing the anger and taking control again—crossed his forearms in front of his face, and wished he had some undetectable poison to take care of this particular problem.

Blocking the punches was useless, and with the first one he fell to the kitchen floor, slid across the filthy linoleum, and moaned, as he learned to do years ago, faking injury.

The big man would surely kill him if he fought back, but that's not all. Jaz was terrified of what else this monstrous being, three times the size of Jaz, would do to his mother, her innocent body lying in stillness in that hospital, hope dangling.

"I don't need no damn dinner!" Jaz stifled the reply on his lips; You sure don't! He let the heavyset man rant on, "I'm goin' to bed! Why don't you get yo'self a job boy, runnin' drugs or somethin'? Get us outta this rat hole? Huh?" He stomped down the hall —after planting a well-rounded kick into Jaz's ribcage—and slammed his bedroom door, rattling walls with his fury.

Get ME outta this rat hole and let the rats have you! Jaz sneered to himself, still lying on the kitchen floor, holding his throbbing head, tasting the salty blood that pooled at the corner of his mouth, feeling the agonizing bruise already spreading at his side. The satisfying thought about thousands of rats nibbling away on that huge body down the hall helped him push to his feet. Temptation to wander dark alleys in search of the nasty rodents spurred his adrenaline.

Only when the Beast tired did the apartment become completely silent, free of yelling, snoring or any sound of slumber. Only then did Jaz quietly clean up the scattered dinner and broken plate. He knew what the morning would be like if he didn't.

Afterward, he slipped noiselessly down the hall to his own darkened room, closed and locked the bedroom door, and opened his closet.

The worn, old bag, still beneath the folded clothing he kept in the farthest corner of his closet—which doubled as a chest of drawers—lay untouched in the night. He pulled it from its hiding place, unzipped it carefully, and removed the hidden treasures of his past.

First, the family photograph that he wasn't allowed to keep out in the open of his room, then the rhinestone encrusted denim jacket, his sister's jacket that his mother had bought for her sixteenth birthday. The few hair ties he kept still held the scent of his sister's hair; he brought them to his nose now, nostrils flaring, taking in the comforting smell. The small bottle of perfume he gave his sister for Christmas last year—now almost empty—she had loved more than any other gift, but it had earned her more than the usual homecoming response from The Beast. He fingered the tiny bottle he had selected so carefully for his sister, and moved it aside.

His change of clothes was still rolled up at the bottom of the bag. Anything and everything he valued was in this bag, especially the silver crucifix his father left him, which now glimmered in the tiny bit of light shining through the one window in his room. The crucifix his grandmother had given to his father the day Jaz was born, the only link to his grandmother that remained. He thought about the pendant his mother had given to Bree, that precious family heirloom that disappeared the night of her d...

A tear dripped into the open bag. He wiped his cheek with the back of his hand before replacing everything into the small canvas bag and returning it to its dark corner.

One day, I'll take that bag out for the last time and never see this closet again! Maybe tomorrow, he thought, before closing the door on his valuable secret and sliding onto his bare mattress for the night. Sleep wouldn't come, though. He lie awake in the dark, listening for The Beast, fearing him, expecting him to awaken any moment and demand that Jaz cater to him. Another sleepless night of fear filled his room, the apartment, his world. He lay awake listening, but the only sounds were the sirens.

"Tommy, get up! Fire! Get up!"

Once Cheater had Tommy fully awake and turned out the door, she ran into his mother's room, only to find her sitting on the edge of the bed, grabbing for clothing, shoes, and a small leather covered book on the bed table.

"What is it? What's all the noise?" She pushed her sleepy blonde strands away from her tired eyes and peered through the dark at Cheater.

Cheater looked down at her apologetically, not believing that this could be happening again, especially to this wonderful mother, innocent Tommy. It no longer mattered whether she discovered the truth about him. Being near him put him in danger.

"There's a fire! Hurry, please, we have to get out of here!" Cheater urged, gently pulling the woman to her feet by her elbow before running to the front door of the apartment, images of a past fire burning through her thoughts, flames engulfing fresh memories from earlier that day. Mrs. Wilkins' footsteps sounded behind her.

Cheater felt the cool door with her slender hands, long fingers groping in the darkness for the knob, and then pulled the door open yelling "Fire! Fire!" down the hallway. How many others live here?

How many others will die this night because of me? She feared they all would.

The three desperate people banged on doors as they moved toward the stairwell. Mother and son pulled on clothing and shoes over their pajamas while hopping and scurrying down the hall. But when they reached the stairwell door, they discovered a heat so intense that they couldn't get within three feet.

"Fire escape!" Tommy ran back toward the apartment. Doors flew open on either side of the dingy hallway; groggy, pajama-clad sleepy-eyed tenants sought the cause of the disturbance, smelled smoke and panicked.

"You'll have to use your fire escapes!" Mrs. Wilkins called out as she moved the kids back toward the apartment.

Pulling the dingy curtains away from the big window above the fire escape, she flipped the latches on either side and pushed the window upward. It moved about three inches and stopped, years of decay holding it in place. She lifted some more, grunting and groaning with the effort, and then she pushed it back down, raising it with force again. No luck.

Cheater ran to the kitchen and picked up a heavy, old, metal diner chair. "Stand back!" She shouted, throwing the chair at the window with all her might. The window shattered. The hissing and popping noises of the burning building filtered through just beyond the closed front door. A loud crash sounded from the end of the hallway, where the exit door to the stairwell had been five minutes ago, its wooden frame melted away like ice cream on a hot day.

"We have to hurry!" Tommy's mom retrieved a dirty towel from the hamper and used it to push out the broken glass. She wiped out the window frame, so they wouldn't cut themselves on the way out. Then she threw the chair back into the apartment, creating a loud thump on the stained carpet.

Once on the fire escape, the night air reassured Cheater that everyone would get out alive. She wouldn't have to relive a nightmare after all. Tommy and his mother would be okay. A desperate bark sounded behind her, and she looked down to find her new friend staring at someone across the courtyard, hackles raised.

"Damn!" She heard Mrs. Wilkins yell. "The fire escape is stuck, too. What are we going to do? We can't jump; we're three floors up. That stupid Super! If anybody dies in this fire…" She stopped, tears of fear and frustration filling her eyes.

"Mom, did you flip the latch?" Tommy moved over the fire escape landing to the drop down ladder, bent over, and flipped a latch out and up, releasing a pin. The ladder dropped, and they scooted down carefully, one after the other, onto the next fire escape below them. The motionless little dog gripped Cheater's shoulder, digging his tiny claws into her shirt for support. Down that fire escape to the next one, but on the last their luck ran out. There wasn't a ladder to drop. And nobody had lived in either of the two apartments behind them in the time since Tommy and his mother had moved in.

"Great! Well, at least we're only one floor up now. We can probably jump and live!" She shouted over the roar of flames already engulfing the building. They could see the fire glowing brightly somewhere in the apartment behind them through the dirty window, the heat battling the cool night air for their attention, hot flames chomping the old wood and flammable materials within.

Cheater looked down from the fire escape, the little dog barked, beside her now, wagging its tail. She turned her gaze in the direction of his.

Sirens blared through the clear night sky.

The tallest of the teenage muggers, muscles straining, carried a mattress over his head, arms spread to the side as if he were trying to catch a strong wind and fly; a larger man in tee shirt and shorts from another apartment followed closely behind him.

The two strangers lay the mattresses side by side below the fire escape and Tommy, like the adventurous boy that he was, jumped before his mother could stop him. He hit a mattress, rolled, stood up with his fist in the air, and yelled, "Yes!" Then he turned his face up to his mother. "Come on, Mom! Hurry!"

Mrs. Wilkins looked down. She looked at Cheater. "You go first. Children first."

"No, go ahead, I'll be fine. I've been through this b...! I mean... I'll be fine!" She stammered, immediately regretting her remark, "Go! Tommy's waiting!" Cheater yelled over the intense crackling of the burning building, trying to draw Mrs. Wilkins' attention from her blunder of truth.

Tommy's mom stared curiously at Cheater for a moment, turned back to the mattress, threw down to her son what few belongings she had grabbed on the way out, and jumped toward the ground, her loose fitting cotton shirt billowing around her waist, her blonde hair streaming upward. Cheater followed as soon as Mrs. Wilkins cleared the mattresses, a silent prayer of thanks for the unfamiliar good ending catching in her throat while she torpedoed to the ground.

She was surprised to see Jaz, below, still there, risking recognition, looking strangely at her before catching the little dog and setting him down.

The tall teen, the neighbor, and the three evacuees moved from one fire escape to the next, looking for people in need of help. They moved the mattresses only once before the fire engines roared to life in the parking lot. Red lights illuminating the grounds, sirens silenced, firemen forcing everyone back away from the building.

Standing in the courtyard, watching the flames lick greedily at what once was their home, shivering from the near danger and the cool night air, the onlookers took in the sight of the firemen urgently fighting an already lost battle, the building too old, the fire too strong. All their efforts led only to the salvation of neighboring buildings, just as old and worn.

Tommy thought about his computer, his MP3 player, and the few clothes he owned. All was now lost as he stared at the charred, flaming remains beyond the third story window; tears suddenly flooded his eyes.

Mrs. Wilkins wondered where they were going to go, how she would find the money for another deposit and first and last month's rent. How would they start over having nothing to start over with? Their burning home reflected fiery wells in her sad eyes, too.

Cheater blamed herself for this disaster, and all those before. She decided it could have been prevented had she not agreed to stay the night, had she not gotten so comfortable with them, or not desired to find out Tommy's true identity.

The parallels of past lives and present ones were too strong to believe it was only coincidence. Her only consolation was that nobody had died, this time.

"Hey, it wasn't your fault. I know what caused this fire. It wasn't you." A deep male voice whispered close to her ear.

She turned her head slightly to glimpse the

speaker's face from the corner of her eye. Jaz, the tall mugger face, aglow with red and orange reflections, a darkening spot plainly visible on his forehead, stood away from the others and just to her left.

Her puzzled expression did not shock him; he looked back expectantly before continuing, "There's a meth lab in the basement of that building. The jerk that runs it probably went off and left something cookin', ya' know? Been doin' it for years. The Super gets a kickback for not reporting him to the police. They'll be investigatin' this time, though, 'cause I called 'em, right after I saw the fire, and gave an anonymous tip just before the fire trucks pulled in." He nodded toward the police cruisers entering the lot.

Cheater panicked when she saw them. That was the last thing she needed. Just play it cool, act like you're with Mrs. Wilkins, one of the family, she told herself, turning her head away from the onslaught of authorities.

"Don't worry. They ain't even gonna notice you. They'll be goin' after the Super first thing. Look!"

"How'd you...?" She stopped, replaying what Jaz had said to her, she faced him, searching his eyes, his sympathetic features.

This was the same boy who had hurt Tommy less than twenty-four hours ago. She hadn't expected him to change so drastically that this display of kindness and justice could be the same person. Was it real or just some act? And how did he know what she was thinking about the fire, about the police?

Before she could question him further, he turned and moved back toward his apartment, a deep, angry voice calling out to him "Hey stupid! Get your worthless, lazy, good for nothin' ass back over here! And bring that mattress back, you little punk!"

Her gaze followed him, watching as he moved swiftly over to the mattress, his bowed head shaking. He hefted the mattress overhead, his muscular arms bulging under the weight; his head bent forward and he carried it across the parking area, easily sliding it through the open door.

Cheater, her back now to the flaming building, saw the enraged, heavily built, man smack the teen in the back of the head. She heard the hurtful words slung in the younger man's direction.

She winced when the boy received a kick so hard that he tumbled forward into a blackened room and was certain the mattress fell atop him.

She fumed when the older man slammed the door on the world in need before him.

Sympathy for Jaz, his situation, welled inside her, and though she still wasn't certain she could trust him, she now understood a little more about him.

"Tommy, we can't. It would just be too..."

"Mom, c'mon! What else are we gonna do? Live on the street?" Tommy regretted the words as soon as he spoke them. He eyed Cheater apologetically. Mrs. Wilkins had already deduced the same of Cheater, but Tommy's look in her direction confirmed it. Cheater didn't have a place to go, either.

Returning to the argument at hand, mother and son glared at each other. One pleaded, the other defied. The three wore the smoky clothing they had on before jumping from the fire escape on the second story of the building earlier that morning. Tommy's mom blew out a long sigh glancing back and forth between the two children across the table.

Cheater felt like an outsider, squeezed between Tommy and the window in the red plastic booth seat. Try as she might, Mrs. Wilkins could not include her in their plans. She didn't know it yet, but Cheater wasn't moving in with them. She already knew what she had to do, and nobody could argue with destiny. No matter how much she had tried herself, it always ended badly when she did.

She let her attention retreat to the interior of the diner she had been too nervous, and too hungry, to notice the day before; the chrome and red leather padded bar with matching stools where she had eaten yesterday; she noted her reflection in the base of the chrome counter. It was so clean.

The rows of bright red vinyl booths with white Formica tables, balanced on wide chrome bases and legs, the black and white checked tiles on the floor that reminded her of a giant checker board, the mini jukeboxes at each booth, one of which her fingers flipped pages now.

It was like one of those diners that her mother always took them to, a throwback to the 50's, a time when her grandmother had been a teenager, a place where they enjoyed root beer floats and burgers when she was little. Cheater felt like she was in a scene from "Happy Days" an old show she had enjoyed in the afternoons at Sadie's after they'd finally left the Home for the day.

Danny breezed through the swinging doors of the kitchen, eyes on Cheater, breaking her train of thought; a large round platter balanced on his hand, he glided swiftly toward the booth.

"Here ya' go. Let's see, eggs and bacon for the little hero, and hmmm..." he searched around the platter, skimming the only plate left, "oh, yeah, bacon and eggs for the big hero!" He set the second plate before Cheater.

Her stomach rumbled as she bit into the steaming, soft biscuit, but it ached, too, with the strange sensation of guilt she always felt after each tragedy that haunted her. Guilt mixed with the soft biscuit and caused a hard lump in the pit of her stomach. She reminded herself that nobody had died in last night's fire.

She gulped some milk to wash down the knot of biscuit and conflicting guilt.

"And what else? Oh yeah!" He slid a key across the table with his fingertip, "A place to live for the lady?" He wiggled into the booth next to Mrs. Wilkins, resting his arm on the bench behind her back, eyebrows raising in question, ears jumping with the effort. Tommy raised an eyebrow at Cheater, giving her an 'I told you so' look.

Mrs. Wilkins began to argue, but Tommy's pleading look and Danny's charming smile stopped her opposing remarks. She sipped the steaming dark coffee instead, eyes staring forward over the top of the cup, across the table at Cheater, probing curiously into the sad face that stared down at the empty fork twirling in her hand, poking and pushing around the scrambled eggs on the plate.

"Okay, but only until we can afford to get our own place again. And that's the arrangement. Danny? Tommy...?"

"Yep. Sure. Okay. So, soon as you young heroes are finished stockpiling the kitchen into your bellies, we'll head over to my place and get you set up. Then we better go find that furry fellow some real food!" He nodded toward the little terrier mix, tail wagging, bottom teeth bared in a doggy smile aimed at the four on the other side of the wall length window, content after his meager meal of biscuits soaked in bacon grease. "I'll call Charlie to come in and cover."

"We can wait, Danny, until your shift's up. Besides, I go on in about an hour. I don't want anybody to get upset, or have to rearrange their plans. I would hate for us to lose our jobs." Mrs. Wilkins sipped the hot coffee again, frowning up at him.

"Oh, I seriously doubt they would fire me. There might be serious repercussions for that. The manager can't just fire the owner you know. And, you, my Lady, are not working today! You covered for Tina last night; she can come in this morning." He slid two quarters across the table to Cheater, and told her play some good old fashioned music, like Elvis or the Beatles, and then he left the booth to make the calls, leaving them in stunned silence: Mrs. Wilkins because as long as she had worked at the small diner she hadn't learned that Danny owned it until just now; Tommy because he had discovered his mom had worked late last night and was not on a date as he thought; and Cheater because she had no idea what kind of music to play. She thumbed the pages of the mini jukebox between bites.

"Wow!" Tommy grinned and nodded. His shaggy hair gave off a scent of smoke with every flip before falling into his eyes.

His life was about to change for the better. It was exactly what he had told Cheater he wanted the night before, well, except, his mom and Danny weren't getting married... yet. Still, he suddenly became the happiest boy in the world. As only a young human vacuum cleaner can, he sucked down his food and smiled dreamily.

"Here, I'll play something!" He reached over Cheater, inserted the quarters and flipped a page in the mini jukebox with a sheepish look on his face while his mother lectured him on the digestive problems he would have if he kept inhaling his food.

After punching some buttons, a song began, and Mrs. Wilkins covered her ears with her hands, playfully mouthing, "Noooooo!"

Danny danced his way back from the phone to the first verse of Girlfriend.

Cheater and Tommy laughed in unison.

Cheater felt a small pointy elbow in her side and felt the whisper move her hair, "Can you tell Mom loves this song?"

"It's not Elvis..." Danny slid in next to Mrs. Wilkins "...but it'll do!" He winked at the kids across from him.

Though Tommy's life was getting better, Cheater's life would remain the same, as it always did, because she was not going home with them. In spite of the comforting thought that Jaz gave her about the fire, she still couldn't shake the feeling that the fire was connected to her. Somehow, her being in that apartment with the Wilkins' had put their lives in danger, even though it seemed to have worked out for them. She consoled herself with the idea that if this boy was Stevey, and Mrs. Wilkins had adopted him, then at least he would be safe and happy now. And she knew where to find him later.

She savored the taste of the cold milk as it coated the remains of biscuit in her mouth, realizing it could be some time before she had the opportunity to eat a breakfast like this again, but the lump of loneliness in her throat had fallen to her stomach with the biscuit. She felt horrible about what had happened, what always happened, to everyone she loved or cared about.

She excused herself from the table and headed toward the 'EXIT' sign at the other end of the diner, but not before Mrs. Wilkins noted the pained expression on her face.

The little terrier mix wagged his tail when they stepped out the door, his toenails tap-tap-tapping musically toward them on the concrete walk.

Cheater picked up the Styrofoam bowls he had eaten and drank from and threw them in the trash can next to the door.

She knelt, stroking the dog's head, purposely furthering the distance between herself, the Wilkins', and Danny who moved toward the car. The little furry body relaxed under her touch. It hadn't taken long for him to trust her, for him to return her love. It seemed animals were the only love she was allowed to have in this life, the only companions she couldn't hurt. He rolled over on the sidewalk and bared his belly to her. She worried about him while she scratched gently.

"Come on, girl. Bring your little friend with ya'! He'll need some things, too," Danny prodded.

Cheater remained mostly still, her sad eyes downcast, petting the dog, a whirlwind of emotions causing her throat to close up and her stomach to lurch. "I can't. I need to get on my way," she choked out. "I'm a day behind schedule already." She shook her head to fight back tears while she swallowed the lie.

She would love nothing more than to stay with them; it would be just like eight years later with her own family, her real family. She had grown so close to the little dog, to the younger boy, in such a short time. It was like the perfect fit.

Loving people easily, finding the good in them, seemed a curse sometimes for her, especially at times like this, and especially when the good was gobbled up by the bad.

Everyone she'd met who harbored any compassion toward her—and there had not been many in this crazy world—had become instant family to her, perhaps because of her own lack of family, affection, love. Yet, she always seemed to end up with a broken, guilt-ridden heart because of it.

Her body straightened up. She took a step backward, a deep breath inward, steeling mind and body away from the trio, the task as difficult as standing in a seventy-five mile an hour wind blowing straight into her.

She took two more pained steps backward.

Bad things had been happening much faster the past few years, and always just about the time she started feeling comfortable with her surroundings.

Those bad things forced her to believe she would be fine on her own, that she belonged on her own, and that a family would keep her from her destiny.

Her final visions of happiness and belonging

triggered an opposite image of these three wonderful, goodhearted people, people whom she had grown to care deeply about in the last twenty-four hours. The picture burned in her mind of three bodies lying in caskets, somewhere in a cold, dark, deep hole, in a neatly landscaped cemetery, and tears pooled at her eyelids.

The trio watched her struggle, a sad knowledge filling their own thoughts.

It was Mrs. Wilkins who spoke up, though. "Cheater, we know you don't have any place to go, nobody to go to. We wouldn't even go through all the red tape with the state. You could just come and live with us, no strings. You need a family, and Tommy needs you. I'm sure Danny agrees that you can come along. We'll work out the details later. But right now, I'm tired, in need of a shower and clean clothes, and I want you to come with us. You belong with us," one last attempt to sway her decision.

Danny knew the impossibility of swaying her. He felt the importance of her decision as he studied her actions. There was something about this young girl, a determination—a mission, or destiny—that he sensed in her. Lightening the moment, making it easier for her, he spoke up, "Look at her, already making up my mind for me, and she hasn't even set foot in the house!"

Cheater laughed.

Tommy giggled.

Danny received a slug in the bicep.

Cheater looked down at her smoky borrowed clothing, and then her worn shoes, the cemetery image still fresh in her mind, a horrible ending to a selfish decision. She wouldn't risk it, not them, not anyone, ever again.

"I can't. I do have somewhere to be, somebody to go to. Tommy helped me print out the map yesterday. If I leave now, I'll only be a day behind," she fibbed.

She didn't know when she had to be in Paradise or why. She just knew she had to go, had to see if this Paradise was the place in the fairytale. What she found there just might make sense out her miserable life.

"Well, why don't you let me pay for a bus ticket, or plane ticket? You'll get there faster, and you can stay longer, and give us a chance?" Danny offered.

"No, thanks, buses make me car sick," another fabrication. "And you all have been so nice to me already. I need to go, now." She looked again at the dog, then at Tommy, realizing the difficulty of finding food for herself, let alone the dog, "But, if you don't mind, you could take this dog. He's a stray. He just started following me around." She left out the fact that he was her only companion, the only one she could have regardless of her destiny.

"Mom, could we? Please?" Tommy begged excitedly.

"We most certainly can! I couldn't deny a little hero his right to a wonderful motley friend! Matter of fact, that's just what my lonely, desolate acreage needs, a little doggy running around watering the trees and little doggy landmines all over the place!" Danny spoke up before Tommy's mom could say no, but not without a burning look from her.

"We may not be able to keep him when we move, though." She glared at Danny.

"Let's cross that bridge when we come to it." He gave her shoulders a gentle squeeze, challenging her again.

"Yes!" Tommy punched the air. "Come 'ere, boy! Come 'ere!" Tommy squatted down and called gently.

The little terrier looked up at Cheater, and she urged him toward the boy with a nod, mentally sending the message to him that it was okay, that he would be happy.

She smiled as he moved tentatively toward Tommy, tail tucked and head down, the same way he had first approached her. The boy scratched his ears, took the small furry head in both hands, and kissed him between the eyes, then picking up the wiggly body, he held him close, ruffling behind his ears.

"Are you sure you won't come along?" Mrs. Wilkins tried again, a deep sadness filling her heart and bursting forth upon her face.

Cheater hesitated, "I'm... I'm sure." She choked out. She wanted nothing more than to go with them, but she knew she couldn't, and she visualized the cemetery for strength.

"Okay, then take care of yourself and call that

number we gave you if you need anything." Mrs. Wilkins walked back and hugged her. "I'll be praying for you, young lady, and whatever it is that troubles you."

Danny came back, too. He handed her a folded up piece of paper, told her to put it in her pocket, and not to lose it.

He told her that it contained several more numbers where she might reach him, if she found herself needing any help.

Tommy put the scraggly dog down, and ran toward Cheater, arms outstretched. He thanked her again and again, and pleaded with her to join their family. He wanted a big sister.

A strange sensation filled her, not having received a hug from another in the past few months, and this being the first and last hug from the small boy she had only helped yesterday, but whom she felt she'd known for a lifetime.

The sensation lingered after Tommy returned to his Mother's side, grabbed up the little dog again, and asked, "Does this mean we get to miss church today?"

Mrs. Wilkins chuckled and rubbed his hair in another moment of normalcy. A sun-born prism of water colored Cheater's vision as she waved goodbye to them while standing alone behind the diner.

If she could pick another family to live with, they would be it, but she knew she couldn't; she watched the car bump down the alley, and disappear at the corner before she turned away, tiny rivers streaking her smoke filmed face.

No dog.

No family.

No home.

Again.

The Interstate, according to Tommy's map, was on the other side of town. She wasn't sure about following the Interstate; there was too much chance of getting spotted by the police, or some pervert.

She took a closer look at the map for other roads, or at least a waterway running parallel to the highway, that would help her stay out of the main view of traffic, but there weren't any. The map wasn't a very good one. The Interstate was her best option.

She walked up the main street, north of the little diner, past a pet shop where colorful parakeets chirped happily in the window, a gift and floral shop displaying a pink and brown teddy bear holding an enormous, floating balloon bouquet announcing 'It's a Girl!,' and some kind of gaming center on her left.

With the bouncing balloons floated a vision, one of her mother holding a tiny baby in the hospital, her brother, his first teddy bear on the bedside table, huge balloons drifting toward the ceiling. The pain too great, she shook the memory away, focusing again on getting out of this city.

She would just have to take her chances following the highway. Maybe she could stay out of sight somehow.

She crossed an intersection at the corner,

waited until the walk sign flashed at the next one, and entered a huge parking lot. A large grocery store lay at the back of the lot. Cars crowded the spaces closest to the store, but there were no cars near her.

She patted her pockets for the nuts she had picked up the day before. They were nestled safely in the pockets of her second hand jeans, right along with the bulky, folded up slip of notebook paper Danny had given her with the phone numbers on it.

She wished now she had let Danny give her some money, so she could buy an apple or something light to carry with her for later.

Oh, well, it's not like I haven't gone hungry before, she sighed. Only after stumbling into a situation in which she received two full meals from a generous person had she thought about eating again later in the day. Two days ago, food was the furthest thought from her mind.

A commotion in the center of the parking lot interrupted her regrets. Turning away from the store to the center of the parking lot, she glimpsed two women, an elderly, silver haired woman cursing and yelling for help, her cries alerting Cheater, and anyone else who might care, to the disturbance.

Cheater looked around for a police car or security to answer the pleas, hoping there were none as she felt a familiar sensation move her. She readied herself to flee if a bubbled car appeared, but she knew what was going to happen instead. As the darkness descended upon her, she hoped this wouldn't be a time when somebody with a good citizen complex, somebody with a shred of conscience, would dial 9-1-1. If she were picked up for questioning, she would never escape again. Not this time. Not after Sadie. She would never find Paradise.

Her body moved closer to the disturbance as her mind slipped into the darkness, into the somewhere else she always went, a place where she couldn't see, or hear or focus on anything else. The place that was nonexistent, as if that part of her was dead.

"I said put my milk down you low-life junky, vagabond!

"I am so tired of you people wandering around stealing from us hardworking citizens. Begging in the streets! It's appalling! I won't stand for it.

"There are far too many of you people in this city. The government should buy an island and move all of you there. It disgusts me to leave my house anymore because your kind are everywhere, begging, stealing, lying around on the sidewalks! Put my milk down and get away from me before I call the police!"

The woman's expensive looking, leather coat, the blue gray, salon styled hair, the flashing, angry blue eyes, and the screeching, high-pitched tone of frustration, drew Cheater's body like a monarch to a sunshine lit blossom.

The frown on the woman's weathered, pale face caused it to crack with tiny wrinkles. She was so bitter and angry that the physical Cheater felt her pain in the darkness, as she always did when someone hurt deeply inside. Opposite the older woman—holding on like her life depended on it to the plastic bag containing a half gallon of milk—was a young woman.

Dirty, stringy blonde hair dangled about her tired, determined, drawn face.

The homeless woman's loose fitting, torn and dirty, cotton shirt hung on her thin torso and ended at the waist of a pair of cut off shorts that were too small and too thin, much like the ones Cheater had thrown away. Her bare feet froze in a snatch and run stance.

"Please, Miss, please! My baby's sick; she needs food. She's dyin'. She's gonna die. Please!" The younger woman begged, pain filled tears streaking her honest face. Fear and frustration projected onto Cheater, penetrating the area surrounding her, pushing into the thick darkness, the unfairness of her situation in this apathetic world piercing Cheater's heart.

Rich and poor was the picture painted in this day.

There seemed to be no middle ground anywhere, no place between the two, no comfortable zone, like the one she had shared so long ago with her own family. Just rich and poor, and they hated each other.

In her travels, she had learned from

conversations she overheard walking by people congregating here and there, and from televisions blaring from open house doors, that the government had cut many programs for the poor, and put so many regulations on them that it made it difficult for people to get help anymore.

The homeless should just die on the street—and many did—was the message sent. "Get a job!" was shouted by passersby, but there were no jobs. Not since the crash. People like Mrs. Wilkins and Danny, they were lucky to find each other, lucky somebody cared.

More and more homeless people, poor people, were unable to support themselves because of the rising prices and all the cutbacks after the huge housing and fuel hike ten or so years earlier, just before the crash. The world economy had fallen and people fell with it.

Cheater suddenly felt a ripple, a tear, as both women exhibited a need for help and in her darkness, the feelings surrounding her, she didn't know which one needed it more, or what was about to happen to solve the problem at hand, but she knew something was happening, because the thick darkness suffocated her senses, removing the smallest of feelings, and then, she was nothing.

"Oh, you people are all alike. You'd say anything to get what you want. You don't have a baby. Where is it? Where, huh? Are you pathetic enough to leave a baby alone? You're just some drug-addicted tramp! Get away from me and leave my milk here!"

"But, Miss, I do have a baby, I do! She's too sick to leave outta the closet we're stayin' in. My boy's stayin' with her.

"Please, I do have a baby. Two of 'em and my babies need it, the milk. Their daddy up and left us out on the street. We got nothin'."

"Well, in that case, there are government programs to help you. Do I have 'Welfare' stamped on my forehead? Do I? Oh, you probably couldn't read it if it was there! Down that road, right there, you go down that road, and about three blocks over you'll find a big building where you'll get help. Now, let go and go find the Welfare people and leave me alone!"

"I already tried down there." The younger woman answered dejectedly, tears shaking her voice, indicating her will to lie down and die if not for her children. Her quivering body clutched the bag tighter. The older woman held firmly to the loose handle, pulling it back toward her, the bag about to split apart.

"Young lady, help me! Get a police officer, quick!" The older woman's high pitched voice crackled out when she glimpsed Cheater on the other side of her shiny new Cadillac, but Cheater was absent from the present place and no longer heard the voices around her.

When Cheater didn't respond, the old woman glared directly into her face with a look that said,

'Today's children have no respect.'

Cheater's glistening brown hair and thin angelic face wavered before the icy blue eyes, though, filling them with loving devotion and curiosity.

Though Cheater remained the same scrawny thirteen year old girl she had been when she walked up, she wasn't what the older woman saw. The vision of the young brown haired girl withered before the elderly woman, transparently at first as the woman could see life going on behind the young girl, and then this girl changed, becoming a 3D picture more life-like than yesterday's memories, the picture of someone very dear to the bitter, pain filled, and aged heart.

"Angelo?" the older voice, husky with time, whispered toward Cheater, and though the girl within the man didn't hear her, the man did; mentally Cheater was gone, in another dimension, space, time. Her body stood there, in the very spot she had unknowingly moved to, strong, silent, and statuesque, an ever-changing vision to the elderly rich woman, but just a strange teenage girl to the younger homeless one.

Cheater spoke no words to the older woman, yet the older woman heard everything she needed to hear from the vision she stared upon.

"Miriam, honey, I left you well cared for. You will have everything you could ever need for longer than you will need it. Look at this poor woman, Miriam. Look at her. She's desperate. Her children need food, Miriam. Let go of the bitterness, honey. Help her. Soon you will be with me, and you won't have an opportunity to do good things. Don't let the evil spoken by him take over your heart, Miriam. Stop listening to the propaganda, the media around him. You always did follow close behind me and my decisions. I worried about that while I was in the hospital. Now you follow him, the wrong one to follow.

"Don't be bitter, darling; be happy, happy to have the chance to help another fellow being become something they may never have otherwise become, happy that you may save not only one life, but three. Think of those children, Miriam.

"I only want you to be happy, honey, and I know helping this young family get back on track will bring you great joy. Do the right thing and let go of your anger. Leave a mark of goodness on this poor, uncaring world. Turn away from him, his teachings, and his beliefs. We'll be together again, soon. I love you, Miriam." The husky male voice, silent to anyone but her, reached out tenderly to the eighty-year-old woman.

The heavy, dark-haired, olive skinned figure, his appearance much younger than Miriam, wavered as the smile on her face grew, the love in her eyes glowed, and the wrinkles seemed to vanish.

"Can you bring him back, again?" The older woman pleaded as Cheater returned before the woman's sparkling blue eyes. "I didn't get to tell him that I..." but Cheater stood solid, unable yet to hear the old woman's request.

Light seeped into her dark world until her vision cleared and Cheater stared blankly at the old woman, blinking, not comprehending the muffled words her ears forced into her wakening brain. Bring... him... back? The old woman was repeating over and again.

Cheater only knew she had lapsed into that unknown place without leaving; she only knew she had mentally blanked out, but physically remained and moved, no longer at the edge of the lot, but to the center. And she knew what would happen next.

Miriam let go of the grocery bag, looked deep into the younger woman's terrified eyes, then down at her basket of groceries. Her hands rummaged the bags in the grocery cart; she stared down at all she had for only herself. She thought about the big, lonely two-story Victorian home awaiting her. She thought about the emptiness in it since her husband died, how alone she had been.

"Take the milk. As a matter of fact, take all of these groceries. I'll get more."

"No, Miss, I got no place to keep it. I got no way to get it back to my kids. I just need the milk."

"Nonsense! I'll take you back in my car, with all the groceries, and we will pick up your children and take them to my house. Then, if your baby needs it, we'll get her to a doctor."

"No, no, Miss. I can't take that. Just the milk,

please."

"I will not take no for an answer, young lady. You will get in this car, and you and your children will come home with me. At least until we can get you back on your feet. That's the deal! Lord knows you probably all need a good, hot bath, and a good, hot meal.

"Ever since my Angelo died, I haven't had the opportunity to make my special lasagna for anyone except myself! Oh, and my homemade garlic bread! That's what we'll have tonight! And the best red wine in my cellar to celebrate! Oh, I haven't made bread in years!

"Now, show an old lady some respect and don't argue with her. Get in! You come too, young lady. I want to see you do that thing again!" Pausing, she turned toward Cheater, but the teenage girl just smiled in the air of excitement that followed, the wave of change and goodness on the breeze, nodded to them both and walked back toward the road, toward her previous destination, leaving the two to their happy dilemma. The younger woman's look of confusion and a faint, "Thank you, young lady!" Sounding behind her.

"Now, how many children do you have exactly? I better know their names I suppose, and yours, too. My goodness, my manners have just disappeared! My name is Miriam..." The older woman's babbling voice grew fainter as Cheater crossed the parking lot in the direction from which she had come.

Engrossed in her curious thoughts of the unknown time she spent next to the car, thoughts of the possibilities that took place during her black outs, thoughts now stealing her concentration and focus, she walked right into the firm body of a person in her path, throwing her off balance and almost to the pavement below.

"You did it, again! I saw you! What makes you do that?" The tall, young man sidestepped back and forth before her, blocking her progress. "I mean, that's like... you know... weird! When you did it to me, I saw my sister. She's been dead for a year. It was great seeing her, again! That thing... it's awesome!" His head shook in amazement, his eyes disbelieving, but it was the astonishment on Cheater's face that changed his expression.

A dead person? I was a dead person? She first assumed the boy was toying with her for some reason, trying to get her off guard, given his display of varying personalities since their first encounter, but when she remembered the man in his apartment, she didn't believe he would toy with her.

"I don't know what you're talking about." She needed time to think about this revelation he had just thrown at her. She tried to move around him, but he slid right and blocked her again, this time stopping her with a gentle touch on her arm.

A slight tingle flowed from the spot where his fingers rested, and slowly moved up her left arm. She peered up into his questioning eyes.

"Sure you do! That thing you do where you

change into a dead person? I mean... don't tell me you don't know?" He spoke as if to a three year old not yet understanding his instruction. He was right; Cheater had never known what happened when she slipped into darkness. She just walked up to the person in need and lost time somehow.

The creeping tingle spread to her shoulder, following a crazy route north at the back of her neck, thousands of tiny feet dancing on her skull. She'd never felt that before, almost like an electric charge running up her arm. She jerked her arm away, rubbing her forearm. "That's not what happens! You're making that up!" She squinted up into his face, searching for the laughter that was sure to follow his comment, but finding none. She would say anything to get him away from her right now.

"Girl, you messin' wit' me?" His voice squeaked back. "You don't know what you do?"

"No." She turned away from his stare, suddenly uncomfortable that someone knew something about her that she didn't know. "And apparently you don't, either! Live people turning into dead people? Come on! I think your brain's been fried or something! I'm beginning to understand how you knew about those drugs in that basement.

"You know what? Just stay away from me, okay? I don't know what your game is, but I'm not playing. I have more important things to do, you know, places to go." She turned completely away, more defensive now than she had ever been. Dead people? The missing brother yesterday? Jaz's sister? Miriam's husband? The bitterness of death? The truth brought burning tears.

He blocked her again, looking down into her face, searching for a glimmer of hidden knowledge, "No, way! How can you not know? I knew I could do this thing I can do when I was little. That's why I know all about my stepdad and sister. The cops, shh..., they don't care about poor people. I gotta walk lightly around that dude." He shook his head in a quick, angry motion.

Cheater couldn't follow his train of thought. His ramblings supported her argument to believe he was losing his mind. The only thing she understood was about his stepdad. She'd seen him in action.

She seized the opportunity to change the subject to allow time for her return from the fog that always lingered after the darkness. She wouldn't have asked, but one statement stirred her curiosity, "That thing you do? The man at the apartment? He's your stepdad?" She reflected on the fire early that morning, him reassuring her about it not being her fault, as if he had read her mind, the aggressive tingling on her arm, the way this young man opened up so emotionally and quickly, his anger about his past, his home life, accentuating his feelings with someone he didn't even know. The connections zapped her brain, firing synapses like a game of laser tag.

She would never tell a stranger, especially this

stranger, about her past. She would wind up right in the middle of big trouble for sure, most likely due to his certain death, just like Sadie.

Confusion clearing, curiosity replacing it, and compassion casting out distrust, she redirected the conversation to the one topic she trusted. "Thank you for helping us out of the fire earlier..."

"Yeah, no prob..." But she didn't get to ask her lingering question.

"Jaz, man, we been lookin' all over for ya'! Hey, wanna come with us over to Juey's to score some... Oh, hey, didn't see you was talkin' to a chick. Ain't that that chick from yesterday? You gonna mess 'er up, man? Need some help?" Cheater's eyes narrowed and she stared into the face of the boy who had kicked Tommy yesterday morning, sensing nothing but hatred.

She felt nothing.

No transition came to her; he must be beyond change, and fear replaced the nothingness.

He was already one of them, the apathetic, the quitters, the menacing. He had no reason; he just was. A prickle of aggression overtook her, helping her stand her ground, work away the fear.

"Be cool," Jaz mouthed. "Don't waste your time on him.

"Naw, man, we just talkin'. Maybe she join us, ya' know?" Raised eyebrows. "Go on over, I'll catch up later!" He called to the two younger boys.

When they were out of earshot, Cheater

responded with fury. "You lied to them. I'm not going anywhere with you, or them. I ain't joining anybody, anywhere!"

"Hey, chill! I know. I just wanted to get rid of them." He smiled, his smile mellowing his hardened features to the point of friendliness. "Since I saw you yesterday morning, and you did that thing you do, I changed, you know, seein' my sister again. Her sayin' what she said..." He looked down at her, a sense of wonder filling his smile, his dark face, his sparkling brown eyes, and then he nodded once, slightly, encouraging her belief of his words.

Could he be telling the truth? Could that be what happens to me? If so, why hadn't somebody told me before?

Because you always leave, stupid, she answered herself.

Cheater squinted curiously at him thinking about Sadie's nephew and his friend, and then she blinked back the thought that popped into her head. He had said, 'I knew I had that thing I got when I was little' and she realized that she hadn't blacked out until she came to live with Sadie, or at least she didn't remember having done it before. She had been shuffled from home to home, city to city, seeming to move slowly in a direction that would deliver her to the one place where long sought out answers to deeper questions waited.

Could I be turning into dead people when I black out? How? Why? Do I do it on purpose?

He seemed to believe his story, and it certainly made sense to her when she recalled all the people who changed after her blackouts, how they reacted toward her afterward, sort of like seeing a long lost family member.

Memories inundated her thoughts, brief but many, reminding her how everyone thought her a strange child, everyone except her parents.

But her brother had been strange, too, so she never thought further about the comments to her mother, her father. Her parents had always marveled at the uniqueness of their children.

They called Cheater, and her brother, special, gifted. Sadie had said the same about Cheater.

"Yeah, I used to get that strange stuff, too. Teachers, family friends, neighbors. I thought I was normal. I thought everyone could..."

The screech of wheels on pavement cut his confession short, and her eyes widened.

An older, shiny, black sedan with dark tinted windows and hydraulic lifts drove by the parking lot, slowed, the skin of the young man before her prickling even before Jaz turned to look.

When the person driving, whom Cheater couldn't see, spotted Jaz, the car slowed even more, drifting to the curb.

Jaz turned nervously back to Cheater, eyes wide with fear as he searched for a way out of the impending danger, moving quickly, pulling her along by the elbow toward the grocery store, weaving in and out of parked cars for cover, until he pulled her to the back of the store.

"Sorry about that, we gotta get outta here. It was them. Did you feel that?"

"I felt something, sure. Something like you nearly twisting my arm off while you dragged me across the parking lot!"

She looked down at the long slender fingers still gripping her arm above the elbow. The tingle returned. It hadn't set off her internal warning lights, and though curious, she found it uncomfortable. She tried to pull free, but he wouldn't let go.

He searched the streets around the lot, "Didn't you feel that... them, when they stopped? We gotta get outta here. They're coming!" His eyes fervently probed hers.

"No, I need to get out of here, away from you and your friends, and you need to stay away from me! I bring people enough danger as it is!" Cheater pulled her arm free of his grip and stepped away.

"Wait..." he grabbed the back of her shirt, "... you don't get it. They saw me talkin' to you. They'll recognize you. If you go, and they see you, you're dead! I know you saw it... felt it! The feeling when they pulled up... the feeling both times I touched your arm!" His eyes widened with fear. So, he felt it, too. What did that tell her? She shook her head. She didn't want to be around him; she needed space, time to process what he had told her about her blackouts, time to piece her puzzled life together.

Besides, she couldn't die, she knew that much. Death followed her around like that little stray dog had in the beginning, coming close, but never touching her. Somehow, she had always cheated death.That's where she got her nickname, the name Sadie gave her.

Not that she couldn't get hurt. She knew that, too, and she had scars to prove it. She bled, broke bones, twisted muscles just like any other kid on earth. She was not a superhero, but she hadn't died, couldn't die, yet. At least not until it was time for her to die, and there was something, someone, some place, keeping that from happening.

"No, you don't get it! I don't care! I should've been dead a long time ago anyhow, many times, but I'm not! I'm invincible!" She blurted sarcastically, the burning tears returning as she moved away from him.

If I can turn into dead people, can I start fires, too? Is it possible that I can crash cars? Planes? Create tornadoes? All with my weird mind? Am I alone because of me?

"I told you, girl, you didn't cause no fire. I don't know what else you can do with your weird little mind, certainly more than I can do with mine. I gotta feeling we're gonna find out, though. Right now, we got to run!"

She whipped around, drawn brows, streaming tears; did I say that out loud? He did that before, right when the car drove up. Maybe, I'm losing it!

Cheater peered into his eyes, her face flushed with doubt, more tears forming; Jaz stared back, a look of satisfaction on his face, not as puzzled by her words as he should have been, answering her mental questions with a shake of his head.

The melancholy in his eyes softened and blurred as he looked at her. He released the twisted tee shirt and raised his eyes to the gathering clouds. "I told you, it wasn't your fault. You didn't do that. What you do is something great, something wonderful, something healing. You do some healing! Mental healing. Emotional healing. You have a great power, so don't go blamin' yourself for that fire or any of it. It wasn't your fault. Far as I know, Mother Nature's the only one who can bring a tornado. And you're not losin' it!" He turned his gaze back on her.

She was mixed up now. Either he was good at reading expressions, or he was reading her mind.

What else does he know about me? She needed to get away from this boy, but curiosity wouldn't allow her to leave. She needed to find out more. The connection she'd felt since their first encounter flowed between them now. She wanted to know why. A powerful surge reached toward her, touched her. Why? Maybe her time on this lonely road had ended.

"That's what you said this morning, but how do you know I didn't start it? I have those space outs. Just because you saw what happened during one, doesn't mean they're all the same. I hurt people. People die around me!"

"Twice, I saw what happened twice. I saw you turn into that fat, Italian man!"

An employee opened the backdoor carrying a bundle of flattened boxes, halting their conversation. His arms were too full to squeeze through the opening; some of the boxes caught against the doorframe and fell to the ground, sliding out in a giant fan shape over the concrete walkway. Jaz ran over to help him.

"Let me help you, man," he said to the timid, boy, whose skin tone changed from beige to bright pink in seconds.

"Th... th... thanks." The embarrassed employee stuttered nervously, lowering his head and bending to stack the boxes, clearly afraid of the one offering help.

Jaz held the dumpster lid open and tossed in some boxes, and then the employee threw in his. "Thanks, again." The employee's painfully shy demeanor caused him to rush immediately back into the open door and pull it closed behind him.

Jaz returned to Cheater. "See? If this was yesterday and that boy dropped them boxes, acted all shy like that, no way I woulda' helped that kid. I'da been laughin' at him, probably makin' his job worse. You did that. What I saw, it changed me. It changed that old lady, too." He looked down into her eyes, a smile lifting one side of his lip.

"Hey, I think we should talk some more, but this ain't the best place, ya' know? If that car comes down this alley, it's over, I mean over! There's some woods out by the railroad tracks nobody ever goes to, and cars can't get there. I used to go there a lot after..."

Recognition lit Cheater's face, "I know where you're talking about; I was there yesterday morning. That's where I got these." She patted her bulging pockets.

"Yeah!" He raised his thick brows and nodded. "I was gonna ask you what you had in them pockets, but I figured it was better not to ask."

"Food for the future," she stated plainly. Proud of her resourcefulness, she pulled out a pecan and smiled like a winter ready squirrel.

The harsh squeal of tires on pavement turning down the alley made Jaz grab Cheater's arm and start running again.

During a fleeting moment between standing still and spinning around, her eyes caught the shine of black metal, chrome bumper reflecting sunlight, and dark tinted windows six blocks down the alley.

Half dragged, half running, Cheater fought for balance. She had no choice now but to go with him, or be run down.

"Run, girl!" was all she heard between what she feared were bullets whizzing too close to her ears.

"Who... taught you... how to run... some girl?" Jaz puffed out between gulps of air as he bent forward, resting his hands on his knees. "Thought... we were... dead back there!"

"Uh, well... I am a girl... and I wasn't too far... behind you... all the way here!" Cheater gulped between words, slightly winded.

"Nah, you sure weren't, only 'cause I had hold of your arm and half dragged you here!" Jaz straightened, smiled and looked up at the tall oak and pecan trees surrounding them, most of their leaves fallen in preparation for the long winter sleep.

"Shouldn't we call the police and report them or something?" Cheater's breath normalized.

"Listen..." Jaz put his hand to his ear while Cheater heard, over her pounding heart, the faint scream of a siren echoing from the direction in which they had run. "Somebody already did. Not that it'll matter. Besides, you have a cell phone? I don't." He spread his arms wide.

Jaz spun slowly in place looking up and around, "Yeah, I remember comin' here... a lot. I've missed this place." They slipped further into the shadows, well out of view of the closest roads. He walked over and leaned on a fallen tree, one hand supporting him, the other digging around under it, brushing away dry leaves.

"After my sister died, this was my favorite spot in the world. The quiet helped me grieve. I felt like she was here with me, sometimes.

"We used to come here and play when we were little, before things changed, way before momma went to the hospital." He leaned back, pulling a stretch of brown nylon handle with him, breathed deeply of the soft scents of earth, trees and grass, drying leaves and dirt, and listened to the quiet rustling sounds in the breeze. After lifting the small canvas bag over his shoulder, he hummed to himself.

"Your sister died." Cheater stated quietly, remembering his earlier reference to her and suddenly identifying the connection she felt toward him. She knew death all too well. Death ruled her life, made her lonely. The fear of death is what kept her alone, so even as she felt the desire to open up to Jaz and tell him her life story, she didn't, for fear that death would take him, too, or anyone else she confided in. And she wasn't ready for someone else, even someone not so innocent, to die on account of her.

"Yeah. She was murdered by that man my momma married and left us with!" A deep frown swallowed the sweet smile of remembrance that lit his features, an angry frown filled with hatred. The soft humming ended. Puzzled and bitter, he didn't stop the vulgar words that slithered out of his mouth like the poisonous infection they hissed, "Got away with it too!" ended the tirade.

Anger distorted his handsome features, brought back the boy he was yesterday while mugging Tommy—his young face familiar to that moment as he thought of the man he lived with—and he stood and moved away from his place of peace, gripping the bottom of the bag as if for comfort, touching the side of his forehead with his free hand.

Cheater hadn't heard language like that since she left the Children's Home and went to live with Sadie. Marlon had been a year younger than Cheater, but he liked to fling out bad words like any adult sailor just coming off tour. His vocabulary included every bad word known to man, and she remembered his words were much worse than the ones she just heard.

Jaz glanced her way, eyebrows drawn, eyes prepared to shoot poison arrows at the nearest target. His expression changed when he saw the disappointment on her face.

One of the most vivid memories of her mother that she still recalled—as clear as if it happened yesterday—was one she thought about now, the memory of the language lesson from her earlier years with her own family.

Her great aunt had used a bad word in front of Cheater and her younger brother, which gave them unspoken permission to try it out, too. She hadn't said a bad word since, for the look it drew from her own mother's smiling face made her cringe to this day. Never mind the lecture after. She loved her mother so much; she hadn't wanted to disappoint her by doing anything wrong. She never wanted to see her mother's face with that horrible, pained look again, not because of something she did. Just thinking of that look made her feel shame now. She felt that same motherly look of hurt dawn her face at the thought.

"Oh, man, I'm sorry! I shouldn't talk like that. Dang!" he shook his head, "I mean... I'm sorry. It just makes me so mad to think about all that and him gettin' away with it, then threatenin' me with Momma's life to keep me there with him. 'Cause' if you leave this house, Boy, if you ain't here to show that CPS bunch we a family, if you don't come on to this here apartment every night, I'll go straight to yer momma's room at that old hospital and slit her throat! You hear me, boy?'" Jaz mimicked. "Argh! Just like that he threatens me. I can hardly stand to look at the old b..." He caught himself, "when I walk in the door, but I go back and cook his stupid supper and make sure his clothes are clean and ironed so he can go to his freakin' maintenance job over in that old run down hotel.

"I ain't never hated nobody as much as I hate him!" Instantly he felt sorrow over the comment. He didn't like hating somebody; he didn't like the turmoil it caused inside. And he didn't like the anger that produced the words that poured from his mouth when he thought of the Beast. He had never spoken to anyone about his situation, his stepdad and his family, and it certainly wasn't like this bit of a girl could help him much, so why was he telling her now?

But somewhere deep down he felt that she could help him. He didn't know how, after all the bad things he had done in the past three months, acts born of that hate eating away at his heart throughout the years. He didn't deserve her help, or anybody's help. He looked over at her again, standing there, slightly puzzled by his words, listening anyway, hearing his pain, his torment, and his indecision. "Is that how you got that bruise on your forehead?"

Jaz touched the tender spot on his head again, not even wincing, "Yeah. He did that last night when he got home, after he threw the supper I made him all over the kitchen floor." He closed his eyes, fighting the angry rumble boiling within his body. "I know how to play him now, though. Know how to get him to leave me alone. I wish I had known when Bree was alive. Maybe I coulda' saved her." His head dropped, bouncing with grief.

"You could've saved her? From what?"

"From him."

"He killed your sister?" she prodded after a moment, "He got away with killing your sister? How? Do you know for sure?"

"Do I know for sure? What... you think... I've been there!" He yelled, spinning on his heels and pacing away from her, memories bubbling to the surface. "I was there when he did those terrible things to her after momma's accident, after momma got put in that hospital.

"I was there and couldn't, no didn't, do nothing to stop him. He broke her! He beat her! But the night she died, she was goin' to the law, she was goin' to find someone to help us. The night she died, I was out, 'cause she told me to leave so he couldn't hold me there and threaten her when she went for the law. He told the law she was out gettin' wasted, gettin' all drugged out with some of her gang friends, that she come home and fell. Her head hit the table, he said. He shot her up with some junk then smashed her head into that table's what happened. I know what happened because he thinks about it every day, and it makes him happy.

"She was seventeen years old, and all I had left after momma went into the hospital.

"He's evil. I can see what he's thinking when he comes home, when he's sleepin', when he's rememberin' what he done to her, what he done to my momma, and I can't be around him, I hate being around him."

"What do you mean; you can see what he's thinkin'?"

"Yeah. I see his thoughts. I see the thoughts of everyone I'm near. Like I saw you thinkin' about the night your house burned down, when that apartment burned this morning. Yeah, I know about the fire. The fire you feel so bad about. I know, because I saw you thinkin' it.

"And like I told you, it wasn't your fault. Neither fire was your fault. My sister's dyin' wasn't my fault, even though I wanna blame myself for it. I don't know why this stuff happens, why we gotta be alone."

He pressed the palms of his hands to his eyes as if keeping all his thoughts from gaining power over him. Talking about the death of her family, about the fires, and thinking about his sister and mom, gone so soon after his dad, triggered an idea, a tiny thought no bigger than a distant star, but still present, and it grew quickly.

The connection, the links between him and this girl, the reasons for their losses; thoughts ricocheted around in his mind, trying to come together into one sensible picture.

Cheater was stunned. She had been right about him. He had a gift, like her. So, besides their losses, they both suffered loneliness because of their gifts. She couldn't believe he knew about her family, though. She hadn't wanted to tell him anything, endanger him with information.

"You know about my family?"

"Yeah, sorry. I understand why you didn't want me to know, why you didn't want to tell me, but I can't help it. What you think, I think. What you dream, I dream. What you remember, I remember. Call it a gift," he huffed.

"A gift or a curse? Sadie used to call it a gift,

too, but I've learned it comes with an awful lot of consequences, too many bad things to be called a gift." She looked away sadly.

"Yeah, maybe when you think about all we've lost and all I see. But there are some good things I see, and I guess I have helped some people. I saw you thinkin' 'bout your family the night of the fire, and just now, while I was talking about my sister, you were thinkin' about 'em some more. That cussin' story, the one you were remembering when I said all that? That was sweet. I don't mind seein' those things.

"My momma, she was like that, too. I hated to do anything to make her look cross at me. She was beautiful, inside and out, is beautiful..." his voice trailed off, then he smiled again. "Wish she would wake up today. Today's her birthday, and she's layin' in that hospital bed, not even knowin' it because of h..." He stopped, not wanting anger to slip in again. Cheater could see it in his eyes, though.

"What day is it?" Cheater hadn't looked at the date on the map printout.

"November twenty-fourth." Jaz peered at her strangely. "Where you been girl? Under a rock?"

"November twenty-fourth?" her eyes grew wider. "Today is November twenty-fourth?" She asked disbelievingly.

"That's what I said. I also said it's my mother's birthday. Did you hear that pa...?" his jaw fell as he looked at her. "Really? It's your mother's birthday, too?" They stared into each other's eyes, searching for truth.

So, he did have a gift for seeing thoughts, memories. Like Jaz, these facts bounced around in her own mind, quickly, trying to form a whole picture somehow that included both him and her.

It was November.

Her own mother's birthday was in November, so was his mother's. Not just the month, but the same day, too. The surge of power she felt earlier when he had touched her arm returned to her. This time she couldn't shirk it away. Her eyes widened, "So do you think it means something?"

But his answer came slowly, hesitantly. All he could force out in light of this news was, "Yeah."

She fell against the fallen tree, biting her bottom lip. "So, what?"

"I don't know." He lifted his left leg and straddled the tree, facing her. "What do you think it means? Us... these gifts... our mother's birthdays... these weird things that happen to us. I think they're all related to what's happenin' in our lives, ya' know?" he nodded, thought some more, his bottom jaw pushed outward.

Cheater was speechless. Completely and utterly without words, this news, these additional puzzle pieces, had silenced her. Finally, she managed a shrug, a few words.

"So, today's your mother's birthday, and it just so happens to be the same day as my mother's birthday. It's not so strange. I mean a lot of people have the same birthdays. It's a big population, you know, and only 365 days in a year? The only way I would think it was anything but coincidence was if your birthday and my birthday..."

His mouth opened in amazement, "It is!" Before she could finish her statement, he jumped off the log. "Okay, this is too much coincidence."

"Yeah, now it's weird."

"I bet it's about to get weirder."

"Why?"

"What time were you born on Christmas Eve?"

"I don't know, twelve something in the morning." She knew, but this much had already scared her, she didn't want to add to the similarities.

"Oh, you know... yeah, you know. I was born at the exact same time, 12:24 in the morning. Mom beat that into my head when I was a kid, made it a big deal, celebrated our birthdays at the exact time we were born. It was strange getting woke up by my dad every November twenty-third at 11:55 so we would be wide awake to celebrate hers!" He quieted, lost in memory, "But, it was kinda cool, too."

Cheater was lost in memories, too, of the first time she'd been awakened at 11:55 the night before to celebrate her mother's birthday, and then her own the next month. It was the only times she and her brother were allowed up after 8:30. She couldn't speak. She couldn't believe this.

"I don't understand any of this." Ideas ricocheting faster and faster, mini rockets in her conscience. "It's just too much. December twenty-fourth, 12:24?" She questioned, disbelieving the numeric connection that popped into their heads at the same time.

"Believe, sister." Jaz nodded, incredulous himself. He always thought it cool that he and his mother shared the exact time of birth, but now he was somewhat scared, because standing before him was a girl who not only shared the same time of birth, but the same day as him, just as their mothers' shared birthdays.

And, they celebrated the same way. So, why? "Whadya think's goin' on? What do you think this is all about?" Fear, interlaced with intrigue, childlike curiosity, rattled Cheater's voice, narrowed her innocent brown eyes.

"Girl, I don't know! Why you askin' me? I mean, you're the one that came here, right? Whydya think ya came here?" He paced some more, thinking. His arms swung at his sides, fists clenched, thumping air with each step.

Cheater returned to her seat on the log, quivering with astonishment. She had always been able to accept what came her way, adapt to what life threw at her. She had always realized she didn't have to understand the meaning of what happened to her, just accept it and go on. But this new information was almost more than she could handle. Why had she come here? How could she explain that?

"I ain't gonna run!" Jaz stopped pacing. "You

know, you been kinda leery of me, and I understand that, but maybe I should be leery of you!" Jaz joked, his chuckle strained, realizing too late the hurt his words caused her.

Yeah, you should. People die around me.

Her eyes darkened, looked away.

"Sorry. I didn't mean..." Jaz started. She waved it off. She'd known what he meant. It seemed, after so much being taken from them both, that suddenly fate was throwing them together. She was supposed to be alone, so she thought. Why was this happening now? Why all of the coincidences?

The winds of her past blew in a story, a fairytale, her mother used to tell her every night before bed. She wondered if that would be another coincidence between them. Would he know of the twelve children, the monster awaiting defeat in Paradise?

After a long silence contemplating their lives, their similarities, Jaz turned toward her and straddled the log again, "Yeah, I know about the story! It was mine and my sister's favorite when we were little. Every night before bed, just like you. Kids from different places, different backgrounds, princes and princesses, heroes, Paradise, the monster!" Story facts burst from his excited voice.

Somehow she knew that he had known. She had always believed it was just a story, but now, she no longer felt that way. Could it be true?

"Okay, maybe. Something big's happenin' here.

Way bigger than us. These ties, the story, I don't understand why."

"Me, neither. Too bad there isn't a way for us to find out, get some information, somebody to ask, some family or someone. But everyone's gone. At least my family's gone. Except for maybe Stev... Well, he wouldn't remember, anyway."

"You think that kid's your brother?"

"Maybe, I couldn't find out. Then after the fire..."

"Yeah, I know."

"What about you? You have family anywhere?"

"My only family is locked up in a coma. Been that way for almost a year. She couldn't give us any in..." He stopped. "Wait. Our mother's would be the likely source, right? The story they told us, the crazy links and celebrations, they would know. Do you think you could become your mother? You know... do that thing you do and channel her or something?"

Cheater thought about that a moment. "I don't know. I didn't even know I could do that until I met you. Until then, I thought I was just having some kind of weird black outs."

"You should try or something? I mean ..."

"I don't know if I can just do it! I just found out that I did it in the first place!" She yelled impatiently. Calming, she continued, "I don't know... it seems that whenever I black out, there's always been a situation, a problem between people, like you and those boys mug..."

"Yeah, do we have to bring that up? Why don't you just concentrate on it and see if you can become your mother. I'll talk to her; ask her what's up with us."

"Well, if I never even knew before that I could do it, how am I just supposed to do it?"

"I don't know, close your eyes and think about it or something."

Cheater's face filled with doubt.

This power, this ability, or whatever it was that she had, was so very new to her on a conscious level. She had no idea how, or if, she could just do it.

"Just try," Jaz prodded.

"Well, why don't you just read your mother's mind?"

He looked away, a deep sadness filling his features. "I tried. I don't get anything from her. I don't know why. Sometimes there are times when it doesn't work. Sometimes I come across somebody that I don't get anything from. Like that boy I was hanging around with, the one who kicked that kid?

"It was kind of nice, not knowing what he would say before he said it. I could actually just talk to him and not know what he was going to say. There was a surprise to the conversation, you know?

"Anyway, I can't reach Mom, but maybe you can reach yours? Be yours? Just try... please?"

After glancing up at him, she squeezed her eyes closed, thinking about her mother. She relaxed, tried to find a different level of consciousness, almost fell asleep, did for a few moments, but no complete darkness overcame her, just gray, the deep gray of slumber. Her eyes snapped open, hoping. "Anything?" She asked expectantly, but knowing otherwise.

"Nah. You tried." He was genuinely disappointed.

"Well, now what?"

"I don't know. You can keep trying. Maybe there's something stopping you. Maybe it's just too emotional for you to do."

She thought about that, about her mother being dead and her ability to channel the dead, become the dead, her emotions.

She thought about his mother, useless to them in her current condition, almost dead, yet mostly in a deep death like sleep.

Jaz turned toward her, brows risen in question. "Hey, do you think you could become my mom? I mean, she's only here physically, like you just thought, in a death like sleep. Maybe you could..."

Her eyes rose to meet his; her shoulders shrugged in answer. "Like I said, I've never done it on demand. I didn't even know I could. Maybe... but in order to do it, it seems there would have to be some reason, some problem, or some drama. I mean, that's how it seems to work. Something happens to someone..." She thought about the morning before, the park bench, the alley, the older woman and the screams.

"Oh, I could give you drama. Lots of drama.

First, we gotta figure out how to get to the hospital. It's across town from here, and still there's those gangbangers lookin' for me... us. Walkin' would likely get us killed."

"Yeah, you're probably right." She thought about the phone numbers in her pocket, the ones Danny gave her. Would she reach them if she tried to call them? But, what if Tommy came with Danny? How could she explain Jaz?

"You could call him, ask him to come alone, give him some story about not wanting to see the kid," Jaz offered.

She rolled her eyes at him. She was going to have to be careful what she thought around him. He smiled in agreement, nodded at her.

She slipped her fingers into her back pocket and pulled out the paper Danny had given her. As she unfolded it, something fluttered to the ground below her. Twenty-dollar bills, five of them, spread out among the moist leaves below.

Jaz jumped off the log and collected them, "Girl, you didn't tell me you had money!"

"I didn't know!" She grinned at Danny's generosity.

"That settles it. We can take the bus, a cab or somethin', get there unnoticed."

She thought about how far that money would get her toward Paradise, how much food it would buy her, and new, Goodwill sneakers for walking. She should conserve it.

"Okay, we'll take a bus. I think we can catch the one I take to the hospital on the other side of these woods, that way. We'll just have to stay low until we see it comin' round the corner, then run out and catch it. It'll be cheaper, so we can save more for the trip to Paradise." Jaz nodded.

"Wait a minute. We?" Cheater questioned.

"Oh, come on, Paradise? The connections? The story? We're supposed to go together; I know that. You know it, too, deep down."

"But... but your mom?" Cheater cocked her head.

"Well, let's go talk to her and see what she says!"

"If it works." She didn't want to get her hopes up. When she did, it seemed something came along and tore them down, shredded them, chopped them into tiny pieces, and scattered them in the wind.

She jumped from the log and followed Jaz toward the opposite end of the woods to the same spot she had hid from the police yesterday morning.

Their shining knight on black wheels in green armor—that would carry them away to the many adventures of the long memorized fairytale—awaited them beyond the trees.

"Can't you just call the police? Turn him in for abuse or something? You got that bruise and all. Wouldn't that take care of him?" She tried to figure out a way to deal with his stepfather while the two of them crouched beneath brush in wait of the bus.

"Well, maybe six months ago I could've called them, but, I've been in some trouble lately. Think maybe they're lookin' for me, too. They wouldn't listen to a troublemaker.

"It's the hope of momma wakin' up outta that coma that keeps me from turnin' to the police, too. But maybe, if this works out, she... you or whoever, can answer our questions, tell us what we should do."

"Hmm... maybe," Cheater nodded, her voice as quiet as her thoughts. "So, what's in the bag?" She glanced toward the worn canvas bag snuggled next to Jaz's leg.

"Oh, that. It's just some stuff from home. I snuck it out here last night, after the Beast fell asleep, and I hid it back there under the log. For some reason, I just had a good feeling about today being the day I needed to take it with me. I just felt like it was a good day to not return. That's why I came looking for you."

"What do you mean?"

"I don't know, just somethin' about the way things happened yesterday, seeing you... Bree, feeling the connection between you and me. I've had this bag stashed in my closet for a long time, just waiting for the moment I could get outta that dump."

"I wish I'da grabbed some stuff from Sadie's before I left. I was too scared, though." She looked between the trees at the mid-morning sun flickering among sleeping branches. Specks of sunlight danced across her face, creating sparkles in her eyes. "So, what about the guys in the black car? I mean, why were they shooting at us?" Cheater dug in her pocket, cracked a pecan between two rocks and pulled out the meat within, not from hunger, mostly from nervousness.

"Yeah, about that. I kinda got some issues with them. They're part of a local gang. They been tryin' to jump me in for several years now, since I moved here. The Beast in my apartment kept tellin' the cops that Bree and I were hooked up to them, but it wasn't true. She had problems with the leader, with the whole gang, but different from mine. Their leader was always after her.

"Fact, she's what saved me from bein' jumped in one night. Leader put out word not to hurt her, 'cause he liked 'er, ya' know, and one night, she was comin' from her job at the library when she saw four of the members surrounded me, ready to beat me up.

She stopped 'em.

"She still kep' turnin' his ugly behind down, and I steered clear of them, so when she died, I became a target. Before, they wanted me in; now, they want me dead, because I said no. They wanna shoot me, just like they did Momma that night."

"Oh. They're the reason she's in the hospital?" Cheater questioned tentatively, reliving the pain of her own mother's death, her horrid screams during the terrifying blaze that seemed to have started on its own. "So, what if they catch up to us before we can get out of town?"

"We just gotta hope they don't."

"Hmm," she nodded again, eyes downcast. "And, where's the hospital your mother's at?"

"'Cross town. We'll be safe on the bus. Too many people on the bus. They won't be able to pick me out. We'll just stay low in the seat."

"Yeah," Cheater doubted, reaching into her left pocket and handing a couple more pecans to Jaz, who was just finishing one.

"Hey, it's okay... I think. We got a mission, you know? Those crazy dudes ain't gonna get us before the mission's done, right?"

"Yeah," Cheater nodded uncertainly. "Just another dragon from the story. Why couldn't one of us have super strength or something, though? You know, sorta like Superman? Or telekinetic super strength!" Jaz chuckled, "Man, 'cause that stuff ain't real!"

“I never used to think any powers were real... until now.” Cheater raised her eyes to Jaz. His shoulders bumped upward in reply.

“Hey, there’s the bus. Let’s head toward the stop!” He jumped up and ran toward the small three sided structure with a roof and bench. After a glance around, Cheater dropped the busted up pecans in her hand, brushed her hand on her jeans, and followed.

The bus was less than half full; the time of day for workers commuting to their jobs had passed. Most of those sharing the bus with them were the very old. Doctor appointments probably, Cheater guessed as Jaz found a seat close to the back, a couple rows away from anyone else.

The rocking of the bus nearly made Cheater fall asleep. As she closed her eyes, her head against the window frame, knees pulled up against the seat in front of her, Jaz spoke very softly near her ear, not wanting others to hear them. His warm breath startled her, the proximity of his face to hers created a sensation of intimacy she hadn't known for a long, long time.

“I should warn you, probably. That drama I told you I could give you will be the Beast. He shows up at the hospital every day on his lunch break. Trying to play the sad husband routine, I guess. We'll likely run into him. At least, that's what I'm hoping.”

It was then that the full plan came to them, during the ride to the hospital, all of the small details of events they hoped would transpire.

The bus ride took the loop around town to the hospital, the airport, and the largest shopping mall in the city. The ride gave them plenty of time to work out the details of how to save his mother's life and land the Beast in prison.

"So, what exactly happened to your mom?" Cheater gave up her dingy city view framed by the grimy bus window. She looked at Jaz; they had thought it best she sit next to the window, just in case. She squinted at him.

"Only I know..." He whispered so the old people around them wouldn't hear.

"The cops said she was mugged, left to die on the street. I know the truth. The Beast took her downtown, where all the dealers hang out, pretendin' he was takin' her to dinner. He went down there to make a buy, and she caused a scene about it, but after that gang leader recognized her as mine and Bree's mom, he shot her in the head, and to cover up his own part in it, the Beast filled a needle and pumped it into her veins, made it look like she was usin'.

"That's what made the cops suspicious; she never had a record for nothin', but the Beast did.

"He dumped her body in an alley for some unsuspecting person to find. All the while, he's livin' it up, gettin' high on his purchase back at the apartment, and she's layin' there in that cold, dark alley, slippin' into a coma because of that gangbanger shootin' her. Cops found her before I could. All he would think about was her layin' in the alley, but never where.

"Doctors think she'll come out of it, but I know

better. At least she's not hooked up on all those machines and stuff, keepin' 'er alive. She just won't wake up. I used to talk to 'er every day; I'd tell her about..." Jaz stopped short, redirecting his shining eyes out the window across the aisle. He pursed his lips and looked off into the distance, "I'd tell 'er the story, the one she told us that gave us so much hope. She doesn't understand me, though. There ain't no thoughts in her head anymore, and I keep thinkin' if she's comin' out of it, shouldn't she be thinkin' somethin'? Other sleepin' people have thoughts, dreams don't they?"

Cheater turned back to the window, gray skyscrapers and brick warehouses filling the horizon. Cars whizzed past on the road below. She wiped at the tear escaping her eye before Jaz could see it. She couldn't wipe away the cold damp trail between her cheek and nose, though.

A beautiful, old, stone church caught her attention; its stained glass windows, featuring baby Jesus in his mother's arms, and Jesus nailed to the cross. Sadness filled her; she realized she hadn't been in a church since Sadie died, which added to the heartbreak of the story this unknown boy from yesterday just told her.

Church was a place she had gone many Sundays in her life, until Sadie's death. Some foster parents took the children, some did not. She wondered what her mother thought about her not going now, what Jesus thought about that, and believed that somehow they understood.

"I told the cops he drugged her, left her layin' out there after getting shot by bangers," Jaz continued with his story. "Of course, they didn't believe me, a kid versus his stepdad. How would I know, right? They asked him, anyway. That's why he's so nervous 'bout me leavin'. He knows I know, and he doesn't get how. Plus, he wants to put on that happy family show. Hmpf!" He grunted.

"At least your mom's still alive, for now. You still have her; there's still hope." Cheater couldn't contain the slight jealousy in her voice, but she quickly regretted feeling that way and hoped Jaz didn't notice.

"Hey, it's cool! I get it!" He looked at her and smiled sympathetically.

"And, hopefully, she'll be able to answer some questions for us. You ever go to church?" She turned back to the image in the windows, sparkling rainbows pouring forth from the colorful prism of glass as the bus waited for more riders to load.

"Uh... yeah. Momma used to take us every Sunday. Get us new clothes for the holidays, dress us all up. "Bree, she use ta' love gettin' all dressed up, ribbons in her hair, yellow, that was her favorite color. I didn't care too much for dressin' up, but it helped to go, 'specially after Daddy passed..." His voice became low, distant, a bittersweet smile crossing his lips.

"My mom used to do the same thing, dress us

up, me and my brother. I always liked the way she braided my hair with ribbons woven into the two braids. I loved getting all dressed up like that too... once upon a time. I went to church many Sundays, then not at all, then every Sunday until Sadie died."

"Yeah, I know." He lowered his voice, smiling sheepishly.

"I guess you know I liked her church best, too."

"Yep." He chuckled and looked away.

"Very funny. But you know, one time, after I started living with her, she tried to take me to a church that was the same as the one my parents went to, and something weird happened." She gazed at the big church, at the crucifix stained into the window. "They wouldn't let us in. One of the Deacons stopped us at the door, asked Sadie some questions, and told us we couldn't go there.

"That never happened before at our old church. Everyone was always welcome. In all my life, I never remember being asked to leave a church."

"You know what? I heard some nurses at the hospital talkin' about something like that happening to one of them. The nurse who was tellin' about it just transferred here 'cause her husband wasn't workin' and hadn't been able to find work back home. He and her family had been visiting different churches, tryin' to find one they liked, and the same thing happened. It was right after Momma went into the hospital. I was kinda' shocked about that, too. I don't know why they would do that. I thought anybody anywhere could attend any church they wanted. I mean, isn't that like, a right or something, freedom of religion?"

"Yeah, I think so. I never heard of that happening before, either. I just remember Sadie mumblin' somethin' about not being rich enough, or somethin' like that."

"Rich enough? Wow! I don't even know any rich people today."

When Cheater turned back to gaze out the window, the buildings outside blended into the next as memories turned in her mind.

One building in particular, an old high rise, about sixteen stories tall, reminded her of a time when she lived in a city this size, the third time she had moved. She'd lived with the foster family when she was eight; the father left every morning at the same time and returned at the same time, late. She never knew what he did when he left. She just remembered him returning, impatient and stressed.

The mother stayed home and took care of the huge apartment and seven children. They had three children of their own and four foster children. The sweet mother baked every day between chauffeuring the kids to soccer, ballet, tennis, piano and voice lessons. That was the first and last time in her life that Cheater had played soccer.

Sometimes, Mrs. Munsen, the mother, had little sales parties and the children would come in from playing outside on a Saturday and find the apartment full of women. Mrs. Munsen would send the children upstairs to play, and they would play hide and seek. Cheater never got caught. It was like a dream, living there with the Munsens— a very busy, happy, city dream. As with most foster homes, Cheater gave up love for comfort.

Then, one night, Mr. Munsen came home late, panicked and desperate. He was angry, yelling slurred words about losing his job. He slammed doors behind him.

Mrs. Munsen, always positive, cried uncontrollably, trying to calm him, telling him it would be all right.

Cheater came fully awake in the big, bright yellow room and slipped out of bed; she had opened her bedroom door a crack and a sliver of light rushed in, along with the view of the foyer.

She saw Mr. Munsen rush by her door, on his way to his big bedroom.

She saw him return with something shiny in his hand, but he was so angry he didn't notice Cheater peeking out the narrow crack.

Her acute sense of intuition made her suddenly afraid, very afraid.

She went to her closet, where two trunks of old clothes were stored. She opened one to examine the empty space, and then closed it.

She climbed on top of the trunks, reaching up to the shelf above the hanging clothes, the pretty Sunday dresses, her new school clothes, the hanging rack of tennis shoes, sandals and dress shoes, and then she climbed upward.

She pushed up with her small hands, on the cut out in the ceiling and climbed up into the attic, where she kept a silver key ring flashlight; the ceiling was the favorite of all of her hiding places. The one she always used during hide-and-seek when she never got caught, her own secret place.

Once in the ceiling, she replaced the ceiling tile, sliding it noiselessly into place.

She lay on the ceiling beam, among the silver air ducts, trembling with fear, and when she heard the first loud bang, her body jumped reflexively.

With a second, closer bang the tears came, but she didn't understand why.

She heard one of the older Munsen boys, Jason, the thirteen-year-old, release a cry, "Dad, what've you done? No!" Then a bang, and she plugged her ears tightly with her fingers, wishing she could have warned the other children because she knew the loud bangs were bad, worse than fireworks.

She could still hear the awful sounds, the muffled screams ringing within the apartment.

She could still hear the door to her happy, bright yellow room open, then close a few minutes later.

She could still hear the sirens blaring, and a final 'bang,' before the doors burst open and policemen filled the top floor, high-rise apartment.

It had been hours before they found her, alone

up in the attic. A female officer heard her whimpering, coaxed her down, gave her a teddy bear, covered her face with a blanket while carrying her out of the apartment, and then sat with her, safely, in the back of a police car, wiping away her tears, shushing her calmly.

She remembered laying her head down in the officer's lap and crying herself to sleep, nightmares of the unseen tragedy filling her mind, the officer stroking her hair, assuring safety.

She overheard the officers talking at the station. Everyone in that apartment died that night, everyone except her.

Jason, Marty, Karen, Aliah, Marshall, Benson, her entire family, gone... again.

They had asked her what she heard, over and over, what she saw; until finally they were satisfied that she knew nothing more. The situation appeared to be exactly what it was. It was then that she realized evil existed, not only outside in the world, but inside of homes, bodies, hearts and souls, and it made her almost as sad as when her own family had died in the fire, but sad in a different way.

"Man! That's brutal!" Jaz almost yelled, unable to refrain from commenting.

He usually hid his secret gift from strangers, but the old lady two seats in front of them glanced over her shoulder and cast him a 'straight from the nuthouse' look. The horrible memory wouldn't allow him to remain silent.

Cheater raised a brow at him, too. "That... um... Didn't you see the way that animal control person back there was handling that dog?"

He continued, slightly embarrassed, in a voice louder than normal, and cast a knowing look at Cheater. He glanced at the back of the old woman's shaking head and turned his eyes across the aisle to the cloud specked blue sky beyond the window.

When they exited the open bus door at the corner and started toward the hospital, Jaz leaned toward Cheater, "Are you sure you can handle this?"

"Well, like I said, I've never done it on demand. I didn't even know I could do it till today. And, as far as I know, you're the only other person who can see what happens.

“Every time it's happened it's always been for good, I believe, because wherever I was, whoever it was seemed nice afterward; like you, they change. Is your stepdad capable of change? I mean, that other kid, the one you can't read, I got nothing from him to help him change. Nothing happened. I'm just worried it'll be the same with your stepdad. I won't get anything from him to bring on the blackout. I don't know if I can just do it."

Jaz smiled, "I meant, the Beast, my stepdad, can you handle him?”

She didn't know. She had seen many forms of evil, felt the evil within all types of people, but she wasn't sure if she could handle him.

What if he struck her like he did Jaz? What if he came after her?

Maybe this wasn't the best plan after all, being at the hospital when he showed up.

Maybe they could think of something else in the next— she glanced at a clock on the wall as they entered the building— fifteen minutes or so?

They walked down a long hallway, Cheater twice as fast to keep up with Jaz's long legged stride, the brown canvas bag bumping against his right hip.

Jaz finally made a left and stopped. He pushed the 'up' arrow on the wall between the closed elevators. Soon, a low 'ding' rang out from one of the carriages and the doors whooshed open.

They entered the mirrored elevator cab and leaned against the waist high wooden railing. Jaz pushed the number 11 button.

The doors slid part way from their recesses when a young, high-pitched female voice sang out, "Hold the doors, please!" and Jaz's strong hand shot forward to push and hold the 'open doors' button.

The doors slipped back out of the wall after the pretty young woman joined them in the small space. Her bright, red hair was tied into a loose bun, freckles dotted her entire face, and her blue eyes twinkled. She was carrying two plastic bags with printing on them. Even though Cheater couldn't see the writing clearly, she could smell the delicious aroma that filled the elevator. Her stomach growled. She couldn't believe, after the huge breakfast she had, that her stomach was growling.

"Well if it isn't Jerome James!" the aide smiled sweetly after entering. Cheater looked up at Jaz, with an arched brow. "Going to visit your mother?"

“Uh...” Jaz flustered, “...yeah.”

“Oh, good. Bringing a friend along?” the nurse’s aide indicated Cheater with a slight nod and glance.

“Uh, yeah... this here’s...” stumbled out.

Cheater looked up at the young woman standing next to her, who she guessed was probably in her early twenties. Images of a crystal blue lake filled Cheater’s mind as she looked into the sparkling eyes. The aide’s lips were pink, as were her round cheeks.

Cheater stole a quick glance at her own reflection in the mirrored wall of the elevator behind the young woman. A couple of inches shorter than the pretty nurse, her long brown hair hung loosely, wavy and was in desperate need of cutting; her thin face seemed pasty and colorless; her eyes appeared dull and sad; and her perfect-fit, hand-me-down jeans emphasized her thin frame.

As the elevator began its ascent, she looked back at the nurse, “Sara,” she finally answered. It was Jaz’s turn to raise his brows.

“Oh, you’re so lucky! I’ve always loved that name! I wanted to be called Sara when I was younger. But, nobody would buy it, everyone, even my friends, still called me Emma!” She pointed her chin toward the name tag hanging from the multicolored smock.

“Takin’ lunch up, huh? Let me take those for you.” Jaz reached out and relieved the nurse of her bags, as if he did it every day. Cheater’s mind found it difficult to wrap around the idea that this was the same kid who tried to mug Tommy yesterday. Her head shook with disbelief at being the one to bring on this dramatic change. Jaz glanced at her and smiled acknowledgement.

"Well, thank you, Jerome. You know, maybe introducing your mother to Sara will help bring her around. It's always good for stimulating the mind, you know, for new people to talk to coma... sorry, Jerome." She'd noticed the hurt in the young man's eyes. "She will come around, you know. The doctors say there's no reason for her to remain that way."

"Yeah, it's okay, Em."

What bothered him most was that he couldn't see his mother's thoughts, couldn't get into her head and find out what she was thinking like he could before the coma... well, at least most days he could. There were some days he couldn't read her. He always wondered why.

As long as he'd been coming here to visit, he hadn't been able to get readings from his mother's sleeping mind, even when he spoke to her. He was beginning to believe she was brain dead, though the doctors told him to keep up hope.

He never gave up either, because they were all so positive, though his better judgment told him to let it go.

Maybe her thoughts were just so deeply buried that he couldn't get to them. Maybe... ding, whoosh!

They stepped out into the hallway and Emma

led them to the nurse's station. A series of "Hey, Jerome" and "Who's your friend?" greeted them, followed by a few teasing winks in his direction.

Jaz rolled his eyes at them and introduced Cheater before leading her down the hall to the quiet of his mother's room.

Before they reached the closed door, a young doctor stopped them.

"Jerome, I need to speak to you a moment, privately." He glanced over at Cheater.

Interpreting the meaning, she leaned into the door and moved through it.

"I've been trying to reach your stepfather, but he hasn't returned my calls. There's been a change in your mother's condition. Do you think you can get hold of your stepfather?"

Jaz peered toward his mother's room, seeking an opening in the drawn window curtains on either side of the door, a look of despair in his eyes.

The doctor wouldn't tell him about his mother; he was a minor; never mind that he was her only living relative, he was still a minor. It didn't matter because Jaz already knew what the doctor wanted to tell him.

"He should be here in 15 to 20 minutes. He always comes on his lunch break."

"Can you wait to go in until he gets here?"

"Naw, I gotta be somewhere."

The doctor glanced at the darkening bruise above the taller boy's eye. "Well, okay," the doctor sighed. "I shouldn't tell you this, but I know your stepfather tells you everything about her condition because you always know what's happening." Jaz shot a knowing glance toward the door, "Just don't tell him I told you, okay?"

Jaz swallowed the fear in his voice. This was the first time the doctors had made any effort to share with Jaz directly. "Sure, man. I won't say nothin'." He looked back at the doctor.

"I know this is hard, Jerome." The young doctor reached up and put his hand on Jaz's shoulder. From the corner of his eye, Jaz saw the nurses at the station behind the doctor all look away from them, pretending they had work to do. "We had to put your mother on life support last night. She quit breathing on her own, Jerome."

Jaz looked away again, the sympathetic gaze the doctor held enough to cause him to burst into tears, rage filling his face, an anger that could lead to the death of another human being.

Cheater felt like a criminal, listening just inside the doorway, but she also hurt very deeply for Jaz.

Moreover, this turn for the worst put a twist in their plan, a plan that was about fifteen minutes from taking place.

"I'm sorry, Jerome. I just wanted to warn you before you went in to see her."

"Thanks, Doc." He turned away from the doctor's consoling touch and continued to his mother's room.

Cheater smiled sadly at him when he entered, then followed Jaz around the curtain to the bedside.

The young girl was definitely not prepared for what she saw as they moved closer to the bed, Jaz flipping the lamp switch on the end table, sending out a heavenly yellow glow just over his mother's face.

His mother, breathing tube taped to her mouth, wires and tubes running from various parts of her body to various types of machinery, beeping, buzzing and humming softly, looked like an angel upon the pillow, covered by a white cloud, under protection of pale sheet and blanket.

Though her eyes were closed, Cheater knew they would only have beautified her features more had they been open.

The same facial structure as her son, fine, delicate cheekbones, nose flaring out gently at the nostrils, covered by a slightly darkened, porcelain-like complexion, and a head full of lustrous black hair, straight and shoulder length, made her the most beautiful woman Cheater had ever seen, with the exception of her own mother, whose face bore different features, but the same beautiful countenance and angelic quality. And soon, she would return to her home in Heaven with Cheater's mother.

The woman before her now could have been a model straight off the cover of a magazine at the newsstand in the lobby. The young girl was speechless in the presence of this sleeping woman, while she marveled curiously at the difference in the shades between mother and son.

"Yeah, she's beautiful, ain't she? My sister looked just like her.

"Bree wanted to be a model, leave here for New York City and try to break into the big time. She was going to after she finished school." He paused looking gently at his mother, a boyish charm filling his face, "Hi, momma. This is Sara." Jaz glanced up at Cheater and smiled, then continued on as if his mother had acknowledged her. "momma, I'm thinking about leavin' here. I just wanted to come tell you, to say goodbye. I want to take you with me, if you wake up. I want you to come along. I love you, momma." He stroked her hair and paused, awaiting a reply, his eyes shining with unshed tears.

The silence was too much for Cheater, a heartbreaking, bittersweet silence that made her cry. "Mrs..." her voice faltered on the last name of the beautiful woman.

"James, that's the name she shoulda kept, my daddy's name," Jaz whispered.

"Mrs. James, it's nice to meet you. I have to tell you, you are the most beautiful woman I've ever seen, like an angel I once saw in my children's bible. Mrs. James, Jaz... Jerome and I are very confused about some things we've discovered recently; we were hoping maybe you could help us..."

Instantly, the scenery before Cheater

thickened, swam, turned to gray and then blackened.

She was gone again, somewhere else in time and space.

The warm feeling enclosed Cheater in the darkness where she wanted to remain, away from the pain of this world, away from the evil about to enter hers. She stayed in the darkness for what seemed an eternity, without thought of the conversation that passed between Jaz and his mother, who now took over Cheater's willing body, made it her own to speak from, to feel and to see her only son for the last bittersweet moments of her life.

Returning to the hospital room with its dim lighting, feeling tired and cold from having been abruptly drawn from the warmth of the dark place to the chill of the room, Cheater trembled, looking down into the tear stained face of her new friend.

She didn't remember sitting down in the chair next to the bed. She didn't remember moving at all; she only remembered the warm darkness.

"Thank you!" Jaz was gripping her hands, kneeling on the floor before her and crying. "Thank you," he said again, before laying his forehead on their moist, entwined hands.

Cheater was confused.

Instantly he felt that and raised his head. "She's gone. She ain't comin' back. Just like I thought. She's been waitin' for you to come, so she could move on, so she could tell me. She told me that, just now. You were her; she was here! She was lying in the bed, and she was standing next to it.

"My momma was standing there, and she was telling me goodbye, and that she loved me, that she hasn't been very proud of me lately, but that she would be," he rambled, tears spilling from his eyes.

"She told me to go... to go with you... that there were more gifted ones... ten more... that we should find them... we needed to get to the place in the story, at the time when we're needed most. It's what we're supposed to do. Battle the monster, take down the monster... we have to.

"It's what she said... just like we thought. And she told me to get her necklace.

"Then she sat down in the chair... you sat down in the chair... and she was gone, and you were here."

The realization of his words was like a slap in the face with a soaked sponge. Cheater pulled free of Jaz's grip and abruptly stood from the chair. Forcing him to his feet, she moved to the side of the bed.

She was waiting for Cheater to get there? Ten more gifted ones?

Is Paradise the place?

She still had so many questions. She looked at the oxygen machine, still forcing air into the body on the bed. "So, she's..." she began.

"No, she's not gone, yet. She's stayin' to help us. But she is going. She said to thank you, too. And that she would see your Mother, the one like her, that your mother knew how much you've grown, how your power has matured. That she's been with you, in spite of the evil that follows you."

He stood next to Cheater, looking down at his mother, his hand resting lightly on Cheater's shoulder.

Cheater felt a tear, a salty trail, roll gently down her face, and drop to the top of her hand that gripped the bed rail, puddling in the crease formed where Jaz's hand touched hers. She wished she could have been the one to talk to Jaz's mother. They needed more information. They needed more answers.

Who is the monster? What is the monster? She silently pleaded to the lifeless form.

"We'll find him, the one that's done this to us, to the world. We'll find him because we're supposed to." Jaz nodded, his eyes never leaving the hospital bed.

"I got to talk to my momma one last time and I'll never have her with me again." He turned his head, and looked down at Cheater. "She'll be gone... forever."

"With your sister." Cheater tried to comfort him, knowing his deepest feelings as if they were hers. "And my family, and you could see them both, whenever you need to, and I have a strange feeling it won't be that long before we both see them all," she added, hope filling the sad words she spoke, a fleeting joy at the possibility of seeing her family mixed with a fear of how exactly that might happen.

"She said for me give you this." He bent forward and placed a shaky, gentle kiss on the top of her head, just like her father used to do, in the exact spot her father would have planted it.

For one moment in time, she imagined it was her father, felt it was.

She turned away from him in her pain, her eyes sliding past the clock on the wall.

"Jaz, it's almost 12:30! What time do you think...?"

"Man! Oh, Man! We gotta get outta the room!" he hurriedly wiped at his face with the backs of his hands, then leaned forward in front of Cheater to remove his mother's necklace, but it was gone. He searched the night stand without luck. He bent forward to kiss his mother's brow and stroke her shining hair one last time.

"I'll check with the nurses about the necklace. You better wait out there, in the hall, to the right. There's a chair. I'll go down the hall to the drink machines and signal you when he's comin'."

His nerves caught up with him, the forgotten plan filling his mind, and his voice shook with grief and panic as he led Cheater outside the room.

"Calm down! It's all right. Everything will work out the way it's supposed to, just like your mom said," she whispered, reassuring him even while her insides trembled.

"If you can't feel anything from him, wave to me. I'll come down here and do as we planned after he goes into her room."

"Okay, go!" She sat in the chair, picked up a magazine and patiently thumbed pages.

Ever since she discovered that she could change heated situations, people, she had relaxed some.

And since their plan had gone as expected so far, she felt she had some sort of control over this mystical power that filled her.

Glamorous young models filled the magazine's middle pages, but all Cheater saw was the map in her mind, the fairytale kingdom, her mother's smiling face.

She had never even turned the page when the atmosphere around her changed, thickened, filled with cold… anger… hate… putrid rushes of wicked.

She knew before she looked up why everything suddenly changed, but she looked up anyway.

The stony-like dark face, brows furrowed in angry disgust, floated toward Cheater, seemingly bodiless as she peered beneath her brows over the top of the magazine.

She wouldn't need Jaz's help.

She felt everything start to darken before he turned into the comatose woman's room.

The big man closed the blinds that the nurses had opened for the invalid woman, blocking out the light, the hope, and he moved over to her bedside, snapping off the lamp next to the bed.

"I despise coming here," he hissed. "You need

to get your fakin' self outta here. I can't stand one more day of disrespect from your stupid son, not to mention his bad cookin'. It ain't my job to be a daddy to that little p...

"Wh... Who are you? You got the wrong room or somethin'! You see any white people in this room? Ain't no white people... holy sh..."

He had turned toward Cheater when she entered the room, her movement fluid and trance like, but she heard none of his vile, race-filled ramblings.

She had been trying to stall the change until she was fully in the room, behind closed doors and curtains, which seemed to work because when she moved beyond the door, everything went dark.

"Stop! Stop! Security!" Cheater lay on the floor next to the hospital bed, waking to a nurse's screams.

Her head ached, and all she wanted was the nurse to stop yelling.

With her fingertips, she touched the right side of her forehead, a small knot forming. The light touch sent flames of pain to the top of her head.

Jaz flew into the room, cleared Cheater's outstretched legs, and hurtled the end of the bed, one hand grazing the mattress for lift.

He placed his stepfather in a chokehold from behind, his long legs wrapped around the large man's waist.

"Let go of her!" Jaz demand adding to the pulsing in Cheater's head.

Cheater pushed herself up from the floor, slowly rising to her feet, only to find a frantic scene. She shook the wave of dizziness out of her head.

Jaz's stepdad, large hand squeezed tightly around his wife's throat, bounced her head against the pillow repeatedly; loose tubes had been ripped free of her body. Clear fluid and blood spattered the bedsheet and the floor. Machines beeped and buzzed. Nurses screamed for help.

Jaz, his chokehold ineffectual against the adrenaline-crazed man, hung on, squeezing his arm tighter, pulling his left wrist with his right hand to gain more of a grip around the thick, pulsing neck of the Beast.

A nurse slapped continuously at the big armed madman, leaving the monitor alarms to continue their furious ring for attention, banging into Cheater's eardrums, increasing the pain in her head.

Two security guards bounded through the door, pulled Jaz free of his stepfather, and used a taser to force the man's release of the dying woman's throat.

The guards fought to get a zip tie around the thick, flailing wrists just before the doctor entered the room. At the same time, police sirens sounded below at the emergency entrance.

Jaz and Cheater were shooed out of the room by the last nurse who entered, and the teens stood down the hall by the vending machines watching the police pat down the burly Beast.

A nurse took Cheater's chin in her hands, called for an ice pack, and told her to go down to the waiting room until a doctor could look at the goose egg on her head.

The guards took out the big man's ID, radioed in his name, and read him the Miranda rights while hauling him toward the elevator.

One policeman who had been talking with a nurse came over to Jaz and Cheater to question Jaz about the incident, his patient face an opposite reflection to Jaz's gritted teeth and flexing jaws.

Jaz quickly rehashed the events that unfolded after he entered the room, his anger rising with each spoken word.

He wanted to kill the Beast.

When the policeman talked to Cheater, she told him the story they had planned out ahead of time, as they had entered the hospital; they had been visiting his mother; Cheater was epileptic and became upset by the tension the big, angry man brought to the room, and she had a slight seizure, crumbling to the floor.

Her bump on the head?

She must have banged her head on the bed rail; she knew nothing of what transpired after her seizure.

Before the elevator arrived, the doctor came out of the room and gave Jaz the sad, yet expected news. His mother had passed during the attack. There was nothing left that they could do to bring her back. Her fragile neck had been snapped.

Jaz became visibly upset, shaking, losing control of his knees and dropping to the floor.

The tears were real; the cries unforced, and the anger in his voice authentic when he shouted down the hall, pointing his index finger at the abomination his mother once thought she loved, "He killed her! He killed my mother, just like he killed my sister! He killed my family! I hope you rot in hell for what you've done to them... to me!" When their eyes met, tempers flaring and heating the room, the tension so heavy that Cheater could hardly breathe, the unexpected happened.

The large man broke free of the hold the two policemen had on him and ran toward Jaz, head bowed, hands held firmly behind him by the hard plastic zip tie, huffing words between snorting pants, a wild bull on the loose, "Just... take... care... of... you... too!"

And then he let loose a terrifying roar as he charged at the teenage boy.

"Stop!" the police officer standing with the teens yelled.

He drew his gun from his holster with speed and ease.

He stepped between Jaz and the bull barreling toward him.

Cheater threw herself at Jaz, moving them both out of the line of collision, her ice pack hitting the floor.

The bull collided with the police officer, his foot coming down hard on the ice pack, jerking his balance away.

The gun went off. The nurses screamed.

Both men fell to the floor, the officer taking the brunt of the fall and landing on his back.

A doctor called over to the nurse's desk and motioned to some orderlies down the hall.

The other policemen, the two who had been

taking the man to the elevator, bent forward with the security guards and rolled the bull off of the officer, his dark blue uniform stained with blood.

The officer groaned, tried to sit up, saw the blood, touching it with his hand, eyes wide.

Jaz and Cheater stepped farther away from the commotion, toward the other waiting room door.

A doctor checked the officer.

Another doctor felt for a pulse on the Beast.

Blood began to pool around the large, lifeless body lying on its back, flowing freely from a wound in his abdomen.

The doctor looked at the policemen and shook his head, "He probably won't make it to the O.R., but we'll try. Get me a gurney in here STAT!"

The doctor barked out orders as the six men lifted the big man onto the platform and raised the bed.

People visiting patients, friends and family members, came out of various rooms on the floor, staring from open doorways in the direction of the commotion.

One visitor peered around the action and down the hall at the two teens as they made their way toward the exit, his fingers stroking a cool metal teardrop pendant in his pocket.

The nurses scurried to move everyone back to the rooms and out of the way of emergency personnel.

Although it hadn't gone as planned—Jaz had

expected his stepdad to get arrested and spend his life in jail—he was sadly satisfied by the outcome. As they pushed the large man down the hallway to the ER where they were more equipped to handle trauma, he heard the doctor's voice, "He's coding! Get some paddles!"

As he and Cheater moved away from the commotion, nearly invisible to all those involved, except for the one who watched them, Jaz looked one last time at the face of the Beast, the heaven seeking, unfocused eyes of the man who claimed to love his family, and where he should have felt a new grief, he felt nothing but sorry for the Beast who harbored so much anger and hatred that he had to take it out on those who once loved him.

It was finally over.

Jaz comforted himself with the thought that the man wouldn't have an opportunity to get out of jail in the future and hurt other people. He and Cheater cleared the waiting room at the farthest end of the floor where a different set of elevators waited for them.

Jaz felt free; free to move on to wherever his life would take him, with Cheater, to unknown places, people and events.

He hadn't expected to feel that way so soon after his mother died.

As he watched from the elevator, the doctor pulled a sheet up over the body and called time of death, another body ready for the orderlies to wheel to the cold room downstairs.

Two nurses had been in the room with his mother when the teens slipped away, disconnecting wires and hoses, and Jaz visualized a doctor pulling the sheet up over her face.

Another tear trickled down the space between Jaz's nose and his cheek as he whispered, "Goodbye, Momma."

He felt Cheater's light touch on his forearm as the elevator doors closed. "Her necklace!" He lifted his bag farther up on his shoulder. "I can't go back and ask now. Not with the cops there. I'm sorry momma."

The teens slipped out of the hospital unnoticed.

Once outside, the bright sun pushed sparse clouds aside revealing blue sky, bringing their low moods higher.

"What now?" Cheater asked.

"They'll bury Mom next to my sister. She had it arranged after my dad died, for all of us."

"Shouldn't you stay? Won't they wonder why you didn't go to the funeral? You wanna go back to the apartment and get some more of your stuff?"

"Naw, ain't nuthin' else there I need. It's all right here." He patted his canvas bag. "Besides, she told me we needed to leave right away. She told me the time is close, whatever that means, and not to worry about the funeral and stuff, it was just superficial.

"And, too many people will be looking for us now, after the services, too many dangers, she said." He turned away until the mist in his eyes cleared.

Cheater remembered her own family's funeral, the plot awaiting her next to theirs, the only surviving family member a five-year-old girl not old enough to understand what had taken place, why her family wasn't standing with her instead of the heavy-set lady in the dark suit who stroked the little girl's head with one hand while dabbing her own eyes with a Kleenex in the other. Two caskets, side by side, lowered by strangers. Stevey was supposed to have been buried with her mother.

“How’s the bump?” Jaz changed the subject nodding toward her forehead.

“What? Oh, yeah, it... hurts,” she nodded.

“Sorry. Wanna stop for more ice?”

“Nah. It’ll be okay, as long as I don’t shake my head.” Just squinting with the pain made it worse, but never worse than the pain in her heart. “So, did your mom tell you anything else, anything that would help us?”

Jaz looked down at the ground, “Not. There wasn’t a lot of time.” He looked solemnly in her direction. “She did mention something about all twelve of us being born at the same hospital, different years. Same month, day, time, all that.

“And right before she left, she chanted, ‘Beware his minions but do not bother with them for each one lost only cuts him at the knees and he grows others.’ ” Jaz thought about that for a moment, as did his companion.

“That’s odd,” Cheater replied, stopping momentarily. “His minions?” Cheater was instantly sorry for raising her brows and winced at the pain. She quickly let them fall back in place.

“Yeah, but there’s ten more of us, with gifts, and she said to find them first.”

“That’s great! Where are we supposed look?”

“We need to find a map. We should catch

another bus to the city limits, get outta town at least."

"Well..." She produced the computer map from her pocket and handed it to Jaz.

He took the map from her, thought to himself a while, and started to move across the parking lot toward an upper class residential area.

Thumping the map from time to time and watching the traffic, taking an alley here, cutting through a yard there, Jaz led them to a park with several picnic covered areas and restrooms.

In the park, enclosed by a chain-link fence, a play area for younger children silently waited for after schoolers. He led Cheater toward a small playhouse building and huddled, hidden, against a wall to keep from being spotted.

They used the time to think. A bus stop stood just down the street from where they sat.

"What's this map for?" He glanced over at Cheater, whose head now lay propped against his canvas bag in the corner. She stared up at the worn and dirty roof of the playhouse.

A few bad words had been scribbled there in permanent marker, a piece of old bubble gum stuck to a seam between planks, and a cobweb hosted numerous small bugs, but no spider.

"It's directions for getting to Paradise from here," she answered, her eyes roving across the ceiling.

"Yah... I got that. Why did you select this

particular Paradise?"

"I don't know."

"There must be a reason."

"The fairytale? Instinct?"

He peered between the worn logs, "Hmm..."

"What?"

"I was just wondering how hard it will be to get there. I mean, pretty soon, my face will be plastered up on posts with yours."

Cheater's head shot up from the bag, just missing a low-hanging rafter; she ducked her head back down and tilted it instead. "You've seen my picture? On a post? Why didn't you say something? Did you take it down?" she demanded.

"Relax. I just remembered that. I saw it before that day you snuck up on me, okay? I would'a taken it down, but why? I didn't know you then. Wonder if it's because some of the other ten are there already? D' ya think, maybe?" he asked.

"I don't know. They may all be headed that way."

"Okay. Well, if this is where we need to go, then it looks like we need to go west from here, outta town, then catch the highway north a little, and then west again here. We just need to wait for the bus."

"Did she say if the monster is a real monster? Like the Giant and Jack, kind of monster, or a Troll?" Cheater wondered.

"No." He laughed.

"What? I don't like not knowing what it is. And

the whole minions thing? Wonder what she meant by that? Like followers, I guess?"

"Yeah, I'm guessing this monster dude from the fairytale has a lot of followers who are not important. They're just obstacles, you know?"

"Yeah, I wonder what we're gonna have to go through to get to that place?"

"I don't know. I just hope we can do what we're supposed to do."

Huddled in the small play building, Jaz found the quiet suffocating. He started thinking, thumping the paper, again, drumming the fake log wall, anything to make noise.

Cheater lay her head back down, exhaustion from the earlier fire wake up taking over, not to mention the traumatic events that followed.

"Hey, don't go to sleep. You can't. Possible concussion. Let's talk, instead."

"Why? All I have to do is think something about me, and you know it. You probably know all about me by now." She quietly retorted, closing her eyes with the thought.

"No, seriously, open your eyes and sit up. Come on!" He reached over and tugged on her arms, pulling her up into a sitting position. Then he grabbed the handle of his bag and pulled it from behind her.

"Oh, come on!" She whined.

"So, how many different homes you been in?" He prompted.

"Um... five... six... yeah, six..." Cheater nodded slowly, a melancholy overtaking her, as she faced her past memories yet again.

"Yeah, tell me about your family, and the fire and all. You were pretty young, huh? Five? Six? Maybe younger? What about your brother? You think that kid is your brother?"

"It doesn't matter. I'm not risking his life, again. Look, I'd rather not play this game. It's bad enough that I hurt physically, you know?" She turned away from his gaze.

"Well, tell me about other family. Didn't you have some? Anywhere? Maybe you have some in Paradise? Maybe that's why you have such a strong desire to go there?"

"You know I don't. We've already talked about this. I've ever known any other family except a great aunt, but she died. My mom was kinda sad when we asked her about our grandparents. We always wondered where they were, 'cause all of our friends had grandparents. Some of them even lived with their grandmas. The way Mom acted, I think they died a long time ago."

"So, what about the rest of the homes? Anybody you get close to? Anybody we could get help from? Any other kids with gifts, older... younger?"

First, Cheater wondered why he was asking about this when he could read her mind and thoughts and feelings, but then she realized he just wanted to keep her talking, keeping her awake until the bus made its way to the stop.

The words spilled out. "No. My second family, the Barterfelds, they couldn't have children. So when they signed up for foster parenting, they wound up with this adorable little five-year-old girl who was very sad and cursed and always asked about her family. They loved me; they wanted to adopt me, and they almost did.

"On the day of the adoption signing—I had just turned six—and the holidays had just ended. We were in their minivan, driving to the agency, and the van was hit by a fire truck. Mr. Barterfeld failed to stop at a stop sign. He was looking back at me." She paused, remembering the excitement on his face.

"The accident killed them instantly, and the rescue men found me in the booster seat without a scratch."

"Man! Awe, man! I mean, I feel sorry for myself right now, losing my family, but you... you lost five of them?"

"Six. They're all dead because of me, somehow, no other surviving children. The bad thing is, I know somehow that if they hadn't taken me in, they would all still be alive today."

"No, you don't know that."

"Well... yeah, I do. And we can't risk being caught on our own and sent to CPS, sent to live elsewhere, away from each other, like..."

"Yeah, I guess we just became our own family, huh?"

"Unless something else happens and you d..."

"Hey, wait a minute! I've got losses, too. Maybe it would be you!" he cracked. She had to smile. It wouldn't be either of them, until it was supposed to be—if it was supposed to be.

"So, what was Sadie like?" Jaz asked, truly curious.

At that moment, Cheater realized Sadie had flashed in her mind with the cheating death comment. She peered between the slats of the playhouse, turning her tear filled eyes away.

"She was special. A fantastic person. Took me in knowing all I had been through, even though it appeared I was jinxed. I loved her."

"What happened to her? Why'd you run?"

"Heart attack, I think. I don't know for sure. I just woke up one morning, and she was dead on the floor, hit her head on the counter. I feel like it was staged, like all the others, like something—someone—controlled the accidents. I guess that's why they're searching for me. Maybe it was staged and they think I killed her and all the others. They probably want to lock me up in a crazy house somewhere, keep me from hurting anyone else."

"Man, you know you didn't cause that stuff! Now, someone else, maybe—to keep you... us... searching," Jaz comforted.

"Bus's here!" She choked out bluntly, getting up and leading the way out of the playhouse, wiping away the tear that escaped down her chin and with it the turmoil of the day, all its death upon death.

They sat quietly in the bus, neither wanting to speak. The bumpy ride out of town wasn't long enough to do what Cheater wanted to do, fall fast asleep, but she couldn't do that anyway.

Traveling in motor vehicles of any kind had always made her sleepy. She lay the uninjured side of her head over on the cool window and closed her eyes, remembering.

Soon, images of her youth filled her thoughts, sweet pictures of what once was and never could be again.

Her mother smiling, waving at her across the yard to come to her, and telling her how special she was, how her destiny was so grand that neither of them could imagine her future. She would be anything and everything, all the joy in everyone's life.

She couldn't figure that one out, because nearly everyone in her life seemed to die. How could she be a joy to any of them?

Just when Cheater began to wonder if her mother had known about her special gift since the day her daughter was born, the bus jerked to a stop, "City limits!" The driver's voice sang out from the speaker.

They looked at the sad little run down

convenience store located just inside the city limits, the last bus stop out of town, its neon 'OPEN' sign blinking on and off. Metal bars covered the outside of the high windows and double doors. Two single out of order gas pumps out front stood sentry covered by a wind damaged metal canopy. They watched as the bus turned around and headed back toward town.

The signs above the pumps boasted Unleaded $10.99, Diesel $15.99 as they creaked on their frames, swinging back and forth in the slight breeze like a lone swing dangling from a dead tree in a horror film.

"Kinda gives you that scary movie feeling, don't it?" Jaz whispered.

"It's a little creepy. Reminds me of a scene from an old black and white film I saw one time, except, they didn't have gas stations back then." Cheater cringed, expecting a monster, perhaps their monster, to burst from the store to begin the chase.

No cars waited at the pumps here. The pump handles adorned plastic bags, out of order, like so many other small stores, the owners unable to afford the higher prices, customers unable to pay it.

The two teens watched the tail lights of the bus as they grew smaller in the distance, their safety net gone. They stood in the open, in view of any passing cars and other vehicles.

"We better get outta sight, figure out the best way out of here without being seen." Jaz nodded at the small store before them.

"Yeah, I was thinking... it would probably be a good idea to get some food and water. From the looks of the map, it's gonna be a long walk between towns. Maybe we should go in and see what they have. We may not come across a place to eat for a long time, and we don't want to spend too much money eating out, anyway."

"Yeah. Yeah let's go in there, but we need to hurry. We're just outta the city, and I gotta bad feeling about being here, ya' know? We better keep it light, too, so we don't have to carry too much, in case we have to run or hide?" They sprinted across the parking lot to the door, keeping their heads bowed.

"So, what have you been doing for food, you know, before the money?" Jaz wondered.

"You don't want to know, do you?" Cheater rolled her eyes toward him. "It's been a little gross."

An image popped into his head, and he made a sour face, "Man, we better not spend too much. I don't think I could do that."

"Yeah, I didn't think I could either, until I about starved to death."

They entered the small store, the little bell jingling cheerfully, a happy contrast to the sad, creepy exterior. Two cars whirred through the parking lot, made U-turns, and headed back toward town, but no strangers lingered in the store.

A short Asian man behind the counter said something to his wife in their native tongue, and they both laughed. Cheater had the feeling they were talking about her and Jaz, but she ignored them and continued to the cooler containing the bottled water.

She pulled out two large bottles and looked at Jaz. He nodded back and held up a bag of chips. She shook her head and carried the water over to him.

"Those won't get us very far. We need something that will last us a while and give us the energy to keep walking. We're gonna be walking..." The bell above the door tinkled and a loud voice echoed from the small building interrupting her.

They hadn't heard a car pulling into the lot.

They hadn't seen the car through the barred windows.

They'd been caught off guard at the panicked tinkling of the front door and the look on the owners' faces as the short, muscular, masked man entered followed by yelling and loud cracks.

"Everybody get down!"

RAT-A-TAT-TAT!

Cheater felt Jaz pull her to the floor before she could finish her sentence as Styrofoam ceiling tile snowed down around her between the aisles.

She leaned to her right, peeking around the end cap, peanuts and trail mixes shielding her, the floor length glass window next to the door revealing what she feared.

Neither had seen the black car with the dark tinted windows.

"Open the register!

"I said, OPEN... THE... REGISTER, OLD MAN!

Or don't you speak English?"

RAT-A-TAT-TAT!

The shots fell much lower this time, cigarettes and medicines bursting shrapnel from the shelf behind the owner.

Cheater realized that they had come out here to rob the store, not because they had seen Jaz come into the store.

It seemed unreal that a robbery like this would happen in the middle of the day, but with rising poverty and prices everywhere, time of day had no bearing on risk.

Violence and evil lurked at every corner of Cheater's life, it seemed, replacing memories of safety, security and stability.

Cheater trembled with fear, her hands moving quickly to cover her ears when the gun went off again, shattering shampoo and aspirin bottles like old mirrors.

If they could just stay down, remain unseen, maybe they would make it through this robbery unscathed.

The gangsters hadn't seen them, so maybe it would be over soon, she thought.

She feared for the elderly store owners behind the counter, though.

"He's gonna kill 'em. We gotta do somethin'. I don't need to know what he's thinkin' to figure that out. When he gets the money, he's gonna kill 'em." Jaz mouthed to her.

She cringed.

"If we get up, they'll recognize us! They'll kill us, too!" Cheater whispered.

The gun went off again, closer to their aisle this time, the shooter aiming wildly.

Cheater couldn't contain the scream that came with a start.

"Who's that? Get up!" the voice behind the mask yelled.

They stayed down, covering their heads with their hands, but it was no use.

In seconds, a different voice came from above them. "What about you? Get up! You got any money?" Jaz gave Cheater a now-or-never sideways glance, and stood up, keeping his hands up, arms stretched out to his sides, palms out, so the robber could see them.

Jaz's downturned face, eyes pleading with Cheater and passing her a paperless, wordless note, like a kid in school, did not raise.

Did he want her to run?

She couldn't run.

She couldn't see the robber, either, because Jaz blocked him from her view.

"Turn around!"

Jaz hesitated, keeping his face toward the floor, attempting to force an 'I'm dead' thought into her mind.

She had worried this would happen, even though Jaz was like her, was supposed to be a part of whatever lay ahead for her, his knowing her put him in danger.

She knew, deep down in the recesses of her shredded heart and soul, that he would eventually be killed, too.

"I said, turn around!"

Louder.

Angrier.

RAT-A-TAT-TAT!

Glass exploded from the dairy cooler.

Milk instantly pooled on the floor and moved downhill as if running from the shooter itself.

Cheater saw Jaz wince at the sound of the gun going off.

He threw his arms up over his head while ceiling tile and glass dusted his head and shoulders, and then slowly turned to face the gunman, his eyes filled with dread.

"Ese, lookee who this is. The Jazboy. Yeah, you not so tough now, hey? Where you gonna run to now, hey, Jazboy? I oughta shoot you down right here, like I did yo' Momma that night she showed up with that fat, stupid man. She still in the hospital, yo' Momma, or she dead now?" The gang member mocked.

The black mask couldn't hide the speech of the gunman, nor the evil glare shining from his eyes, and now Cheater knew why Jaz looked so angry and scared.

"Yeah, I should shoot you down, right here and now, in the very spot. Spray your little white girlfriend there with blood and brains, all over her pretty brown hair. Maybe she find out how you such a coward and come with me, hey baby?" Jaz shook visibly with anger now. The gunman jabbed Jaz in the chest with the gun and forced him back into an endcap, almost causing him to fall on Cheater.

"Man, let her go. She ain't my girlfriend. Look, I'll go with you; I'll join your gang. Just let her go on about her business man, just jump me in right now! I'll help you with the robbery."

"That chance has come and gone, Jazboy. You be nothin' but a punk, now. And a dead punk at that!" He raised the muzzle of the rifle level to Jaz and aimed it inches from his forehead, his finger moving forward to wrap around the trigger, squeezing a little at a time.

"Man, we ain't got time for that bullshit! Just shoot 'em. We gotta go, now!" The robber by the counter yelled, shaking a paper bag as he filled it with money and cigarettes.

Cheater stood up and moved from behind Jaz into view of both robbers, following her instincts, finally realizing what Jaz meant with his pleading looks.

She moved slowly, broken glass crunching below her sneakers, looking into the evil glare of the one holding the gun to Jaz, until his eyes join her in a curious glare.

"B, whatchu doin'? You ain't gonna try to be no hero, now? Get down!" His head bobbed toward the floor, and he swung the gun around on her, but as their eyes held she began to sink into the darkness, the transformation quick and painless for all, and the anger in the dark eyes, the evilness, dissolving to curiosity, disbelief, fear.

The other robber, his gang brother, stood transfixed upon the scene unfolding before him. A person he never thought the gang would see again, a member killed in a shooting, materialized seemingly out of nowhere, right before his eyes, speaking words only the two, and Jaz, could hear.

Then another figure, and another, slipped into view, all speaking in turn, all ghosts past shootings or gang strikes.

One melted into another: Black, White, Asian, Hispanic, old, young, tall, short, fat, thin, babies not yet old enough to speak, yet speaking plainly, great-great grandparents of the two young men, grandparents they had never met, who had suffered so much during the civil rights movement and fought so hard in history, for freedom, for integration, and equal rights to make the lives of future generations better.

People from all walks of life, in a short time, appeared right before the gangsters' very eyes, halting their actions, confusing their thoughts.

One of those people, the gangster standing before them had killed, with the very gun he held now, the nine-year-old body lying in a bed in a chilly, dimly lit hospital room, calmly awaiting his return to the life he left for deep sleep—little league, birthday parties, fishing with his dad.

Sirens wailed a few blocks from the store. Yet, the two gang members stood transfixed by the images and words brought to life from their own actions, not realizing that while they stood shaking their heads, eyes white with fear, at those before them, though not physically, the store owner's wife had set off the alarm under the counter.

The lady did not understand the scene before her, neither did her husband, but they watched the transformation of the robbers as they lowered their guns to their sides and listened to words of forgiveness that flowed from the ghosts of the past, words only three people in the store could hear, coming from faces only the same three could see. The storeowners watched as the four stood still, frozen in time.

With an absence of forgiveness for past actions, the sheer amount of such now overwhelmed them.

The robber holding the paper bag of money let the bag slip from his hand, softly landing on the floor near his left foot in a crackle.

He had just seen the very person whose death brought him to this horrible life, the one person in his life he had loved more than anything, the one who had been gunned down by a rival gang member, his hardworking, innocent father, the one man who never wanted this life for his son.

Jaz searched the outside window for the police

cars he knew were coming, wishing Cheater would stop so they could slip out before the police arrived, yet hoping she could keep it up long enough for them to arrive.

They didn't need to get questioned by the police now, after slipping out of the hospital, and he sure didn't want to hang around for any other reason that would compromise their quest.

Jaz didn't need for these two to come out of their trances and shoot him or Cheater, either.

As the sirens blared, lights flashing, into the parking lot, Cheater began the return to herself, and Jaz led her by her shoulders out of view.

The owner's wife silently waved them toward the back of the store. Her thoughts pouring into Jaz, she quickly opened a door labeled "Employees Only" allowing Jaz to push Cheater into the dark storage room.

"Put down the weapons!" was the first thing Cheater heard as she returned from the total darkness.

21

Minutes passed like years as the teens huddled silently while waiting for the arrests and police departure, Cheater slowly coming around to the muffled noises beyond the storage room door.

An angle of light crept into the room as the door opened. A woman's soft, high-pitched voice called, "You come. It okay. You come out now."

The teens stood, following the woman's voice toward her nodding head and waving hand.

Flipping the light switch, she grinned as she pushed by them, every wrinkle in her tiny face enhanced by her smile; she patted them both on the arm, first Cheater, and then Jaz.

"Store close; you shop now. Popo gone. You take. Free." She spread her arms wide indicating the undamaged merchandise throughout the storage room.

Her broken English cleared the fear filled haze in their minds, and they blinked in confusion. One word they clearly understood was "free".

To Cheater at that moment, the word free had a different meaning.

It meant freedom, the freedom that came with not having to worry about anyone else, about hurting anyone else—accidentally or otherwise.

She had been in two dangerous, traumatic, events with Jaz and he had not died.

He was alive and well.

Would he always be there?

Perhaps she couldn't settle down and live with a family, but she believed she now had a companion, and as he'd said earlier, her new family, someone to travel with her to that destination, someone to talk to, to joke with, to help her out of jams. Someone she didn't even need to speak to aloud.

She didn't have to be completely alone anymore; Jaz wasn't going to die on her, leave her alone, like everyone else seemed to do.

And there were others like them.

"You the ones." The storeowner said to Cheater, breaking into her hopeful thoughts. "You the ones." She repeated, nodding and smiling.

Cheater turned to her, catching her twinkling dark eyes, her toothy smile before she bowed her nodding head and Cheater glimpsed the tight black and gray bun at her crown.

The storeowner stepped over to them, shook their hands and offered a long, broken dialogue about the constant robberies plaguing their store. "Take... take what need." He handed Cheater an old empty backpack, "Fill."

"For trip!" His wife smiled and nodded again, eyes wrinkling in joy at the corners.

"For reward!" The husband handed Jaz another pack and patted his arm lightly.

Cheater and Jaz looked at each other, understanding that this couple sensed something about them, knew something about them.

From the fairytale?

Did everyone know the fairytale? Does everyone know the monster? What did they know, exactly?

Cheater wanted to find out more.

Jaz shook his head at Cheater's thoughts to stay and talk to them more. "We gotta get outta here. Once word gets out about those two guys, the rest will be huntin' us." He leaned into her hair and whispered.

"Yeah, you should know," Cheater huffed.

"Yes, you leave soon. You drive." The storeowner waved one hand toward the back door and touched Jaz's arm with the other encouraging Jaz to follow.

Jaz shrugged at Cheater and followed the shorter man out the door, but he had no intentions of taking the man up on his offer. "We can't put you in that kind of danger."

"You in danger. We take. Come."

The store owner's wife walked the storage area with Cheater and helped her load the backpacks quickly with food items: a jar of peanut butter, saltine crackers, fruit cups, bottled water, beef jerky, peanuts and sunflower seeds, canned lunches that didn't need cooked or kept cool and plastic silverware, all items untouched by the shooting.

By the time they were finished, the backpacks

weighed about twenty pounds each.

On the other side of the backdoor lay a different world. Covers in all shapes and sizes hid vehicles of variation. Mr. Store Owner apparently enjoyed a hobby that died with the rise of gasoline.

"Help!" the older man nodded toward the other end of a car.

Jaz grabbed the car cover at the back bumper helping the older man flip it up and off the vehicle.

"You drive?" The man pointed toward Jaz. "No. No, I'm not old enough." Jaz shook his head.

"Okay, we drive." The older man opened the driver's door and leaned forward digging around under the seat. Next, he started the car and pulled it up to the backdoor. Jaz walked back to the building, afraid of what might happen to this sweet old couple if allowed to help them.

They returned to the dismal, broken store, the shorter, older man patting the shoulder blade of the taller boy.

Cheater stood at the counter arguing with the wife about paying for the food.

"No! Reward! You not pay. You help. You save us. Police come. Reward!" She nodded her head more dynamically than ever and pushed at the Cheater held folded in her hand.

The younger girl argued, shaking her head in refusal. She needed to pay for the food.

"But I have money. It's not right for me to take this food. Please, take the money." Cheater forced the money back at her.

"No. You take!" In a motherly way, she folded Cheater's hand around the money. "You need, later."

Not wanting to make Mrs. Store Owner angry by insulting her generosity, Cheater resigned herself to folding the money and returning it to her pocket.

The store sign was off, as it had been when the police were there.

The yellow caution tape blocked the entryway, and the broken glass and burst chip bags, sundries and milk still coated the floor.

It would be some time before the store opened again. Mr. Store Owner, out of habit, went over and locked the door, set the alarm and turned out the lights.

"Come, we take you, now!" He motioned to Cheater and his wife to follow he and Jaz out the backdoor.

The light blue Nissan Sedan—a fully electric car—sparkled in the sun that peeked between thick gray clouds.

Electric cars had become a replacement car for gasoline versions years earlier, but there were still some vehicles that couldn't run as electric, and there were some vehicle owners who couldn't afford the switch or the gas.

The two teens sat comfortably in the back seat, their bags between them on the seat and floor. "We take to next city, okay?"

"North," Jaz spoke up, anticipating the man's

question.

Cheater shot him a cautious look.

“Two cities North.” The older man repeated, nodding and smiling.

Hesitantly, the teenage heroes nodded their heads and tried to return the smile.

The car was comfortable, the soft back seat hardly used.

It was a quiet, reflective ride, no talking, no music, just the soft hum of tires on the highway; no normal motor sounds filled their ears, as when the black car slipped up behind them before they fled in the alleyway, or with the bus ride to the hospital and the store.

Occasionally, the Asian couple spoke to each other in their first language, the two teens becoming less insecure about their conversations.

Cheater worried that something bad would happen on the way, or perhaps when the two returned to their store.

She felt a light touch on her shoulder.

Jaz was shaking his head, his eyes telling her not to worry, to relax. Her pessimism was well grounded, though.

After all that had happened in her life, she automatically expected the worst. However, she also learned that after the worst had passed, something better lay waiting, except in the case of her own family; nothing could replace her own family, and she always wished she had them back.

Every day she wished for them.

She acquiesced to the idea that all would get better, and her fear for these nice people subsided.

Cheater wondered how they seemed to know so much about 'the ones,' and she was curious as to what they meant by that, and exactly what they thought they knew about Jaz and her.

The question popped out of her mouth before she could stop it, "Do you know about the monster? What is the monster?"

The woman looked back over the seat and smiled, "No monster, silly girl! Just a dream. You sleep!" She turned back to the front.

She knew about the dream? So there was not a monster like in the fairytale? Cheater wanted to speak to them about their knowledge, but they apparently didn't know any more than 'the ones'. Besides, she was afraid that they might actually know something that she didn't particularly want to know.

She pushed her dark hair behind her ears, leaned her head against the cool back of the seat, and glanced back and forth over her cheeks at the two heads in front of her.

Soon, her eyes closed and she fell into a deep, uninterrupted sleep.

Her past surrounded her; a blanket of green blossomed up from a gray beginning, her mother's garden filled with leaves and blooms of future vegetables, the old tire swing rotating slowly in the gentle breeze, the hammock swaying lazily between two trees.

Cheater was five years old, digging in a mound of dirt, making mud pies, a dripping water hose at her side. She glanced over at the hammock, swinging gently, and in it, her mother napped.

Long, dark hair poked through the netting in patches. Her mother's arm, bent at the elbow, covered her shining, sea-blue eyes. A white sundress flowed over one side, back and forth, following the rhythm of the hammock, barely sweeping the grass below it.

A paperback novel lay open on her flat stomach. Her slender body disappeared in the bowed hammock. Long, narrow, bare feet one across the other below crossed ankles bore collected dirt from her recent gardening.

Five-year-old Sara Lee stared in wonderment at her sleeping mother, remembering a fairytale about a sleeping princess.

To her, the woman lying on the hammock was the sleeping princess and the handsome prince would *come out any moment and kiss her tenderly, waking her from her deep, peaceful sleep.*

To Sara's right stood the two-story house where they lived. It was an older country home, white with blue trim, and spacious, high-ceiling rooms. Smoke billowed toward the sky, gentle and white, the smell of hamburgers filling her nostrils with each breath. Daddy was cooking at the barbecue grill. The picnic table was set with makings for dinner, a checkered tablecloth topped with dishes full of hamburger fixings, potato salad and garden fresh vegetables.

Sarah's father closed the cooker lid—just seconds after Sara had looked at her mother and compared her to Sleeping Beauty—then he jogged silently, sheepishly, over to the hammock, hooked his fingers in the netting on one side, kissed the sleeping mother of two playfully all over her porcelain-like face, and then pulled upward. The swaying hammock stretched and dumped Mother book and all to the soft grass below.

Sara's mother stood up, shocked, feigning anger. With hands on hips, grass stains on her sundress, she shook her finger as Sara's father grabbed her and kissed her again.

She turned her head away, "Do you know how hard it is to get grass stains out of white clothes?" Her loud question filled the backyard, and she pulled out the sides of her dress looking first at the stains, then back at her husband. Sara's father smiled playfully, and her mother smiled back, "Don't you dare!" She shook her head and stepped backwards, moving away from him, but before she could turn and run, he tackled her in the coolness of the lush green grass, covering her white dress with more green stains.

As Sara watched and laughed, a flash from the corner of her eye caught her three-year- old brother, Stephan—Stevey to family—running toward them, laughing happily, "Momma! Daddy!" He screamed, falling atop his father's back, shrieking and bouncing on his father.

Well, that wasn't how it went in the fairytale, but certainly it was exactly what happened after the prince and princess got married. Sara shrugged her tiny shoulders, then joined her family, rolling and laughing in the sweet smelling grass, adding muddy handprints to the already stained clothing. Her father tickled her and Stevey until their sides ached, the hamburgers cooking slowly on the grill, the aroma filling their senses and bringing growls to their stomachs.

Later, after dinner, while her father relaxed in the hammock, her mother lay in the lush grass with both of her children, one small head on each of her shoulders, looking up at the high floating clouds.

Clouds of bears, dragons, dogs and other animals filled the sky.

"Tell us the story, momma, please," Sarah begged.

And she did.

She told them the story of the kingdom and the

gifted ones for the millionth time while she stroked their hair, the sun setting behind the trees, cooling the warm air.

Sara loved hearing the story, the story her mother made up, much better than any story read to her from a book, better than the sleeping princess stories, because one girl in the story looked just like little Sara. The five-year-old girl covered her tiny ears with her little hands at the mention of the evil monster who tried to ruin the wonderful kingdom, though. She didn't like the scary parts of stories. She didn't think it was right how the monster tricked everyone into helping him.

Sara fought sleep, eyelids popping like toast, until her mother told of the twelve gifted ones, how they found each other in spite of all the perils, fighting dragons and sea monsters and giants, how they joined together to protect the people, but some people fought against them, by the advice of the monster.

Sara always fell asleep before the end. Always, no matter how hard she tried, her little eyelids closed, and she would miss the ending. That was okay, because she always felt the ending was not good and happy like in other fairytales, because this wasn't just any old fairytale.

Thirteen-year-old Cheater, known then as Sara

Lee, smiled in her sleep, the sweet smile of an innocent, happy five year old, but soon awoke to a gentle shove on her arm. Jaz hated to wake her, but it was still too soon for her to sleep. He glanced over at Cheater's puzzled expression, a bittersweet smile of understanding emanating from his face, tears pooling in his lower lids.

He had always fallen asleep before the end of the story, too.

What will happen at the end of our story? He wondered.

In spite of the older couple's promise to take them as far as San Marcos, it was almost two hours later and several cities away from the old convenience store when Jaz and Cheater stood beside the blue Nissan and said their goodbyes to the sweet couple who had helped them so much. Cheater hadn't asked them the daunting question regarding how much they knew about 'the ones.' She had lost that opportunity to dream filled sleep.

As the car pulled away from the ghostlike mall parking lot where they requested drop off, they waved goodbye before digging out the new map from a donated backpack. It was then that they noticed the couple had taken them much farther than they had intended.

"We still got a long way up the highway; we keep north for a little while, then looks like a hundred miles." Jaz pointed at where they needed to cut west toward New Mexico. "I sure wish I could I drive. He was gonna let us take the car."

Cheater shrugged, "It woulda been great. But you probably would have been stopped and we would be caught. I wish I would've had the courage to ask them some more questions."

"That's okay, Sleeping Beauty." Jaz smiled as

he referred to the dream Cheater had had in the car, "I took it upon myself to ask them, and what they didn't tell me I learned from their thoughts, and you're gonna be just as weirded out as I am about it."

"Somethin' tells me I don't want to know right now, but go ahead."

"Yeah, well, maybe we should wait till we settle in for the night, sister, 'cause it's... Let's just say, you're not gonna believe it."

"I'm having a hard time believing anything that's happened in the past two days. Just tell me this: how does it end?"

"Just like the fairytale."

"But I never..."

"Exactly! Me neither."

"So, there was no ending?"

Jaz nodded. "Apparently, it was never written. That part's been left to us, 'the gifted ones.' But we're right about the monster, which isn't really a monster. He's bad news, definitely. And, apparently, he has many followers. A strong network of followers."

"Did they happen to say or think his name? Do we at least know that much?"

"Girl, there was so much negativity surrounding this dude that they didn't even want to think about him! I did learn that there are few, and I mean few, people who do not believe him or follow him, people from all walks. They don't make it known, though.

"And there's like, this faction of people against

him..." He paused, reading her next question, and shook his head, "No, I didn't happen to get the name of the group or anything like that."

"Then how did you find out about them?"

"Mr. and Mrs. Store Owner are members... very, very secret members. They wouldn't even tell me their names or think it. They knew. That's what they were talking about in their own language."

"So, we know this monster's a person, then? Not a real monster. We don't know who he is or what he looks like, but we know people are turning against him. We don't know how to find him, or where, but we do know he's part of the fairytale that we have no ending for because we write the ending.

"Since we seem to be living the fairytale, that means we will connect with the other ten!" Cheater looked hopefully at Jaz while she worked her way among the tall, tangling grass on the right of way, tripping when the flapping sole on one of her worn shoes got tangled in the grass.

She tumbled forward, and the weight of the backpack she carried rolled her over onto her back like a stuck turtle. She couldn't help but laugh.

"Here, I'll carry the packs!" Jaz chuckled, and offered his hand to help her up.

"That's okay. I can carry one. I just tripped over that clump of grass. You already have two bags to carry."

"Girl, you can't even carry yourself. Probably our luck, everything in that pack will be crumbs when we open it!" He joked.

"Ha, ha!" Cheater brushed herself off and checked the bag to make sure nothing leaked. "You have two, and I have one. We'll see whose gets crumbed up!" She teased, giving him a shove that caught him off step and sent him tumbling.

"Hey!" He laughed from the ground.

"Hey, yourself!" She stretched her hand down to his uplifted one and pulled. "You never told me what's in that bag you're carrying, anyway.

Everything you need is all you said. Does that mean you got something that's gonna give us a little help figuring out all this stuff? Some high-tech gizmo or gadget?"

"Yeah, I'm a miracle worker! And a freakin' genius! When we stop for the night, I'll show you all my magic stuff in here!" He patted the bag.

"Oh, sure, you'll show me when it's dark outside and I can't see!" Cheater mocked.

Jaz laughed again. He smiled down at her, his happiness at knowing her evident. She felt like a sister, and he just realized how much he had missed that feeling in his life.

They walked on the right of way; the heat from the afternoon sun emanating from the paved shoulder on the road and warming their bodies as the evening sun descended.

Clouds formed to the Northwest, thick, black, ominous clouds that bore lightning and rumbled softly in the distance. The clouds had been gathering since noon, forming and growing into darker clumps throughout the sky.

Above them, lining the side of the highway, billboards advertised everything from food to hospitals. One in particular drew Cheater's attention. A handsome, charismatic, friendly-looking face stared down at them. The man looked like someone she should know; kind and caring, someone familiar and helpful, but she couldn't place him.

At the same time, there was something about the man that sent thousands of tiny nerves prickling from her neck to her spine. She stared so hard at the huge face of the man as they walked up to the sign that she almost drifted onto the shoulder of the highway, a very dangerous mistake. Jaz grabbed her arm, pulling her back to the grass.

"Girl! You sleep walkin' or what?"

The billboard called out to passersby, "Join us in our mission of peace! Become a worker, not a loafer! We have a duty to cleanse the world and prepare for the riches that await us! The end is near! Join us today!"

"Look at that." She pointed toward the sign, a creepy feeling filling her soul. "Who is that guy? You ever seen him?"

Jaz looked up, "Nah, never seen him before. Looks like an actor or somethin'. I don't know. Do churches hire people to advertise for them, 'cause that looks like a church billboard? Guy gives me the creeps. Look at his eyes. Probably some model."

"Yeah, his eyes creep me out, too. Like they're following us, watching us. He seems so nice on the outside, but his eyes, they look... "

"...dark." Jaz looked away from the sign; Cheater followed suit, not wanting to think about the man staring down at them from his perch far above the average person, or his mission, not listening to the nagging feeling in the pit of her stomach that pushed and prodded its way upward to her memories.

A heavy, thought provoking silence fell upon them while they walked into the oncoming autumn storm.

Cheater remembered how her mother enjoyed thunderstorms, and especially how she helped Sara and Stephan overcome their fear of the loud cracking booms during storms as the wall clouds passed over the old country house, heavy rains pelting the metal roof and lightning flashing between rumbles, as if its electric arms could reach through the windows into the room where the two huddled together for safety.

One night both little Sara and Stephan screamed after lightning struck near their playhouse in the old oak tree behind the garden. They played in that tree all the time; this time of year the almost bare branches were easier to climb.

The two children had covered their heads with blankets, screaming and screaming, until their mother and father came into the room.

Cheater remembered her mother's explanation

of storms; her mother's soft, dark hair swinging back and forth over the tiny faces of the children as she animatedly explained how storms were a drummer band in the sky, one set beating softly, the rain, and the other set beating loudly, the thunder.

Sara could almost hear the music that night.

The band even had its own light show to entertain the eyes as well as the ears, and every so often the light cast across her mother's face, bouncing off her excited eyes, calming Sara.

"How can you be so afraid of such beautiful music?" Mother had smiled brightly; eyes riveted on the storm outside the window. Her long hair, now swept away from their faces, flowing down her bare shoulders to the back of her night gown.

After that, thunderstorms made Cheater sleepy more than anything, because the beautiful music they made soothed her into a deep relaxation, all her fears vanishing along with the symphony.

"Man, your mom loved you two a lot, to get outta bed and make up a story like that just to calm you down.

"Mine would've done that too, I guess, if I was ever afraid of thunderstorms," Jaz teased, jarring Cheater back to the present time and away from the coming storm. "My mom always looked at the good in everything... everyone... too. I'm gonna miss momma... been missin' her. I been missin' my sister, too, but I'm gonna miss my mom. I hope I can remember the good things like you do, and not feel sad and angry over their ending. I kinda got a thing for angry." His eyes flashed at the horrible memories of the last hours, at having his last hope removed from his life.

"You will remember the good things. Not right away. It took me a while. I mean, your mom taught you how, and she let you know what had to happen."

Was Cheater ever going to get used to this mind reading stuff? "It's difficult, getting used to your family being gone, though. Almost as difficult as getting used to you reading my thoughts, and making fun of my childhood fears." She rolled her eyes towards him and drew her thin brows together.

"Sorry," Jaz ducked his smiling face sheepishly. "I can't help it, especially when you have such great memories like that, or like that cool dream you had earlier about the picnic in your backyard."

"What picnic?" She shifted the backpack to her left shoulder, walking more swiftly, more assuredly, setting an even pace.

"On the way here, in the backseat of the car? The picnic dream?" he prodded, shaking his head and spreading his hands, as if the motion would help her remember.

"Picnic dream?" a deep horn blew from the highway to their left, and even though they had moved ten feet away from the shoulder, walking in tall, browning grass, they both jumped and turned.

The tractor trailer sailed past them, whirling a wind toward them, blowing strands of brown across

Cheater's face and snapping brown whips into the shoulder of the tall, slender boy walking next to her. He brushed at the cobweb like feeling it left on his shoulder.

"Man, don't you ever tie that stuff up or nothin'?"

"I would if I had a rubber band or something. Of course, my hair never bothered anyone else before... " she pushed on a little faster, watching the clouds over them collect and roll, feeling the humid, yet cool wind against her face, inhaling deeply the oncoming storm.

"Uh... maybe because you've been alone for the past few months. Who's gonna complain when nobody's there to complain? Here, slow down!"

Jaz slowed, dug into his canvas bag and pulled out a purple Scrunchy, handing it to her. With one raised brow, she took it, turned it over in her hands a few times, scanned the cropped head of her fugitive friend with curiosity, and then wrapped and twisted her hair until she had pulled it into a loose bun at the back of her head. It felt much better to have her hair under control.

"Uh... thanks?" She questioned with a raised brow as well as her voice. "So, is this one of those miracle things that's going to help us figure out our puzzle, or do you just carry ponytail holders around all the time in case you, what... need to tie up your hair?" She glanced up at Jaz's head again.

"Yeah, ha, ha, you're funny. Nah, it was my

sister's favorite hair tie. She had hair like my momma's. She almost always wore that hair tie 'cause she loved the color purple. It's one of the few things I have left of her, that and the picture I carry of the three of us."

Cheater reached up to the elastic band holding her hair, took it out and offered it back, "Here, you should hang on to this. I don't need it."

"You do too, to keep that spider hair off me! Besides, I have a few others. They're easy to carry, you know? And you and me and that hair band are all goin' to the same place, right? Since we're all three goin' to the same place, you can borrow it until..." he paused, not knowing how to finish that statement. "You want me to carry that other backpack now?" he nodded down at her humped shoulders, her strained, forward position, and her slightly bent knees. "Nah, I'm good."

"I can carry all three of them."

"I got it!" she snapped.

Between the tall coastal grasses and vine like weeds, they walked in silence, only the sounds of early evening surrounding them amidst the few automobiles on the road.

The quiet felt good to Cheater after the eventful day, but she soon realized that she had spent too much time in solitude and silence in the past few months. Having someone to travel with made her want to talk, even though she knew she didn't have to speak her mind to Jaz. A question raised her brow, and she waited to see if he would answer before she asked, but he just stared ahead and waited, submitting to a normal conversation.

"Those two guys at the store, would they have shot you? Us, I mean?" she looked up at him.

"Oh, yeah, no doubt. They were gonna shoot that nice couple that owned the store, too, if you hadn't stopped them. They're some bad ones.

"Funny thing is, one of them used to be my best friend. Long time ago, in grade school," he reminisced. "Yeah, we were tight back then, when my dad was alive, and things were good. 'Course, we lived in a different part of town back then, both of us. Dad would take us to Spurs games, then Anton would spend the night with us. We always talked about going pro back then, basketball, me and Anton. Bad ending to a great friendship.

"After his little sister got hit in a drive by, by a different gang— she died like, right then— he got real angry. His mom wanted to move to a different city, but his dad grew up here, wanted to stay, make a difference, change the gang situation. Her death tore them apart. His mom walked out on them, and his dad turned to drinking all the time instead of helping.

"Anton jumped when he was 12, just to try and get the guy who shot his sister, tore his family apart. Forgot about all those good times, the basketball dreams, the games with me and my dad. He tried to get me to jump, but I never would, and he kept gettin' madder at me for sayin' no. We grew further and further apart. I couldn't stop the flow.

"I missed him, especially when my sister died. I could 'a used a friend, especially one who'd been there.

"I'm glad he got busted back there, and saw everyone you showed him, especially his little sister. Maybe he can get some help now, ya' know, change. Maybe what you did will set him on the right track. Maybe."

Cheater listened patiently to his long dialogue with one question fixed in her mind, "You think after all that that he would have shot you just like that?" she asked tentatively.

"Yep. It's the life."

"So, we get more and more alike? Nobody left? You're sure you don't have any other family anywhere?" a change was needed; she could tell memories of his friend were getting to him.

"Well, supposedly I have an auntie someplace, but momma never speaks... spoke of her much, so I don't even know where she is now. momma never talked much about other family. Daddy either."

"Yeah? That's weird, 'cause my mom and dad were the same way. I don't know any other family members that may be living, and nobody ever showed up to claim me after the fire. Sometimes I wonder if there is anyone else, but then again, I don't want to show up on their doorstep and have them die shortly after like everyone else. You're the only person I've been around who knows so much about me who hasn't died, yet. It kinda' scares me, you know? Bad things always happening to the people I'm around."

"Yet? Oh, yeah, that's comforting. Thanks. Yet." He repeated, shaking his head.

"Sorry. It's true, though. I've been worried about what might happen if you stay around me, keep following me around, ya' know? I can't help it," Cheater frowned.

"Wh... Followin' you? Girl! I ain't..." Cheater grinned and Jaz gave her a playful shove, then he became somber again. "Hey, after what's already happened, I think I'm pretty safe. After what momma told me... you told me... We're cool. For a while, anyway. We've barely begun to live the fairytale, ya' know? Think we'll be around for a while."

"Yeah." Cheater puzzled over her life, their lives, looking somewhere for the complete picture, trying to figure out the last piece.

The sun retired behind a blanket of dark clouds, and the evening grew cooler, the storm much closer. When they looked back, the distance they had gained up the long highway appeared much less than expected.

"Hopefully we'll figure it all out. I mean, apparently we ain't s'posed to die, right? I guess we'll just have to stick together till we find out what's goin' on? Right?"

"Yeah, looks that way," Cheater agreed.

"Besides, I gotta hang with you! You got all the

money!" He lightly punched his new friend's arm and chuckled.

"Ow!" she playfully whined and rubbed her arm, like a tattle tale sister. She fooled him, but he took her pain seriously.

"Oh, Man, my bad! You okay?" he stopped beside her.

She walked on, throwing her head back, laughter filling the space between them. When he caught up, she slugged him in the arm much harder than he had.

"Ouch!" He rubbed the tender place on his arm, "I guess you better go easy on me with those punches, little sister! I didn't hit you nearly that hard!" He threatened her with another fist hiding his grin.

Already, in this short time, with all of the action of the day, they had become much closer. The thought of walking on this right of way without a companion crossed Cheater's mind, and she realized just how much a difference it made to have him taking this trip with her.

"You know, I'm glad..."

"Yeah, me, too!" He nodded, wondering what it would have been like for him, not having been truly alone a day in his life. "It's nice to have an experienced hobo girl along for this trip," he chuckled.

"Ha, ha, ha!" she mocked.

The dark deepened with the cloud filled

horizon. Lightning lit the sky brightly from time to time, but mostly dusk surrounded them; besides lightning, the only other light sailed past with the rarely seen traffic.

The smell of rain threatened, and Cheater looked toward the wooded area to the right for any sign of shelter. Though the storm seemed quite far away yet, being caught in the rain a few times, thunder and lightning surrounding her, had taught her to seek refuge well before the storms approached.

"Yeah, we probably got about... hmm... a half hour?" Jaz assumed. "Wanna keep walkin'? I think I see car up ahead. Maybe it's abandoned. At least, I hope it is!" Jaz pointed up the right of way to a car parked in the grass at the side of the road.

"And maybe there's some creep sleepin' in it?" Cheater doubted.

"Won't know till we get there?"

"We should run," Cheater suggested, glancing at the overhead clouds.

"Nah, real rain's still a ways off." No sooner had Jaz spoken, when a big raindrop smacked him in the middle of his forehead.

A few seconds later, one hit Cheater on the shoulder, and they both raced toward the car at top speed. "You gonna hafta run faster 'n that!" he laughed.

"You're the one that said 'a ways off'! Remind me not to listen to you, Mr. I'm-So-Wrong-Weatherman! I bet you've been a couch potato for the past twelve years and never even seen the weather!"

"Man! I didn't have time to watch TV!"

The two reached the abandoned car just as the rain began to fall heavily around them. They peeked inside the dirty windows and jerked the shiny green doors open on the passenger side. Their damp bodies squeaked as they situated themselves on the green vinyl seats. Just before the storm hit in full force, they slammed the wet world out. Fortunately, for them, the owner hadn't cared about locking the doors as most others did.

"I'll camp up here in the front, 'cause, ya' know, I'm oldest. Oldest sits in the front, right?" he smiled at her over the back seat as they adjusted themselves, replaying the age old riding game of seniority shotgun.

"Yeah, so, how do I know you're older than me?"

"Girl, look at you! You can't be more than eleven, right? Am I right?" he teased.

"Eleven! I'll have you know I'm almost fourteen! We're probably the same age!"

"Nope. I was born two years before you, so, when you're fourteen, I'll be..." he waited for her to do the math.

"Oh, shut up!"

"I hate that we have to stop because of this storm. We haven't gotten far. It's kinda hard to walk in the rain, though. I don't care for wet sneakers." Cheater's face saddened as she watched water rivulets race down the windshield. Her socks and shoes were soaked—what there was of them, anyway.

"Hey, we'll get there. And technically, we did get pretty far. I mean, we did catch a ride, remember? We don't even know if that Paradise place is the right one.

"Hey, gimme one of them Granny bar thingies out of your bag or somethin'; I'm gettin' really hungry."

"It's called a granola bar." Cheater handed Jaz a granola bar, and he handed her a bottle of water. "You don't think a cop will stop and check on the car, do you?"

Jaz squinted at the orange sticker on the driver's side window, "Nah, they tagged it today. Got two days left on the side of the road. Hopefully, the rain will let up, and we won't be stuck in it for those two days."

Cheater glanced at the orange sticker on the driver's window, sheets of water sliding over it, a background of thick, black clouds beyond that. "So they shouldn't stop, then?"

"They might if we fog the windows. Better crack the passenger side windows a little. It won't let in much rain; it's coming down from the other direction. Good thing this is a cheap car without electric windows." Jaz turned the crank a quarter turn. "Besides, cops ain't likely to stop while it's rainin'." Jaz looked over the back seat, "Hey, don't worry, this won't last long. We'll be able to leave in less than an hour."

"Yeah, okay, Mr. Weatherman," Cheater snorted, turned the window crank a quarter revolution, scooted around on the seat of the old Buick, and looked out at the extra glass-like layer of rain running down the back window, obscuring the view of oncoming vehicles.

At least if she couldn't see them well, then they couldn't see her looking out. The rain was coming down harder, and she wondered about Jaz's forecast.

Since near total darkness was upon them, and the storm clouds covering the barely risen moon made it completely dark, Cheater resigned herself to staying the night in the car.

That being the case, she would rather lie back with her head facing the traffic, so the lights of slowing cars could be easily spotted. She rested her head on the passenger side armrest and kicked her feet up on the driver side armrest, relaxing while staying hidden.

Jaz still lingered over the back of the seat, chewing and gulping, eyes adjusting.

"Yeah, we can catch some sleep in two-hour watches. If it doesn't stop raining, I mean. I'll take the first watch, if you wanna rest," Jaz offered.

"No, I'm not tired. I slept a little on the way here. Remember? The picnic dream that you remember I had? Besides, it's probably not okay for me to be sleeping, yet, is it? I don't want to dose off, and have you pushing and shoving me awake!" she touched the tender bluish bump on her forehead.

"Yeah, you're probably good to sleep. I mean you already have, and you woke up. Besides, it's been well over an hour." He chuckled, "You were cuttin' Zs in the backseat, all droolin' down your chin and talkin' to yourself! Bet that couple thought you were crazy by the time they dropped us off!" During a brief flash of lightning, Cheater happened to catch the facetious look in his eyes and the slight smile lifting the corners of his mouth. He was joking.

"Ha, ha." She rolled her eyes and made a lunatic face at him, then turned her gaze back to the seemingly double pained glass in the window. "I wish I remembered it, the dream."

"Hey, by the by, I was wonderin' where you got them fancy Trainers. Sharp lookin' shoes!" Jaz took a drink from the bottle of water, swished it around in his mouth, and then washed down the last of the granola bar. He twisted the blue cap back on the bottle.

"Oh, aren't you the comedian! I guess you musta tried out for that Reality Show a few years back and didn't make it, so you went solo."

"Girl, I told ya'. I don't watch no TV."

"Didn't have time, huh? Too busy doin' other more important things? Like reading everybody's minds?"

"Nah, truthfully, didn't have a TV."

"What? Didn't they have TV connections in that apartment complex? I noticed Tommy and his mom didn't have one either."

"Tommy? Tommy, who?"

"The boy you tried to mug?"

"Oh, yeah." His smile disappeared behind a long face showing remorse, shame. "I feel bad about that.

"All the TVs in the complex got stolen. The last Super. Only a few people living there could afford to buy new ones. We couldn't. We weren't allowed to watch it much before that anyway. momma didn't like television.

"The kid's okay, right? Tommy?"

"Yeah, he'll be okay. Don't worry about it. It's the past, already."

"That was the last bad thing I'll ever do." Jaz nodded, promising himself more than her.

"So, the Super stole all the TVs? Jeez! I guess Sadie was right. She used to watch the news every evening, and she would just shake her head, back and forth, and keep repeatin', 'I don't know what is happenin' to this old world, but it's gettin' worse and worse, girl. People all over turnin' bad.'

"Then she would go into one of her 'When I was a chile' stories. She had some real good ones. I loved listening to her stories."

"Yeah, she sounds like a cool person. Wish I had known her. She's the one started callin' you that? Cheater?"

"Yeah, because..."

"I know why, remember?"

"Oh, yeah. So where'd you get the name Jaz, Jerome?"

"Watch it, Sara! My mom started callin' me that when I was little. Her and Daddy would listen to Jaz CDs, and I would sway to the music. She said it was like I was in a trance or somethin'. Couldn't hear nothin' but the music. Cutest thing she ever saw."

"Oh, I'm sure! You? Cute?" she teased.

"Hey, when I was five, I was a babe magnet. Got my first kiss in kindergarten! So, ha!"

Cheater laughed. "So, did you ever learn to play? Music, I mean. Not kindergarten girls."

"Oh, who's the comedian now? Well, I can answer your question, but if you ever tell anyone else, I'll have t' kill ya'...

"I took piano lessons till I was nine. Never told my friends or anyone. Bree always held it over my head, like sisters do, always tryin' to make me do her chores and stuff, but she never told anyone.

"I remember once, for a recital, Momma dressed me all up in this loose fittin' black suit and combed out my hair, so it stuck out all over my head like a giant plant, a 'fro. She thought I was so cute, but I knew how I looked, like some seventies, pimp, piano player!"

Cheater squealed with laughter. "Were you any good?"

"Yeah, once."

"I bet!" She giggled again.

Silence filled the car as did each thought about

their past, their younger years and all they used to do before they lost everything.

"You know what I miss about bein' little?" Cheater remembered.

"Christmas lights?"

"Dang! Would you stop it, please? Yes!" Frustration filled her voice. "Besides a normal conversation... I miss the decorations and stuff. While I was walking into town yesterday, I didn't see a single Christmas decoration, not even a hidden one. It's kinda sad, you know?"

"Yeah, well, I guess people don't wanna risk gettin' arrested for decoratin', you know?"

"What gets me is not even being able to celebrate in your own home. That's the odd part.

"I remember when they used to light the big tree on the White House lawn! That's one thing we always watched on TV. Now, nobody even says 'Merry Christmas' to anyone."

It was Jaz's turn to be silent for a moment before continuing, "Yeah, I remember the year they passed the 'No Christmas' law. Momma was upset. It was the first holiday we actually felt like celebratin' after Daddy passed. Momma couldn't believe it. No tree, no lights, no plastic Santa or Baby Jesus for neighborhood pranks, or anything else like that. I dunno, it was strange, totally outlawin' Christmas."

"Yeah, they did basically. I remember that year, too, our last Christmas together, the one before..." She couldn't say it aloud. "My mom cried. She just kept sayin' how it was a terrible thing they were up to. I didn't know who they were, but I cried with her. We celebrated without all the Christmas decorations and stuff anyway. She ended up makin' that the best Christmas ever, somehow, totally without decorations. All we had was food, music and presents, but it was the best."

Cheater heard a zipper, and then "Man, I forgot to grab my toothbrush this morning! I hate dirty teeth." Jaz threw his head back into the window with a loud thunk!

"Toothbrush!" Cheater choked out in fits of giggles. Here she was, without change of clothes, shoes, little food and money, having spent the last two months eating wherever she could find, and washing wherever she could wash.

There he was, about to embark on the same type of misfortune, and thinking about a toothbrush? It was humorous, him only thinking about a toothbrush, but it made Cheater remember when she first started out, after she'd left Sadie's.

"A toothbrush?" she repeated. "Did you grab your toothpaste?" she teased. "One thing I've learned is, when you travel the way I've been traveling, you figure how to make do with what little you have. Less to carry, less to worry over, less to replace, especially without money."

"So, like, how do you brush your teeth? Oh, man! Worse, how do you take a shower? Where do you use the bathroom?"

Cheater burst with laughter then, at his afterthoughts, and the shocked look on his face as he sat bolt upright, thinking of all the everyday things he did at home, things he might not now be able to do. She knew exactly what he meant, but she couldn't stop laughing about it.

Eventually, her laughter reached his ears, his thoughts, and flicked a switch deep inside of him that made him join her; a tired, delirious roar rocked the interior of the car. Tears dampened the seats, washing the emotional strain of the day away as the rain outside washed down the dust on the old tree sedan. Hysteria set in upon them, releasing tension, anger, fear.

All they had been through in the past sixteen hours left them with the natural high of laughter. They lay back into their own seats, wiping at their eyes as roars became chuckles. "You'll learn," Cheater softly commented, a smile still on her lips, a giggle slipping between them.

The quiet in the car contrasted with the natural explosions in the sky, and the pellet-like rain pinging the metal and glass was too much for Jaz, too. He had been quiet, hiding, running with the wrong crowd—alone without friends or family who cared—for too long.

It felt good to have someone to talk to, joke with, laugh with, without inhibitions; someone who acted like a real friend should act. He hadn't had a real friend in many years.

"You know, a shower ain't a bad idea for you right about now. You could do me a favor and step outside; roll around in the wet grass for a while; let the rain rinse that smoky smell off you. You'd probably feel a lot better, too."

"I could say the same for you Smokey the Bear!" Cheater smarted back just before a half full water bottle flew over the front seat toward her head.

She reached up, caught it, and threw it back, listening as it rattled to the floor beyond the expectant catcher, laughter again exploding from deep within her.

A lull passed over the car, inside and out, as the lightning moved out of the area, leaving a gently drumming rain to set a rhythm on the hood, the roof, the trunk. “So, what happened to the other families? Yours died in the fire, that young couple was in a car accident, Sadie had a heart attack, that dude killed everyone. That’s four what about the others?” Jaz’s quiet, hesitant words carried over the front seat, breaking the silence, soft and low.

“I’ll tell you if you tell me. What’s in the magic bag?”

“Oh, yeah. A change of clothes, a jacket, a picture, some other things.”

“A picture of your family?” Cheater sat upright.

“Yeah.” Jaz dug around in the bag and passed a framed photo over the back seat. “You probably can’t see it well right now, but it was taken a year after my dad died. Me, my mom and Bree.”

A distant streak of light touched the earth allowing Cheater a glimpse of the picture she held, three, bittersweet smiles staring back at her.

“That’s a nice picture, but I can see you’re all sad. Your mom and sister, they’re pretty. So, what happened to you?”

“Oh, yeah, here we go again! We should go on

the road together!" He snatched the picture from her and put it back in the bag.

"Uh, we are on the road together!" Sarcasm momentarily returned the humorous tone to a melancholy conversation.

"I wish I still had pictures of my family. Somehow, with all the home changing, the one that survived the fire disappeared. That and my mom's favorite necklace. What else do you have? You said other things. Life changing miracles, you said, right?"

"Well, no cracks, oh Funny One, but I got what's left of a bottle of perfume I gave my sister for a present. She loved it. Every time I smell what's left, it reminds me of her."

"That's sweet. It's funny, you know, how smells remind you of people. My mom always smelled like baby lotion, or baby powder, and every time I'm near a baby, I think of her. Sometimes I smell it, out of the blue, no babies in sight. It's just kinda there, you know?"

"Yeah, that happens to me too. Okay, your turn. What happened to the other two families?"

"Well, they all died, in some way or another."

"I know that, but how? I mean, if you don't want to talk about it, it's okay."

She didn't want to ruin the good mood they'd discovered, the playfulness that transpired between them. It seemed such a long time since she had laughed. "I don't... I mean... you can read minds anyway."

Cheater closed her eyes, trying to avoid the subject of the others, driving the past from her mind, but the memories came anyway: Sadie and her heart attack, the horrible day Cheater had found her, lying there on the kitchen floor, coffee mug shattered and coffee pooling toward the living room carpet, speckling the tiny kitchen floor.

The Norfelds drowned that summer weekend when they all went camping and the boat capsized in the quickly changing weather. Cheater, the only one wearing a life jacket, floated to shore and was rescued by hikers.

The Barstons leaving their niece's birthday party—where Cheater had had a great time with the other kids in the family, jumping on the inflatable moonwalk and swimming in the pool—just minutes before that drunk driver rammed into their SUV at the intersection.

The Munsens and the horrible shooting, where not only their entire family, but all of the other foster children living with them had died—except her.

The newlywed Barterfields, so happy to have her in their new life together that they wanted her to be their own child, killed by the fire truck on the way to the adoption agency, leaving her alone again.

And then of course, the one that hurt the worst, her own family, and the fire that killed them after her desperate father went back into the frightening flames to save his wife and son; both had fallen down the stairs while her mother carried the younger sibling, her father, her hero, saving only Cheater, and dying with the other two in an ensuing explosion, leaving her completely alone. At least, that's what she always thought, until now... until Tommy.

Tears of guilt flooded her face as she turned her head to the back of the seat, glad for the darkness surrounding her, stifling sniffles and sobs. No matter how long it had been since the tragedies occurred, she remembered them as if they had happened yesterday.

Knowing Jaz could see her thoughts, she realized that she had just answered his question about her past life, and the dam broke free when she felt a light touch of compassion on her shoulder, and heard him whisper, his warm, breathy words floating over the seat and falling against her cheek and ear, "I'm sorry."

He gently stroked her shoulder while her sobs came faster, grew louder, over the pain of her past. She hadn't had the time to grieve, hadn't taken the time, since Sadie. Tears fell and the thought of whether a time would come when she wouldn't cry anymore, tie it to the dream that would likely haunt her again tonight, like every other night. Would she see the face behind the laugh finally, the face of the one she believed responsible?

She heard the click of the glove box button, some rummaging noises, and a small package of Kleenex appeared over her shoulder.

She sniffed and took the open package, pulling one free, blowing her nose. "No sense snottin' up these fine seats or those fancy designer clothes." Jaz attempted to lighten the mood, the way he had always done with his sister.

Cheater sighed a thin smile, choking back more tears, and looked toward his voice, the dim silhouette of his head, chin resting on the seat. "Thanks. How'd you know these were in the glove box? X-ray vision?"

"Hey, old as this car is, clean as it is, must have belonged to some little old lady. Old ladies carry Kleenex." He chuckled.

The predawn light shone pressed into the water specked windows, barely lifting the dark from the inside of the old car, when the two teens awakened to three sharp raps on the driver's side window.

Both started.

They had stayed up late talking which caused Jaz to fall asleep during his early morning watch.

Neither had seen, from closed lids, the glare of headlights behind the car. Having stayed up for several nights in a row, only to catch short naps away from home during the daytime, Jaz had been exhausted. He woke Cheater once out of a nightmare during the night, just before she saw the face.

Rap, rap, rap!

The second set of sharp knocks straightened the two fugitives to a sitting position, eyes wide with fear of the person making the noise, staring in at them.

From inside the dampened window, they viewed a wild gray beard, and long gray hair under a tattered straw hat. Their relief that it wasn't a highway patrol was short lived, though.

Beneath the bushy gray brows angry, cold, dark eyes glared. The man stuffed his hand into the pocket of his old denim overalls while bending down to peer inside the car.

He wore no jacket, though the air that filtered into the car was chilly. A red flannel shirt covered his arms beneath overalls.

He removed his hand from his pocket, wiped his sleeve in a circular motion over the window, and cupped his hands between his face and the window, peering in for a better view. He closely examined Jaz, and then Cheater as best he could in the early light, as if searching for someone, then, after a sudden realization, immediately turned red faced and angry.

Cheater and Jaz checked the locks on the doors behind them and found them still secured from the previous night.

The driver side doors were locked, too.

RAP! RAP! RAP!

The loud, sharp knock sounded again, and the fuming face glared back and forth between Jaz and Cheater.

"Open the door!" The heavy, raspy voice yelled through the window. "Open this door, right now!" He strained to make himself heard beyond the thick glass.

Cheater grabbed up the backpack, stuffing two empty water bottles back into it, ready to make a run for it.

Jaz hurriedly zipped his canvas bag and grabbed for the other backpack.

Cheater watched Jaz for any sign of quick flight out the passenger side doors, afraid the man might be some pervert and have a gun or something, but Jaz didn't move.

Instead, she saw him squint his eyes, staring at the old man, reading his thoughts. She could feel the man's rage, but she waited for Jaz to move first.

Beyond the back windshield, she glimpsed an old Ford pickup with a trailer behind it, but it was the rifle mounted in the back window that her eyes focused on. He owns this car, she thought, and she saw Jaz's head nod slightly in agreement.

It never occurred to either of them that the owner might actually come to pick up the car, as so many cars today were left for tow trucks to haul away. They had only been concerned about the police checking on their overnight hideout.

Quietly, Jaz spoke to her, barely moving his lips, "I think it's okay. I think we should open the door and listen to him. I don't think he'll turn us in."

Before they could make the decision whether to stay or fling the doors open on the other side and run for it, the man jingled a ring heavy with keys, poked one in the door, threw it open, and stuck his tanned, wrinkled old face into the driver's side of the car.

Eyes wide, Cheater and Jaz looked at each other, pressing farther into the passenger doors, frozen in time and space by the terror this concerned old man forced on them.

"What are you doing in my car? Do you know my grandson? Where is he? Have you seen my grandson?"

"Y .... your grandson?" Cheater stammered.

The old eyes turned on her, "Yes, girl, my grandson. You don't think I have a grandson, or somethin'?"

"No sir, I... "

"You must know the boy, you're in the car he stole from me!" he interrupted.

"Stole from you?" Jaz repeated.

"Yes! Good Lord, what's wrong with you two kids? Are you slow or somethin', repeatin' ever' thing I say? All I want to know is where my grandson is and why he left this car on the side of the road with you two in it!"

"Uhm, sir? We don't know your grandson." Cheater spoke up tentatively, trying to melt into the car door behind her, hand grasping the lock, ready to pop it and run.

This was it! They should have run when they had the chance. They still could, though. The man was too old to catch them. He probably just wanted his car anyway. Of course, then he would report them to the police and they might be caught.

"Well, if you don't know the boy then what in tarnation are you doin' in my car?"

Jaz looked over the seat at Cheater; they both

looked back at the man, and in unison replied, "Sleeping?"

"What? Sleeping? Oh, oh I get it. You two are runaways. Well, let me go back to my truck and get my telyphone so's I can get you two back where you belong."

"No!" They both contested, louder than necessary.

Not the word, but the desperation in the synchronized voices, made the man freeze. "Say, what's goin' on here? You two do somethin' agin' the law, like that boy o' mine?"

"No sir, we haven't broken any laws. We were just travelin' together, to the same city, and it started raining, and the car was unlocked and..." Cheater rambled the explanation.

The old man's face softened when he saw she was telling the truth, "Unlocked? Dang that boy! He just plain ain't got no sense! Boy couldn't take care of an ice cube!

"Well, I think I understand. Same city? Goin' home, then? And you don't know nuttin' of the boy who took off in this car?"

"No, sir," Jaz answered.

"Good God Almighty! I don't know what I'ma do with that lyin', good fer nothin' boy! Like to take a switch to his behind, but I never even raised a hand to my own children!" He ranted, pacing the length of the car.

"Well, where you kids goin'? Supposin' I give

ya'll a ride if you help me git this here car hooked up to that car hauler, so's I can take it back with me to Paradise."

Cheater and Jaz passed each other a look. "Uhm, yessir, I can help you with that," Jaz volunteered, popping open the passenger door.

"Well, I dunno what ya' done, but yer a right sight more polite than that rascal grandson o' mine. Come on, boy." He gestured for Jaz to follow him to the truck.

"So where is it you kids need a ride to?" Cheater heard the old man ask as they rounded the back of the car. She slipped her wet socks and shoes on, grabbed up the three bags, opened the backdoor —stumbling out under the weight of the bags—and carefully scurried in her floppy soled shoes to catch up.

The old truck bounced down a rough area on the highway, Jaz in the passenger seat, and Cheater in the back seat with the bags at her feet. "So's I git a call yesterday evenin' that my car's sittin' out here along 35, and then find it was left unlocked to boot. They tells me if'n I can't come get it, they're gonna tow it off. All this time, I been thinkin' the car's out in the barn, right where I left the darn thing, covered in the same tarp I've had on it since Gayle died.

"Gayle, that's my late wife, God rest her soul." He said looking over at the two teens. "So's anyway, I go out ta' the barn, and low and behold, the danged ole tarp is lyin' there, bunched up, where the front of the car sat. No car. Right then, I'm thinkin' to myself, somebody done stole Gayle's car. Who in tarnation would do that? Well, by 10 o'clock, I knew. That boy din't come home, and I knew. Whoever hearda such? I mean it's a good thing, kids aknowin' how to drive by the time they kin reach the peddles on the floor, but in my day, I'da never thought about stealing my grand pappy's automobile! I wouldn'a been able to sit for months! But that boy, I jus' don't know!"

"Not to doubt you sir, but are you sure it was your grandson that stole it?" Jaz, having been accused of things he hadn't done so many times the past year, played devil's advocate for the missing teen.

"Am I sure?" The old man chuckled, coughing in between. "I will forgive you that as you don't know the boy. Am I sure?" He laughed again. Jaz thought that was an odd response. "Well, that boy been trouble since he come to live with me and my late wife two years ago. Twelve years old when his parents died in a plane crash. Angry, angry child, it just bubbled in his blood. Hated livin' in the country, away from his friends. Hated life! Hated me and his grandma!

"Strange boy, too. Somethin' very strange about that boy, especially when he turned thirteen. Never could quite figure out what it was about him, though." Jaz looked over his shoulder at Cheater, who wondered the same. Could this man's grandson be one of the ten they were trying to find? Was this more than a chance meeting?

It couldn't be this easy, Cheater thought, noting a slight shrug of Jaz's left shoulder just after her thought. Of course, it isn't going to be that easy. The boy is missing, she communicated to Jaz. A slight nod revealed his understanding.

The tires hummed on the black pavement, no radio played in the background, and silent, deep thought filled the truck.

The old man stared out the windshield, driving carefully, slowly, evenly.

"Yep, that boy's strange," he repeated.

"His parents died?" Cheater prodded. Another sign of being one of us. Parents, grandmother, next grandfather? She worried.

"Oh, yeah. Two years ago. My beautiful girl..." he shook his head sadly, "spittin' image of her momma, my own Gayle. Shiny black hair, twinklin' brown eyes, olive skin. My sweet baby, Maria, our only child..." His shaky voice trailed off into memories. A few silent moments passed, and he continued. "Married a good man, too, Hector. Good to her and the boy. He was takin' her on a second honeymoon down there ta Cancun, Mexico. The boy was supposed to go, but he come down with that Strep throat stuff right before they left. Had to stay with me and the wife.

"Yeah, she was a good girl, just like her beautiful mother. Always called, checked on us every day. Never missed a birthday card, or a holiday call or visit. Her momma would git down with that kidney problem and Maria'd be there ta help out. Loved her momma. Loved her family. Good, good girl. Who'da thought that second honeymoon would bring her death?" He sniffed and turned his head away from Jaz just enough that he could still see the road before him.

Silence filled the rumbling truck until the next city came into view; fast food and regular restaurants, convenience stores and shopping malls lined the highway, some open, most permanently closed.

"Hey, you kids hungry? I could do with some coffee, maybe one of them there biscuit sandwich thingies. Don't normally eat junk, but it's pretty convenient sometimes, 'specially since I don't cook much. Gayle did all the cookin'. Now, that boy, he can cook. Surprised me. Don't know how he done it sometimes, not much in the way of groceries in the house while Gayle was sick, but he could produce a meal from thin air, seemed. Often wondered if he was stealin' food, but word about that woulda got back to me."

The two teens glanced at each other, then at him, and nodded agreement. He guided the truck into a fast food restaurant with an orange W on it, parking the truck and trailer around back so it wouldn't block anyone else. The morning air still held a damp chilliness as Jaz pulled open the door and held it for Cheater and the older man. "Thank you, son." The older man nodded his approval.

They sat together at the table awaiting their order, the two thanking the old man for paying for their breakfast.

"Ah, I got some money stashed away. You kids got any money? You need to hang onta what y'all got if ya' do. By the way, the name's Johnston, Jeb Johnston. Friends call me JJ. Kids call me Mr. Johnston." He looked at the two teens with a smiling twinkle in his eyes.

"Um, I'm Sara, and this is Ja... um, Jerome," Cheater offered their given names over their nicknames, as the old man was already somewhat suspicious of them.

"Sara, Jerome." The man nodded at each in response. "You two have kinfolk in Paradise?"

"Yes," Cheater lied.

"No," Jaz contradicted.

"Yes, no? Okay, I understand. I mebbe old, but I ain't dumb. Ya' got secrets. Shoot, most kids today do. I guess I had a few in my day." He smiled and sipped his coffee.

An employee brought the order out to the table.

Jaz unwrapped his bacon, egg and cheese biscuit, and then stopped midway, glancing at the elder man and Cheater. He hadn't realized how hungry he had gotten. He tried to eat slowly, but wound up scarfing down his meal in silence.

"You know, I jist can't get over that boy running off like he done. And just before his momma's birthday! Not to mention just before his own. Say, you think maybe that would trigger it? You kids are about his age. What would make you do something crazy like that?" Mr. Johnston asked before sipping his coffee again, noting the sideways glance between the two.

Feeling compelled to answer out of respect, Jaz gave his reasons, "Well, Mr. Johnston, sir, maybe anger? Maybe he was mad about something? His parents, his grandmother, that's a lot for a kid to handle. His grief and all that happening right there where he lived? Maybe that's why."

"Heck! That's a lot for an old man like myself to handle, staying in that big ol' empty house. Mebbe yer right there son. How 'bout you young lady?"

"F... yeah, I agree." Cheater started to say fear, but couldn't for the life of her explain that without giving her own life, away.

"Fear? S'that what you started to say? What in the world would make him afraid? Not his grand pappy, for sure. I loved that boy!" He raised his brows at Cheater.

"Well... maybe... I...." Cheater quietly stammered lowering her head and peering at Jaz from the corner of her eyes.

"Sir, would it be all right if I explain?" He waited until the older man looked his way before continuing. "Perhaps he was afraid because everyone in his life seemed to be dying and he didn't want to lose you, too. He was afraid he would, and then he would be alone."

"Hmm. Yer a pretty smart young fella, aren't you? You two grow up together? Raised together in one of them there foster homes? You answerin' her questions ain't that kinda like you been together for a while?" His brown eyes darted back and forth between the two teens curiously, and then, to their relief, he changed the subject.

"Well, my wife, she was a Martinez. Grandparents helped farm my grand pappy's place. They were illegals, but not her. She was born here, right there on his farm same year as me. I fell in love with her the first time I saw her, when we were six years old, but we didn't know it yet. Used to play together when I visited in the summers, then worked side by side when we were teens.

"My daughter was the spittin' image of her momma. Beautiful, beautiful, beautiful. Grandson looks just like 'er, too. Good lookin' boy. Charm the skin—and rattlers—off a snake. But no good sense. 'Bout to buy that boy an old truck for his fifteenth birthday next month for me and him to fix up while he's waitin' to turn sixteen. Done the same with his momma. She'da made a pretty good mechanic, had she not turned so girly on me." Mr. Johnston nodded in reminiscence.

"Well, see we're all done here. You grab this here tray young lady, and take it over to that trash can yonder, and we'll skidaddle outta here. Git back on the road."

Cheater followed the command, curious about the date of the grandson's birthday next month. The two met her at the door and they were on the road soon after, where Mr. Johnston continued.

"So your grandson's birthday is next month, sir?" Cheater heard Jaz ask during a break in the story.

"Hmm? Oh, sure, sure, next month is his birthday, December 24th. Christmas baby he was."

Jaz glanced over his shoulder at Cheater who bit her lip to quiet her questions.

The look was not lost to the old man who checked her expression in the rearview mirror, "Why, one of you got a birthday next month, too?"

Jaz stumbled a reply, "Uh... well... you know... December 24th, it's just... well... yeah."

What harm would it do to let the old man know about his birthday? They wouldn't be in contact with him or anything. He was just a kind old man, a ride to their destination. It wasn't as if he knew anything about them or their mission. To him the birthdays were just another coincidence, so Jaz just blurted out his answer before thinking, drawing a surprised look from Cheater. Jaz left it at that, allowing the old man to continue.

"Daughter married a Bartholomew. Nice boy. Good family man, always takin' care of what needed done. Hard worker with a good job. Yep, he was a good man." The gray head bobbed with pride, continuing his ramble as if Jaz hadn't spoken.

Cheater listened from the back seat as best she could, over the rattles and roars of the old truck, but she quickly gave up and nodded off. Jaz listened intently. He found Mr. Johnston's family information very interesting, knowing he might need to remember it later.

Mr. Johnston didn't realize that Jaz's intuition and gift of thought invasion gave him a little more information than the rambling the seemingly lonely old man now produced. Jaz listened, letting the man continue, finding it difficult not to finish the man's sentences or correct him when he misspoke. He had never listened to a person whose thoughts were so in line with his speech, right down to the rhythm and tone.

"Anyway, that grandson o' mine, he and I get into this big argument. All I asked the boy to do was stay home with his grandmother; keep an eye on her just one day! For Pete's sake, the boy was always skippin' school anyway! That principal rang my phone more than anyone, callin' to check on that boy! I's always havin' to hunt him down, take his scrawny butt back to the school like I din't have nuttin' better to do but sit 'round the farm waitin' on that dern phone to ring.

"The wife, she caught some new bug, turned into pneumonia, bad case. That hospital sent 'er home, danged insurance, whilst she was still sick. Had to tend to 'er night and day, make sure she took her medicines and such.

"Those medicines, they cost too dang much, if you ask me, for anyone on a fixed income. So's I find I need to sell some of my cows in order to pay fer her medicines and oxygen and such, those danged breathing treatments three times a day!" He shook his head, scratched his bearded chin, and went on.

"One day! That's all the boy had to stay there to watch 'er whilst I went to sell the cattle. I called the school, tole 'em he was stayin' home with his sick grandma, got it all cleared up so's neither of us would get in trouble. I come back that afternoon, she's dead, my Gayle's dead.

"I ask the boy what happened, he says she told

him to run down to the Pates', our nearest neighbor, borry some butter fer supper, so's he did. I ask him did he take 'er temperature, see, 'cause she's talkin' crazy. We don't need no butter. Did he check the icebox before he run down there?

"'Well, no,' he says. Aw, I went ta yellin', and he went to cryin'. I thought he was lyin' see. After all that skippin' school, thought he just took off for the day like he does. So's I take care of Gayle, call the funeral parlor and all. Next couple days, after the funeral, we still ain't spoken t' each other, but I git up and find the boy gone already. Figure he took off to his friend's or somethin'. Don't know the car's gone, yet, see? Not till that afternoon. Boy done took off in the car. Fourteen years old and thinkin' he kin just take off an' go joyridin'!"

Mr. Johnston flipped the turn signal to exit the highway. When Cheater started awake with the stop and go motion, she noticed a highway sign for US 81 and 287.

Realizing, from the image of the map in her mind, they had been on the road for a couple of hours, she hoped it wouldn't be much farther because her legs were beginning to get stiff and cramped from all the sitting. She wasn't used to sitting so much after two months of walking everywhere; she missed walking now, and she rubbed her thighs.

Cheater wondered if they had made the right decision to catch a ride with this man who lived in

Paradise, whether it was the one they were searching for and if the others were there.

She thought about the grandson. It still seemed too easy for her. Nothing in her life had ever been this easy. The man in the front seat fell silent after his recent life-story telling, and they rode in a slightly tense quiet period for what seemed an eternity to the teens.

"So, I realize, mebbe, I's a little hard on the boy. Mebbe you're right, son. I mean, he done lost his parents, now his grandmother, and to be so young to boot. Mebbe he is 'fraida losin' me, too. I am an old man. Boy's bound to be a little wacky in the head right now—more than usual, I mean. Sure hope I find that boy, make it up to 'im."

The old man stared out the windshield, silent again, nodding his head with the rhythm of the bouncing cab on the rough road, lost in the past, or future, wishing he could change either or both.

Sometime later, the truck slowed, and the old man broke the silence, again. "Well, here we are kids, the grand city of Paradise, Texas, USA. Where kin I let ya' off?" he fished.

Cheater panicked, looking down both sides of the street, eyes wide with a question she hadn't anticipated. She spotted a convenience store on the left, "Over there... at that store... that would be good. There's some phones; we can make some calls." Jaz looked over the seat at her, a who-are-we-calling look in his eyes. The old man grinned.

"Okay by me, if ya' say so." He turned on his signal and pulled into the drive, going along with the charade.

He leaned over, pulling out a notepad and pen from the glove box, and scribbled something on it; then he handed it to Jaz. "This here's my cell number. If ya' happen to run across my grandson someplace, call me will ya'? I know he won't call; he's a proud boy, like his grand pappy."

He looked Jaz in the eyes, and the younger man understood that he offered his number to them, too, in case they needed help. The look left Jaz a little uneasy, perhaps because if the boy was one of them, they wouldn't be calling him soon. He might never see the kid again, given the fairytale.

"Uh, sure, and thanks for the ride and breakfast!" Jaz took the paper from him and hopped out of the truck, pulling the upper seat forward, so Cheater could hand him the bags and step down. They waved at Mr. Johnston as he moved the truck back onto the main road and drove slowly on, the old brown truck rattling, the trailer bouncing and bumping behind it, the back of the green sedan bringing up the rear.

"Now what?" Cheater checked out the quiet, empty street.

"Well, I think we need to find that boy, the grandson. He's one of us, one of the other ten, no parents, and Mr. Johnston said he was strange. I think maybe he's got a gift, too. Maybe we're supposed to help him, them?"

Cheater looked up at Jaz raising a brow, "Gee, that sounds familiar." She rolled her eyes. She had thought the same while she listened to the grandfather talk about the boy. How were they supposed to find some kid they didn't even know, though? Where could he possibly have gone after dumping the car?

Cheater flung the backpack over her shoulder and they started walking down the main street looking for a smaller side street with no traffic.

At an intersection, a few yards from the drop off, a small poster on a telephone pole drew her attention, and something familiar pulled her toward it.

"Oh, crap!" She said, grabbing at the poster, ripping it loose, paper corners still stapled to the post.

She held it before her with trembling hands, staring down at a picture of herself, above the small paragraph, "Wanted for questioning in the death of..." Jaz read over her shoulder, took the poster from her trembling hands and balled it up, squeezing it tightly into his fist; his knuckles whitened with effort.

"Hey, don't worry. We just gotta stay out of sight."

He slipped his arm behind her and patted her shoulder to calm her while leading her forward. "But do you think he saw that?" She looked up at Jaz.

A familiar sound filled their ears as Mr. Johnston's old truck came back up the road toward them.

Jaz slipped the paper into a nearby trashcan next to the old gas pumps just as gravel crunched under the tires, and the truck came to a stop alongside them.

The passenger window slid down, and Mr. Johnston raised his voice over the big motor of the truck. "Okay, so's I git halfway home and realize I can't git this danged car off by myself. Ain't as young as I usta be, see?" He smiled pleadingly out the open window at the two. "Whyn't y'all hop on in and we'll jist go back to my house and git this thing off. You kin jist throw yer stuff in the bed, heck, you can hop up in there yerself. Nobody gonna say nothin' out here in no man's land."

Jaz and Cheater shared an uncertain look between them, the poster on their minds.

"C'mon, ain't got all day. Gonna have cows ta feed shortly!"

If they ran now, he would surely call the local sheriff and turn them in; they'd be caught. He had been so kind to them already; it would be disrespectful to take off or refuse to help.

Reluctantly, the teens threw their bags into the back of the truck and climbed over the side, sitting comfortably on the wheel wells facing each other across a space filled with scraps of barbed wire, old buckets, and feed bags.

Neither had ever ridden in the back of a truck before. The breeze lifted loose strands of Cheater's hair, tickling her face and arms. Jaz found the ride liberating, refreshing; he felt as if he hadn't a care in the world.

In minutes, the two found themselves at an old, paint chipped farmhouse surrounded by rambling seeded and plowed acres, cow patty dotted pastures, and a long limestone driveway that nearly bumped them out of the truck bed.

Looking back the way they'd come, they realized just how far back the house sat from the gravel road.

A couple of well-fed, medium-sized, long haired, black and white dogs rose from the porch, standing guard as the old man's truck rolled up the driveway.

Although the location hinted of safety from discovery by the outer world for the two teens, it was not their safety that concerned Cheater.

Everything happens for a reason, she kept telling herself. Everyone plays a part in the story. She closed her eyes as fear for Mr. Johnston crept into her heart, and slowly made its downward to her stomach; she reminded herself again that there was a reason they were here.

As for the reason, it would surface eventually. It always did, but she sadly expected that this nice, old man with the missing grandson would not be alive long enough to find the boy, and if he was, this farm could be devastated by some disaster or another, like another fire.

That's why she hesitated in the bed of the truck after Jaz easily jumped over the side.

That's why she turned back toward the end of the long driveway, headed back down the road, after she finally jumped out.

The two dogs growled as Mr. Johnston approached. "Here, now!" he commanded, holding out his hands, one to either dog, the dogs sniffing his palms uneasily.

Jaz feared dogs that feared him. Perhaps they could smell that he was afraid of them, because they growled again.

"Git on out to that pasture, you gonna be unfriendly!" The owner ordered.

One dog whimpered, the other ran in front of Jaz as the boy came around the truck, looked up at Jaz with an odd expression, and then ran out to the pasture.

Cheater, lost in her own thoughts, hadn't noticed the exchange, the uncertain look as the dog hid, and then ran away. She had been too worried about being caught, about being the cause of someone else's death.

No matter what she told herself, what belief Sadie had tried to instill in her heart regarding her gift, no matter what her destiny, she couldn't take on any more guilt.

She couldn't let anyone else die because of her.

But there's Jaz, she told herself, biting her lower lip and glancing back at him.

Jaz who at this moment wrapped his long fingers around her thin elbow and pulled her toward the house.

Jaz was still alive.

Jaz who was right this instant reassuring her, yet again, with his eyes that she was not at fault for all the deaths in her life

Jaz was still here with her.

Jaz who she had known for little more than two days and with whom she had survived near fatal incidents already was still here, by her side, warm with life.

Perhaps, just perhaps, Mr. Johnston and his grandson were part of some bigger plan, and Mr. Johnston's life, or death, would play out as part of that master plan regardless of whether she and Jaz stayed or not.

She hoped beyond hope that that fate would choose life for him as she halfheartedly followed the two others toward the house, the border collies whimpering and whining just beyond the barbed-wire fence.

She stepped cautiously around cracked boards on the porch, not wanting to embarrass herself by getting one of the flapping soles of her shoes stuck in a hole and then tripping, like yesterday in the grass.

With great caution, she found herself standing behind Jaz in the dim quiet entryway of the run down farmhouse.

"Now, I'ma show ya' where ya'll 'r can stay. Then, we're gonna go sit down in my kitchen and have us a little discussion about things." Mr. Johnston led them up a stairway and down a hall to a room on the left, both of them confused about his actions.

"I thought you wanted us to help you with the car?" Cheater hesitated at the bottom of the stairs.

"Yes, that is correct, Missy. We'll do that later. I figure you kids ain't got a soul around here to he'p you, no place to stay, 'cept cars and benches, cold ground, so until you figure out what ya' gonna do, and I find that danged kid, mebbe ya' better just lay low here.

"This here was my girl's room. Young lady, you stay in here. Feel free to go through that closet. Might be some better shoes in there for you!" He pointed to the far corner of the room. "Over there..." He nodded across the hall to the first of two doors on the opposite side, "...is that boy's room. Young feller, you go stay in there. And down there..." His strong, wrinkled finger pointed to the door at the end of the hallway, "...is the bathroom. There should be clean towels and whatnot in the cabinets there. If'n ya' need me, I sleep downstairs, as my old knees can't handle this trip up and down much anymore.

"Now, why'nt you put yer things in the rooms and meet me down in the kitchen after ya' freshen up or whatever." He turned and grasped the railing, making his way down the stairs, disappearing beyond an archway to his left.

Cheater's mind filled with questions and uncertainty, causing Jaz to answer with a shrug of his shoulders.

Jaz turned and disappeared into his assigned room, leaving Cheater alone in the long hallway. She looked at beautifully striped paper walls, filled with family pictures, the grandmother and the mother, the mother, father and very young boy, the grandmother alone, unfaded rectangles surrounded by the old wallpaper where pictures had fallen—or been moved or removed? Cheater thought, searching farther down the hallway for the exact shapes and sizes of the missing pictures without luck.

One picture in particular caught her eye, the young boy. The grandson, in his school picture, sat staring at the camera, a solemn look on his face. She searched it for a connection like she had experienced with Jaz, but the photo didn't even tickle her intuition. Maybe it would be different if she met him face to face. Now, at least, she had an idea what the kid looked like.

She looked around, anticipating that tomorrow morning, when she awoke, the view would be charred, smoldering walls harboring buried, water-soaked treasures.

She hoped—yet suspected the opposite—that the grandson would have a home to return to. If he were one of the other ten, he wouldn't.

Jaz appeared again, gesturing at her to put the backpack into her assigned room, a look of doubt in his deep brown eyes. He wasn't sure about the upcoming conversation, either.

"What should we tell him?" He wondered aloud, following her into the room.

The room held pink hues, curtains, bedding, dusty lampshades, all in pink, walls a lighter shade, the mopboard in white. Cheater had once wanted a pink room like this, a princess room. Before the fire, her mother had made plans for just such a room.

She turned in one spot, stopping to take in the canopy bed. She turned another circle, disbelieving that her dream room could become a reality now, as if it were made for her. The room had been well cared for, too. Not a chip or scratch anywhere, just dust.

"Hey, forget the room for a moment. What do you think he wants? What should we tell him? We already messed up once answering about having family here."

"I know. Better to not say too much. Let's just see what he has to say. And just answer one at a time. Do you think he'll turn us in?"

"I don't know. His thoughts didn't indicate that he would; they were mostly directed toward our safety, concern and curiosity for what might have happened to us, what put us on the street. He thinks differently than anyone I've read. I can't figure it out. It's odd... unnatural. I guess it's just because he's the first old person I've been around since I learned I could read minds."

"Something odd? What do you mean?"

"Ah... I don't know. Just weird. Like he's reading it out of a book."

"Well, do you think that has something to do with why he cares so much about us, strangers? He doesn't seem to care so much about his grandson, and everything that's happened to him." Cheater turned back to Jaz after dropping the backpack on the floor near the bed.

"He seems to care about him. He just can't show it. Maybe there's too much hurt surrounding the kid... I guess. We know about that... hurt. He can see we hurt, but maybe he can't see past his own hurt to his grandson's because of his wife. Maybe because the kid reminds him of his daughter... and his wife?"

"Maybe. Yeah, you're probably right. It's weird, though. There seems to be pictures of all the family out there on the wall, but he isn't in any. Pictures have been removed."

"Eh, maybe he was taking the pictures. Maybe he doesn't like pictures. Maybe he's one of those people who believe a picture can steal your soul." Jaz half smiled at Cheater's imagination. She shook her head.

"Well, ready? Just remember only one of us

answer at a time." In contrast to her confident question, as if being led to her own execution, Cheater dragged her floppy soled feet down the staircase and into the kitchen.

"Root Beer's all I got; s'all I like. Sit down, we need ta have us a little chat." Mr. Johnston nodded toward the two chairs opposite him, sweating glasses of the sweet soda sitting on already damp paper towels. Jaz took one chair, Cheater the other.

"Now, 'for we go git that car unhitched, I wanna know what you kids are about here.

"I know the story 'bout family ain't likely. I ain't never seen you around. I kin see loss when it's 'afore me, and I know you kids have lost people. And you..." He nodded once at Cheater, "...seen yer face on a poster at the post office th' other day. Somethin' 'bout a woman dyin' and police wantin' t' question you. So's mebbe we better start with you." Mr. Johnston noted the fear in Cheater's eyes as she looked between him and Jaz, down to the table top, and back up at him again.

"Ya' ain't got nuttin' t' be afraid of. I ain't called the law er nothin'... yet. Even though my cousin's the Sheriff here. I got reason t' b'lieve you kids need help, so spill it. Besides, at my age, I can read a person pretty well. You ain't no killer."

He took a sip from the glass before him, nodded, and then gave Cheater a patient look. Judging by that look, she knew he would sit at that table the rest of the day and into the night waiting for her to speak, but she stalled by taking a long drink of her soda, and then another.

She glanced over at Jaz again. He shrugged uncertainly, and nodded, then turned his cautious gaze toward Mr. Johnston.

"Well…" Cheater stumbled.

"Just spill it, girl. Ain't nuttin' t' fear."

She began by telling the man about Sadie and the Home, and how she met Jaz, careful to leave out the whole mugging, and then Jaz proceeded to tell about the hospital, intentionally leaving out any information about their gifts, his step dad, and the murder of his mother.

Mr. Johnston nodded understandingly, closely watching their expressions, their glances toward each other, and listening, his gaze turning back and forth between the two teens, the Root Beer in his glass disappearing with each nod.

Cheater couldn't read his eyes very well, so she glanced to Jaz for reassurance of his thoughts.

Although Mr. Johnston passed the thoughts test, Cheater still felt uncomfortable telling him more than what she already had, reliving the pain that came with her past.

Several parts of her past were left unsaid, including the nightmare that awakened her from every sleep. So he knew about Sadie, and she told him what had happened, the heart attack, the Home, her fear of returning.

She didn't have to tell him everything, about every family she had lived with, about all the deaths that followed her as that little dog had.

She didn't have to give him all of her story, and maybe, just maybe, telling him only enough to appease his curiosity would keep him alive.

Maybe what she did tell him was all he required because sitting here worrying about his life and thinking about the outcomes of those whom she had come in contact with was increasing her flight sense.

"Well, that there's some stories," Mr. Johnston nodded. "But I feel yer leavin' somethin' out.

"See, wisdom comes with age, and Lord knows I'm old enough to be wise to the stories of kids. I also see's things in ya' that ya' prolly don't realize. But, seein' as that was so difficult fer ya'..." he nodded at Cheater, who seldom cried in front of strangers, but whose face now gleamed with moisture, "...I'll let yer trust build up, trust in me that is, and we'll have us another talk later on. Meantime, we got a car to unhitch, animals to care fer, and some rules to set down. 'Sides, mebbe when that boy gets back, you two kin help 'im see things a little different."

Mr. Johnston pushed his chair back from the table, rose, and went to the stainless steel sink with his sweaty glass, gesturing for the two to follow.

The old man's future was not theirs to know. They were taking a risk staying with him, divulging information to him, a risk that harm would come to Mr. Johnston, this farmhouse, the animals on the property, and Cheater and Jaz wouldn't be able to stop it because they had no way of knowing what would happen until it was too late.

Cheater knew they needed to leave again, to fulfill their purpose, to discover why they were connected, why they had been given such gifts as the ones they bore, to find the faceless man, but there was the grandson—possibly one of the missing ten—and all Cheater and Jaz could do was believe that they were meant to be here, to find the kid, before they moved on.

And if he wasn't one of them? Cheater only hoped she was right and nothing would happen to either the old man or the boy because of another wrong decision to stay when she should leave.

She was finding it ever more difficult to trust her own instincts regarding her destiny, but she had another gift she had forgotten, one buried deep in her roots, in her soul, one that seemed to have died more with each person in her life, because it had appeared to have lost its power.

Yet, the gift tugged at her heart when they passed the church the day before, and she stilled it. She only did that, buried the gift, when it came to important matters like this. Had she forgotten how to hope, or had she just given up on it?

Her faith had always been strong.

Cheater's mother had made certain of that, and Cheater wanted to believe that all would be well here, as she had so many times, but doubts crept in, a thick, murky fog stifling her gift of hope, carrying away her thoughts, her words, in the heavy vapor, leaving them to disappear in the dreary destination of doubt brought to her by the faceless man.

Three nights of sleeping like a princess passed before Cheater dropped her guard. She realized that if anything were going to happen, it already would have. The first few nights in the room, she laid awake worrying most of the night, but that was a week ago.

She began to relax, enjoy herself, and felt as though she were home. Perhaps the fairytale would have a happy ending and the old man, if he survived, would be grandpa to them all? She wondered what he would think of that, twelve grandchildren. Hadn't he mentioned that he and his wife had wanted a houseful? She couldn't remember for sure. He was old—and a little gruff, sometimes. Still, he might make a good guardian.

Although the dogs scattered when the old man came into view, he seemed to have grown fond of Cheater and Jaz. She wondered why the dogs reacted the way they did, slinking away from her relaxing hands in the middle of ear scratches whenever the old man banged out the screen door.

"Them's working dogs. They ain't bred for playing and caterin' to kids' needs! You be spoilin' 'em from workin, you keep that up!" The man grumbled in answer to her unasked question.

Cheater took the hint, getting up and climbing

back up the ladder, paint scraper in hand. The two teens had been helping Mr. Johnston around the house and farm, awaiting news about his grandson; Jaz sat high atop a second ladder, paint brush stroking back and forth as the man had instructed. The weather had been unusually warm this early December.

Cheater worked and scraped on boards to his left, above the front porch.

They had worked almost a week, replacing worn porch boards for Mr. Johnston, while he supervised and instructed them on how to complete the tasks that they had never learned to do.

Cheater's doubts and fears slowly diminished as the first part of the week sped by. She whistled happily while she scraped old paint away, baring the wood beneath for Jaz to paint over with the bright white primer Mr. Johnston had picked up the day before.

It was Jaz who had suggested they repaint his home. It was the least they could do; he had told Mr. Johnston when the old man argued against it.

"You two should stay outta sight. I know I'm out here off the road, but somebody might see ya'. We shouldn't risk it."

"Come on. Nobody'll see us. We can't just sit around all day. We've done all we can do cleaning and dusting on the inside. Let us help you repair the outside," Jaz had pleaded.

Mr. Johnston acquiesced, and now here they

were, working away, whistling, happy to be doing something besides worrying.

Almost two weeks without news, a week without monsters, except in Cheater's dreams, and a week of normalcy brought relaxation and relieved fears. Though still concerned about timing, the two stayed on, waiting for the boy, trusting fate.

"I'ma go bring us some soda out. You two take a break. Come on down them ladders."

A sickly, coppery scent drifted on the breeze toward the two.

"Pyeu!" Jaz exhaled sharply, "What's that smell?" He wrinkled his face in distaste.

Cheater knew what it was. She had smelled it several times in the past few months, in alleys, in wooded areas, along roadsides. It was the smell of rotting flesh just after it burst from swelling gases.

"Ah, probably a dead cow. Gotta go check on 'em later, I reckon. Sometimes calves is born dead, left to rot if I don't go find 'em." Mr. Johnston's matter of fact reply concerned them, but he was used to those situations. "Now, come on down."

Jaz wiped at his forehead with the back of his hand and stepped his way down the rungs, bouncing to the ground from the second one up.

"I'd be happy to give you a hand looking for it," Jaz offered.

"Oh, no, no. Could be up there by the road. Don't want ya' to be seen by some nosy neighbor. It can wait."

Cheater climbed down more cautiously, laid the scraper on the porch rail and positioned her exhausted body on the recently painted steps, a look of doubt filling her face.

It did smell like an animal, she guessed, but there was something different about the scent. She'd smelled it yesterday, too. And the day before, but today it was strong. Must be the wind.

"Hard work!" Jaz exhaled, trying not to inhale too deeply the scent traveling on the breeze.

"Yeah, glad you suggested it." Cheater answered sarcastically, pulling the collar of her shirt up over her wrinkled nose.

The two relaxed until the crunch of tires speeding down the gravel road alerted them.

Too late for the mail car to be delivering, they both jumped up and headed for the house, almost bumping into Mr. Johnston on the way in, stopping just short of dousing him with root beer.

"Company!" Jaz sounded and moved passed the elder man, taking the stairs two at a time toward his room.

"Hey, take these drinks!" The man ordered, shoving two of the glasses at Cheater, who carried them up the stairs with her, but instead of entering the room which had become hers, she turned toward the room Jaz had disappeared into, handing him his soda.

"Oh, thanks." He gulped a quarter of the dark liquid, ice tinkling lightly against the side of the glass, before setting it on the dresser next to him and listening for sounds, focusing on thoughts.

Cheater put her ear to the crack she had left in the doorway, wondering who had come up the driveway.

Perhaps it was a delivery.

Maybe it was just a neighbor, yet even that didn't satisfy her doubt.

In her heart, she knew this was bad; her intuition told her it was time for a change.

A long silence passed before both of them heard a voice. Cheater motioned to Jaz.

Neither said a word with ears pressed to the slight crack between door and jamb, the noise of pounding hearts filling their ears. They had gotten too comfortable, spending days working, nights searching maps, trying to discover the whereabouts of the boy, locate one like them.

"Yeah, come on in, cousin!" Mr. Johnston announced, slightly louder than necessary.

Cheater looked at Jaz.

Cousin?

Sheriff?

Jaz nodded, drawing a picture of a star in midair with his index finger, indicating a badge.

Cheater looked down at the floor, concentrating on the words, a slight tremble overtaking her.

Mr. Johnston had warned that his cousin, the sheriff, might stop in unannounced with news of his grandson. They had planned in advance how to handle the situation if that happened.

“Doin’ some paintin’ J.J.?” The deep voice questioned suspiciously.

“Uh, yeah, ‘bout time, doncha think? Glass o’ root beer?” His voice sounded forced, but he attempted a cheerfully normal tone.

“Sure. Sure, thanks.”

Cheater heard them move to the kitchen below her feet. She couldn’t hear as well from the door, now. Looking at Jaz, she jabbed her finger at the floor on the other side of his room, quietly laid down, and pressed her ear against the hardwood.

Muffled words filtered through the old flooring.

“Got somethin’ stinkin’ up the place out there, cousin!” The sheriff commented jokingly.

“Yeah, yeah, I know. Gotta take care of that.”

“Sooner the better, I’d say.”

“I ‘spect you’re here with news of that boy?” Mr. Johnston asked.

“Well, actually, might be.” The other voice suggested before making another observation, “You gittin’ up on them old ladders out there and paintin’ this house in your condition, J.J.?”

“Me, ha! Yer a funny one, Joe!”

Laughter.

“Well, reason I asked, Tilly, down ta’ the post office, said she saw a black fella out here other day way up on a ladder while she’s deliverin’ mail. Handyman?”

“Well, heck yeah, Joe! I ain’t aimin’ ta climb a ladder and die any time soon. Leastways not till I tan that boy's hide for stealin' that blamed car!"

Chuckle, chuckle.

The entire conversation sounded odd to Cheater.

Perhaps it was difficult having a cousin who worked for the Sheriff's department. It was probably very difficult to lie to someone you grew up with that now worked in an authoritative position, especially when harboring two fugitives.

Something was definitely wrong about the words, the tone, and the slight mocking overtones.

Perhaps she had just forgotten what it was like to be suspicious. The conversation between the two seemed stiff, scripted, planned.

Maybe it's just lies. She glanced at Jaz's face opposite hers on the floor. He wrinkled his nose in reply, his shoulders bouncing up, then down.

"So, what news ya' hear might be about the boy?"

"Well, you ain't gonna like it, J.J. You ain't gonna like it a'tall.

"News come over the scanner this mornin' 'bout a elderly woman found dead in 'er kitchen. Blunt force. Head wound. Whoever done it, she had her granddaughter livin' with 'er... girl had some problem.

"Anyway, girl's gone. Kidnapped, they think. Boy fittin' Nate's description was seen at the house just before the Sheriff over there arrived. Can't say it was him, but both kids disappeared."

"Lord A'mighty! What in the world could that boy be thinkin'? What has he done now?"

"Now, Jeb, first of all, may not be Nate. Second, if it is, he may notta done nothin' but he'p that girl, which ain't bad... Lessin' she killed 'er grandma?"

Cheater, who had been lying quietly listening to every word, sought the face of her friend again, a concerned look in his eye, panic in hers.

Perhaps they had made the wrong decision to remain here and wait for the grandson. If he could take another life, surely he couldn't be part of the fairytale mission, part of the greater plan. On the other hand, the girl could be one of the ten, too. Something wrong with her could mean a gift. The conversation downstairs continued.

"So, Jeb, where'd ya' find this handyman, or should I say, these handymen? Two ladders, two people."

"Uh... oh, well... ya' see, they's some of them, uh, boys lookin' fer work ta' make money fer their own cars. Never could get one over on those eyes of yers."

Cheater could hear the struggle of words in Mr. Johnston's voice, the difficult explanation, just as she had struggled when asked about her life. He was definitely hiding something.

"Uh, huh. They help ya' with Gayle's car?"

"Yeah, yep, that's right."

"Well, Jeb, shouldn't they be in school?"

"Ya' know, I ain't never asked 'em 'bout school.

Thought they's old 'nough ta be out. Guess, I should. Ask I mean. Been a while, since I had ta deal with the schools and such. Maria never was a problem. That boya hers? Totally different. Guess I shoulda thoughta that after him gettin' in so much trouble. Could be the kids I hired in one o' them there work programs?"

"Could be. Be sure to ask 'em. Don't need no truancy problems with another kid associated with you. You could wind up in jail. Know how you're set in them old ways. School's the law, though. Got to learn the new ways, ways he wants 'em to think, ya' know?"

"Yep, yessir, sure do."

"Where they gone off to?"

"Who? Oh, the kids? Uh... oh... they went... on downtown... to git 'im somethin' ta eat."

"Old soft heart ain't feedin' the help?" The sheriff grunted.

"Don't keep hardly 'nough fer me around anymore."

More laughter.

"Ah, the single life! Happin' to notice if them two came around with a girl? Maybe 13, 14?"

"Uh ..."

Cheater heard a glass set down hard on the counter, "No, no can't say I saw any."

"Mm, hmm, but you will keep an eye out for her? She may be workin' somewhere's else in town. They might meet up after they make enough money."

"Well, uh, is there somethin' I should know about this here girl, case I do see 'er?"

"Ah, she's jist a kid the local authorities down there to the south are lookin' for. Somethin' 'bout the death of a foster mother or somethin'. She's last seen with a tall black kid wanted for somethin' to do with the death of his mother and stepfather, as well as some gang activity, or somethin' or other. That's why I stopped, 'cause of Tilly's description of your two helpers."

Silence.

"Gang activity? My heavens!" Mr. Johnston exclaimed.

"Oh, yeah, well. Anyways, be wise, Jeb, to gimme a call if ya' see those two?"

"Oh, sure, sure. What in tarnation is wrong with these here teenagers today? Killin' people, stealin' cars, runnin' off 'n' hidin'? I jist don't get what is happenin' in this here world o' ours! You, Joe?"

"Nope, no I sure don't. Sometimes think o' retiring soon. 'Fraid one day one o' them there kids with a stolen weapon claiming to hunt is gonna end it for me 'fore I can take my retirement and that extended fishin' vacation down to the Gulf!"

More chuckling.

"Well, mebbe that feller fix all this mess, huh?"

What feller? Cheater thought to Jaz.

He shrugged back.

"Mebbe." Mr. Johnston didn't sound so sure in

his answer.

"Got some good ideas, he does. Well, gotta get back ta work at the station. Got ole Pop down there, again. Walkin' down the street half lit, tried to walk in front of a car, pulled out his pretend rifle and commenced to shootin' the driver. Gotta git the papers started fer rehab ,again."

"Shame. Hero like that bein' treated the way he is and not gittin' the help he needs."

"Yeah, well, there some stories 'bout that, too, but that's a Sunday after church one. Someday. See ya' later, Jeb."

Footsteps crossed the floor, the closing of the door, another glass clinking on the counter.

Cheater pushed up from the floor, quietly went to her room and grabbed the still packed backpack.

Jaz threw his dirty clothes into his bag, reached under the pillow, and pulled out his picture, putting it in the protective pocket. He frantically grabbed at the perfume bottle on the bedside table, almost knocking it to the floor in his rush before tucking it away in his bag.

Packing done in silence, they met in the hallway.

No words passed between them, only a look of understanding in their eyes.

No sounds made as they stepped lightly down the hall.

Silence down each step of the stairway.

Not a sound across the living room floor.

They would sneak away, so Mr. Johnston wouldn't have to lie to the law, since the law was family.

Their life was taking the turn again, and they intended to change it before someone got hurt.

Side by side, feet stepped to the threshold of the front door.

Two hands reached out for the screen door knob.

Four eyes searched the screen for a car in the driveway, which they hadn't heard leave, but nevertheless was gone.

"Now, jist where do you think you two are off to? You ain't done paintin' yet." A gruff, familiar voice, once muffled from the kitchen, now filled the hush left behind by the teens.

They had only heard the sounds of pounding hearts in their eardrums while fleeing.

They thought they'd heard the door open, close.

They hadn't heard the car leave after the that; they hadn't heard anything until this moment—this moment of dread as their eyes found each other, afraid to turn around, hoping to see what they knew they would not see, the smiling curious face of the old man.

They had gotten too comfortable here, dulling their street senses, instincts lost in gratitude, their interest in the boy, the puzzle that entangled their lonely lives, all senses momentarily forgotten.

Run or turn around? Cheater passed the question to Jaz's seeking mind, but the look in his eyes held no hope.

The look told her that this was the end.

The look in his eyes said, 'Run, die', 'Turn, die.'

Either way they were without choice, without plan.

As they turned around to face their ending, Jaz noted the sadness in Cheater's eyes, too.

No blank stare, no changing of her form, she could not save them, the two old men. No choice remained for the teens.

They turned completely, looking first into two dark holes directed at them. They peered up the long black barrel, and into the old, wrinkled face smirking beneath the tan hat, the Sheriff.

"Sorry, kids, had to keep ya' around, keep playin' the role, till we found somethin' out about that boy, Nate." Mr. Johnston raised his brows, his head bobbing at them.

"Soon's we can bring 'im back, he'll be joinin' ya', him and that dumb girl, as will the rest o' you kids. Yessir, you'll all be together all right, just like the plan, the age-old plan. 'Cept, it ain't gonna be the same age-old ending wrote for you Gifted Ones."

The young girl shot a desperate look at her companion.

Mr. Johnston hadn't died, she told herself.

He was part of the plan; she revisited her earlier belief as she faced the once kindly old man.

The scent of death drifted from outside.

Nothing terrible had happened to him since she'd arrived, the benevolent old man looking over the sheriff's shoulder, the look of deceit in his eyes.

Now she knew why he was still alive.

He wasn't Mr. Johnston.

The smell, the dogs, his questions, all churned in her mind, tumbling along with the events of her life, of the past week.

As a last resort, she glanced up at Jaz again and still found hopelessness, defeat, and despair.

All lies? She silently questioned; his head bobbed once in reply.

Not once had Mr. Johnston, or whoever he was, thought about this plan, until now.

Not once had the boy picked up on the hint of deception that now glowed from the weathered old face.

How did he block the truth from you?

Another shrug in answer, minds' wheels churning, searching, formulating a fruitless plan of escape.

"I got jist the place fer you two, while we wait for that other boy and girl. The beginning of the end. Your end. Let's go!" A jerk of the shotgun set the teens in motion, out the backdoor, past the barn, and through a wire gate, a short walk in thickly shrubbed land, the smell of decay strengthening, a sheriff with a shotgun aimed at their backs, and two hands tightly gripping each other.

Mr. Johnston's imposter opened doors and gates as they moved out of the backyard, solemn silence, except the crunching of leaves beneath their feet, the pounding of blood within their ears.

Jaz squeezed Cheater's hand with his own, tighter still, neither alone as they entered the dark place.

Please take a minute to review Paradise Rising on the site where you purchased this book, on Goodreads, and on Amazon.

TIME
OF
DREAMS

First, Nathan noticed the blood on her hands.

He didn't have time for this. The last time he tried to help someone in trouble, he was thrown in juvenile hall, and he never saw his parents again.

"Get away from me! How many times I gotta tell ya'? Quit followin' me! Go home!" He spun around and pointed up the path. "What is wrong with you? You stupid or what? You can't go with me! Just go back where you came from!" The anger he'd felt for weeks released in a rush of spittle filled words.

For the third time since this problem arose—and by this problem he meant her—Nathan jabbed his finger in the direction from which he had just come, speaking as if to an unruly puppy. He could tell, even before their eyes briefly met, that the girl didn't have it all together upstairs. He didn't know what frustrated him more, that she wouldn't (or couldn't) talk or that she didn't seem to understand what he was telling her. In spite of his annoyance, deep inside guilt welled from the harsh words he had just spoken. He hadn't been raised to be rude to others, and never had he bullied anyone, especially a helpless girl.

She created a dilemma, though. *"It's a rock and*

hard place." His grandpa's voice urged. *"Figure it out, son."*

Maybe he could call the cops anonymously. Hope gleaned while he patted his empty pockets, yet he knew full well he had used all his money to fuel that monster, gas-guzzling boat his grandpa called a car. Inside his pockets, his fingers collected flat blue lint.

He should never have run away in the first place. He should have stayed and fought it out, found a way to protect what was rightfully his. What could he have done, though? After all, he was just a kid, a kid on a farm he loved and now missed. Thinking about the farm brought back the night he left.

"Nathan! Nathan!" The teen rolled to his stomach and pulled the covers over his head to smother the sound.

"Not yet, Mom! I'm so tired. I worked hard with Grandpa yesterday."

"No, Nathan, I'm not your mother. Wake up, Nathan. You have to wake up!"

Nathan squeezed the blankets in his fist and mashed them with his knuckles against the pillow. "No," he may have replied. A slight, sleepy smile turned the corners of his lips as a cute girl with long, brown hair filled his dreams. Her hair gently blew back from her face in a delicate breeze, just like the supermodels he'd seen briefly on TV. The girl's soulful eyes reached deep into his heart. He had the urge to hug her, comfort her, make her smile.

She looked so familiar, yet not.

Nathan's brows drew down in concern.

Why wasn't she smiling? She should smile.

The wind whipped tendrils of her hair around her face; stronger and warmer it grew, spiraling the long strands upward.

Her mouth opened, "Get up, Nathan! You have to leave now! You're in danger. Get up! Get your Grandpa and go!"

Grandpa? What about Grandma?

Her urgency confused him, and he rolled to the other side keeping his covering at his chin.

Why should he leave Grandma?

"Now, Nathan!" She yelled, her eyes turning angry. Then the fire erupted, the hot wind growing.

"No—no—no," Nathan mumbled in his sleep, tossing to the other side. "Not him. Not this, again."

The heat rose around him and Nathan began to sweat beneath his covers. He threw them off seeking cool air.

A loud noise downstairs jolted him from the damp sheets and jarred his body upright.

He listened.

In his sub-conscious state, semi awake now, she tugged at his flight sense. "Now, Nathan! Leave, now!"

After what happened, that girl in that stupid dream he'd had the night he left turned out to be right; it had been a matter of life and death and he chose life.

Yet, his selfish desire to sleep brought him more guilt as he thought of his grandparents.

He shook it off. There wasn't anything he could have done. It had been too late. He didn't even have time to try before—

He shook his head again; his too long, greasy, black hair swung side to side around his ears, and he scowled angrily at the poor girl who had been following him. He'd tried getting through to her with motions instead of words, but she continued to stare blankly someplace beyond him.

She would surely bring him death.

For the first time since their encounter, he took a long look at her, at the stringy, unkempt golden hair, half still in a ponytail from the night before, half poking loose, looping wildly out of its tie. Her filthy, thorn-torn pajamas covered her thin frame. House shoes, two sizes too big, donned her pale feet, and her thin hands dangled at her sides, long fair fingers smeared in a deep red blood.

The boy scanned her again, inching closer; her blank expression static while he searched for the source from which the smears had come, hoping to find a bleeding wound, but his instincts told him otherwise. A fleeting hope that the blood came from an animal dispersed with his intuition. It was never something that simple for him.

He knew.

A long, sighing circle around the girl only brought a curse to his lips, “Dang it!” He truly had a dilemma: a not-right-in-the-head girl with blood on her hands who wouldn’t let him leave her.

In his rock star dreams, he’d always found girls fawning over him and following him, but not like this.

What was he going to do?

How was he supposed to handle this situation?

How could he make her understand that he couldn’t help her right now, and that she couldn’t go with him? More importantly, how could he quell the desire to find out what had happened to her?

It was all about the timing, and no matter how much he wanted to help her, he didn’t have the time.

“Rock and a hard place, boy…” The gruff old voice echoed in his thoughts.

No, she would slow him down and he had to return to the farm, finish what those killers had started, and avenge his grandparents.

Contemplating, he turned and walked away from her again.

Hair in need of washing slapped his cheekbones in refusal. His clenched fists bounced in front of him with each “No!” he uttered. Each step more like a trek in thick, sucking mud.

Taking her back to her house wasn't an option.

It would take too long.

He didn't know where she lived, and she couldn't tell him.

But... there is the blood on her hands. Momentarily curtailed by that thought, he stopped, then continued.

He stumbled over a stump, catching his balance before he injured himself.

The blood...

A mystery it was, but he couldn't get involved in her problems. He had his own. Every time he'd involved himself in someone else's problems, or caught himself up in a mystery, or simply tried to help someone in the past, it turned out bad for him.

"Okay, okay..." he turned, taking a few steps toward her. "Listen. I need to go home, back to my grandf ...? You have to stop following me and go home. Do you understand me? You have to go home. Somebody else will find you." His voice softened with empathy as he moved closer to her; her head tilted sideways. He gazed into the absent stare of her blue eyes. His grandmother's motionless face replaced her image. No! "Home. Go home. Do you understand?"

She issued no response or recognition of his request, no response to his compassion.

Standing inches from her, well within her personal space, his chest puffed in desperation for an answer or some kind of acknowledgment.

He waved a hand before her vacant stare. He smiled, "Hello? Anybody in there?"

Finally, she turned away shuffling her slipper clad feet across the autumn dried grasses and leaves.

"Good. Thank you God!" he spoke the words sarcastically spinning on his heels in the opposite direction. He needed to get out of this town and its weird happenings, back home to Paradise. Though content with the recent outcome, a vengeful scowl creased his forehead at the thought of his last night at the farm, of the killers.

The crunch of dead leaves behind him halted his steps again.

How long did he have to play this ridiculous game until she understood?

His shoulders drooped in defeat as he turned, trying to hide his annoyance. She was following him again. His angry eyes flashed.

"Look, I thought we had this cleared up! You were going home! You can't go with me!" his voice held firm as he reduced the distance between them to less than two feet.

He wanted to grip her shoulders and shake her, make her understand. Before he could act on his urge, she turned away, moving down the same path where they had first bumped into each other.

"Good, good. Let's try this again. You go on home and I'll go home, t..." how could he refer to it as home, now? His grandparents were gone. He had to stop referring to them. He didn't know what he would find when he returned to the farm, but a desperate need to return fueled his anger and he took it out on her.

He waited warily, watching her walk away until she was twenty paces from him, then he spun, ran, but the dragging noise of her feet behind him followed, shoocrunch... shoocrunch... shoocrunch.

"No!" he screamed in a whirl of rage.

Run, he told himself, but his body wouldn't respond. He dropped to his knees, his gaze falling to the leaves before him. She couldn't fend for herself. She'd get lost in this place and die, or worse, some out-of-town crazy, some perv would find her wandering the town in her torn pajamas.

"Please, keep going, please! You can't go with me!" He begged her.

On the verge of indecisive tears, he stood again, charging toward her, attempting to scare her away by waving his arms like a lunatic. "Leave me alone!" His arms shook.

She turned calmly and walked away, not in the least frightened by his torrent of emotion. When he didn't follow this time, however, she stopped and turned back toward him, head never straying from its slightly cocked angle, the forever blank stare taking her thoughts somewhere in the distance behind him, the thin shoulders sagging the message, "Well, come on then."

He thought he saw a championed flicker buried deep in the calm sea of her gaze, the tiniest of taunting motion in her narrow hand.

His weariness played tricks on his vision, that was all.

No, that wasn't all.

In defeat, he finally caved.

She wanted him to follow her, most likely to her house, where the source of all that blood on her hands lay waiting for an answer. Silently without much conviction, he prayed it was not human blood.

This disaster would get him in more trouble with the law, like all of the other incidents since his parents died; the turned-over headstones, the vandalized school, the burglarized cars, all events he tried to prevent in his friend's life. He hadn't participated in any of them, hadn't even touched a can or slipped through a door with malice; he just wanted to help the only person he considered a friend, but it hadn't worked out like he planned.

His grandpa told him to let it go. *"Some people can't be fixed, son,"* he'd warned. He didn't understand, though.

Nobody understood.

His parents were the only ones who knew anything about him, about his lack of trust because of his abilities, about his knack for turning people in the right direction. Now he was the only one who knew… well, except the girl in his dream.

He didn't have time to deal with this problem before him, but he would anyway; his conscience wouldn't allow him to leave this girl to herself. The blood on her hands, the way she waited for him to follow, the sense that she understood more than he gave her credit for, all left him no choice but to help her. It was the right thing to do. Regardless of the trouble it would bring him, he always did the right thing.

She needed help.

He would help.

He let her lead him into more trouble.

From behind, he watched her closely as she stayed some distance in front of him, walking into the leafless, near winter brush without a thought for pushing it aside and protecting herself from cuts or scrapes. No wonder her clothes were so torn.

Before long, a small, white, wood frame house appeared at the end of a narrow driveway perpendicular to the lonely road they crossed. The girl moved straight into the front door, so he gulped air assuming this was it.

She paused at the door, holding it open for him to enter, a statue, staring at the doorjamb opposite her.

Trapped—that's how he felt. He knew for certain now that somebody in that house was hurt, but he didn't know how badly, didn't know what he could do to help them, or even if he could. After the last incident with his friend, he no longer believed in himself.

What if he couldn't help the person waiting in there? What if this was a trap?

Reluctantly, he stepped onto the porch and reached for the screen door. As his hand touched the cool metal, the girl pulled back her bloody hand—leaving no smears behind—and shuffled into the house.

Cautious eyes followed her into the gloom, all curtains and blinds closed tightly, all present rooms lightless. Other than the gaping triangle of light left behind by the door they had entered, there wasn't a beam of sunlight filtering into the house reminding Nathan of another dark building.

"Jake, what're you doin'? Get out of there! Come on!"

"Oh, don't be such a baby. The door's open. I just want to look around, maybe see if the science lab is open, too."

"The door wasn't open, Jake. Come on; let's go to my house, hang out until my parents get home. It's dark in there, and creepy."

"Yeah, schools are creepy at night." His voice grew fainter as he moved farther into the darkened halls. "Come on, Nate! Hey, the science lab is open! Come on."

The loud crash of breaking glass drew Nathan through the door, though he knew it was too late. He had to stop Jake from doing anything else foolish. He'd already been to Circle Court twice. This time he'd go to Juvenile Hall.

"Jake! What are you doing? You idiot! Let's get out of here before the cops get here!" Nate surveyed the room of broken glass beakers, smashed computer monitors, toppled computers.

"Teach him to fail me..." Jake mumbled as he bent, gripped the bottom of the teacher's desk, and straightened his legs, forcing the desk on its face.

"Man, Jake, you're already in enough trouble! Let's go!" Nate turned from the room and into the chest of a security guard just before he switched his flashlight on.

"Run, Nate!" Jake said as he flipped the latch on the nearest window, pushed upward, and slipped out the opening.

"Too late." The security guard's downward grimace forced Nate's frightened features to pale.

Visit thegiftedonestrilogy.com to find out when you can finish reading Time of Dreams, or become a patron of my work at https://www.patreon.com/PGShriver to read it online now.

About the Author

P. G. SHRIVER lives in Texas with her family of two and four legged beings.

She has been writing since the age of seven and was first published in a local newspaper. Some of her hobbies include gardening, reading, sewing and cooking.

She is a retired Developmental Education instructor and 4-8 teacher. She enjoys writing, traveling and presenting, but due to being rear ended twice by drivers on phones in the past two years, she now presents and reads from home. She has also established three private Facebook reading groups for children 3-5, 6-8, and 9-12 called *Socially Distant Readings* where young readers can interact with her books safely, watch recorded readings and live videos, read her books, take quizzes, complete writings, and create critical thinking projects based on books.

Visit her website today at pgshriver.com! Follow her on Amazon, Facebook and Twitter.

PG Shriver on Amazon
https://amazon.com/author/pgshriver
Gean Penny on Amazon

https://www.amazon.com/author/
www.geanpenny.com
Facebook
https://www.facebook.com/SociallyDistantAuthor/
Twitter
https://twitter.com/AuthorPGShriver
Patreon
https://www.patreon.com/PGShriver

Lightning Source UK Ltd.
Milton Keynes UK
UKHW022133070620
364543UK00013B/583/J

9 780996 377829